THE
RAISE

THE RAISE

A NOVEL

Ali Kriegsman

Cashmere Street Press

This book is a work of fiction. The names, characters, and events in this book are the products of the author's imagination or are used fictitiously. Any similarity to real persons living or dead is coincidental and not intended by the author.

The Raise

Published by Cashmere Street Press

Photography by Eva Zar
Book Design by Alison Golcher Stone

Copyright © 2025 by Ali Kriegsman

All rights reserved. Neither this book nor any parts within it may be sold or reproduced in any form or by any electronic or mechanical means, including information storage and retrieval systems, without permission in writing from the author. The only exception is by a reviewer, who may quote short excerpts in a review.

ISBN (paperback): 9781662962493
eISBN:9781662962509

For us.

"It ain't what you don't know that gets you into trouble. It's what you know for sure that just ain't so."

Mark Twain

1

September 17, 2019.

I got a call from Darcy's mom Cecilia about three hours ago. Apparently, the wig options are pretty limited at the funeral home. They've got a cherry red bob or a copper cut with bangs, and Cecilia, who has been micromanaging the beautification of her daughter's corpse, would much prefer Darcy's signature long locks. "It's how she'd want to be remembered," she said coolly, before urging me to arrive by 3 p.m., so the mortician would have an hour to glue the wig onto Darcy's scarred, bare scalp. I threw my makeup in my bag, called an Uber, and rushed to the beauty supply store.

Darcy has been dead for fifteen days. And, just as in life, her body's preservation, and presentation, is of the utmost concern. After the accident, Cecilia called for an immediate embalming. They drained all the blood from Darcy's veins and plumped her up with Formaldehyde, a necessary procedure to ward off the ruthless sulfuric gases that bloat the body so severely it can double in size. An open casket meant keeping Darcy at her taut size two.

The Raise

In life, Darcy looked like a grown-up Shirley Temple with delicate, doll-like features and luscious, curly hair she dyed religiously. Despite knowing her for nearly a decade, I could never pinpoint her natural hair color. She never let her roots grow in long enough—not even when we were fundraising for our company, Savvy, or in a hiring sprint, or pulling back-to-back all-nighters ahead of our launch seven years ago. She'd put fake meetings on her calendar and sneak out of the office to go touch up her reddish highlights in SoHo. I couldn't quite figure out how to make time for "maintenance," like manicures or facials or Juvederm. Her mom, Cecilia, sent me subtle messages that I could be *so pretty* if I *just tried*, like when she'd leave piles of Crest Whitening Strips and self-tanning pads on Darcy's pillow at home in Syosset. When Darcy returned to the office, she'd pour them out of her beat up Goyard and we'd divvy them up like kids rifling through Halloween candy.

As I stare down the sparse wall of wigs at the beauty supply shop, I come to the horrifying realization that the real hair SKUs are out of stock.

I *cannot* bring a synthetic wig to Darcy's funeral. Cecilia would snap. Like, pull-her-own-hair-out-and-wail-in-front-of-the-entire-funeral-party kind of snap. And I don't blame her. A corpse in a costume wig feels a bit too dark.

I stumble toward the checkout counter and ask if there's any inventory hiding in the back. But the sole employee is being held hostage by some girl who's hysterically crying.

"The glitter triggered my rosacea!" she sobs. "Who *cares* if I don't have the fucking receipt!"

Honestly, they should just eat it. The girl's face really does look like shit.

My iPhone alarm goes off. *Fuck*. I have to leave for Penn Station if I want to make it in time.

Darcy taught me that trick. After getting gridlocked on the Brooklyn Bridge and running twelve minutes late to our first board meeting ages ago, she snatched my phone and scheduled a "LEAVE NOW" alarm for our investor breakfast the following day. I got there ten minutes early, convinced I'd be the first to show. But she was already settled into our Balthazar booth with two oat milk lattes, wearing a knowing smirk.

If I don't book it now, I won't make it in time.

I am bringing a synthetic wig to Darcy's funeral.

I rush back to the hair aisle and rifle through the discount bin, eyes scanning for anything red. I pull a dry, tangled mermaid wig up from the bottom and rush back to the counter. I buy a tiny comb and leave my receipt.

It cost me eleven dollars to hide Darcy's re-sewn scalp from the people who watched her die, and the ones who thought she'd live forever.

As I stash the wig in my backpack and sprint toward the C train, I wonder if Cecilia hired her at-home tanning lady to give the corpse a quick spray before the service. A nice bronze may offset the cheap sheen of the acrylic strands, help make Darcy look more like a real person and less like a Little Mermaid mannequin. But then I remember: Darcy spent her last few days at Burning Man, dancing and drinking under the blazing Playa Sun.

Does a sunburn peel into a tan, even if you're dead?

The train to Syosset is packed. My seat smells like mildew and Shake Shack grease, as if a hamburger crawled inside a wet wool coat and died there. We're in the thick of fall, when each passing day gets shorter and darker and the sky sheds rain to cool down the clouds. The floors are still damp and streaked with dirty footprints, residue from passengers who trekked through yesterday's heavy downpour.

I comb out the last knot in Darcy's wig and carefully slip it back into its plastic liner. I tuck the liner into my backpack and pull out my laptop to put the finishing touches on my eulogy. Remembering that Darcy said her family struggled with "vulnerability," I had offered to draft a tribute for the Lyons family to deliver. Cecilia kindly declined, instead instructing me to write one and dictating a length requirement: five whole minutes.

It's not that I don't want to give a eulogy. Darcy was like my older sister—my *only* sister. I have so many things to say. So many things I wish I told her. I wrote them all down, like Cecilia instructed. But the thought of standing in front of everyone, of speaking to all those people, makes me want to slip my neck inside the train's radiator fan. I hate the sound of my own voice. And all those eyes staring, expectant and anxious, praying I don't stumble. Hoping I'm eloquent enough, and confident enough, to give a performance that spares them the discomfort of pitying me. I worry they won't get what they want. Because I know that as soon as I hear my hot breath hit the microphone, my insides will collapse.

If Darcy were here, she'd tell me to push through it: to reframe it. She'd insist that I'm not inherently "bad" at public speaking, that my stage fright comes from intrusive thoughts, not some genetic mutation. She'd remind me that if I just change the way I talk to myself, I can take on any challenge. Darcy's encouragement was the only thing that could choke out my inner critic. Now that she's gone, I can feel it gasping for air, coming back to life to terrorize me.

Before I met Darcy, I'd just escaped a hostile internship in fashion media. The one nice and equally broke person I befriended at *The Magazine*, Kevin, quickly proved to be a fucking loser. He'd affectionately call me his "work wife" and invite me out on lunch dates to the local Quiznos like he was doing me a favor. The first time I went, he spent the whole meal complaining about how hard his boss rode him. What a "massive bitch" she was. How he was meant for so much more, but no one could see his potential. All while chewing through his three-dollar blue cheese and roast beef sub.

Later that day, I found out his boss "rode him" because he broke the copy machine, didn't tell anyone, then demanded the IT department rush up a new one. The delivery guys carted the new machine into our fanciest conference room while she was kicking off her biggest pitch of the year, wheels squeaking, men grunting. From then on, I hated Kevin. For his clumsiness. For his incompetence. For his inability to think things through.

In that moment, I felt a sudden urge to take myself more seriously. To differentiate myself from him, and everyone *like* him. I wasn't going to get anywhere in life, especially in this city, if I wasted my career hobnobbing at Quiznos with the "Kevins" of the world. There's a saying my mom always uses: *"You're the average of the five people you spend the most time with."* In an instant, spending less time with Kevin felt like life or death.

I started eating alone at my desk and thinking about who I should be. What I should become. I stalked everyone at *The Magazine* on LinkedIn and studied hundreds of copywriters, salespeople, marketers, "analysts," trying to find myself in their profiles, hoping one of them could offer a blueprint for my own vague ambitions and take me under their wing. But trudging through the buzzwords and gibberish of what they all did for a living, "optimizing key results for our shareholders," "bringing value and rigor to the accounting discipline," "leveraging data and insights to improve sales productivity," felt like wading through a grimy ocean polluted by candy wrappers and radioactive goop.

The Raise

When a full-time position finally opened up at *The Magazine*, the "massive bitch" told me I "wasn't eligible for it" because I didn't "convey the brand ethos" in my Forever21 blazer and crunchy pleather pants. This, after reorganizing their entire subscriber database, project managing the launch of their first-ever influencer activation, *and* decoding pages of Xerox jargon to fix Kevin's broken copy machine. I realized they'd never appreciate me. They'd never see my worth. I may have had grit, but I didn't have status.

Not anymore.

That same night, in my bed at my mom's, where I was living at the time, I stayed up scouting LinkedIn for open positions in anything, at any company. My goals were modest. I was seeking a salary, benefits, and a corporate culture that felt slightly less elitist and didn't require a fifty-thousand-dollar wardrobe. I was looking for job descriptions with words and sentences I could understand. And in an ideal world, I'd find a role model or two, professionals who would mentor me into success, money, and power, three things my mom and I had growing up, then lost in an instant. That's why I worked so hard. I was always crawling back to my life in "The Before," a time when I felt secure about money, about my future, about everything. Continuing to pick up chicken salad sandwiches and Diet Coke for my boss and becoming a Xerox expert weren't going to get me back there. I had seven hundred dollars in savings, thirty-eight thousand dollars in student debt, and pulled an annual salary of twenty-eight thousand dollars, which is unlivable for New York City—let alone anywhere.

I was hoping to pole vault out of my misery and away from what I'd done, the fateful decision I made right after my Bat Mitzvah that sank my entire family. I needed someone, something, that could get me jazzed about my life again—a Hail Mary to reignite my sense of possibility.

Right after hitting "send" on my thirtieth job application that night, I did one final scroll on my main feed and noticed an old classmate's boss promoting a few openings at Jetto, an e-commerce startup that helped small businesses with guaranteed two-day delivery. I did a quick search on the company and stayed up for another hour stalking all their current employees.

That's when I first saw her.

Her profile picture showcased a cascade of loose red curls framing a welcoming yet detached smile. She was a few years my senior and studied business in college, then went on to work in sales at various startups in New York. She had won Salesperson of the Year at two of those companies, and was even featured in a Forbes article, "Ten Women Doing Big Business in the Big Apple." I read the article in full. I watched hours of her panel appearances on YouTube. I listened to her podcast features. I disassociated a bit, and by the time I returned to my body, it was 4 a.m. I could hear the birds chirping outside my bedroom window, my mouth crusted over with morning breath and saliva goo.

Darcy's most recent LinkedIn post indicated she was part of that big Jetto hiring sprint; she was looking for a Junior Sales Rep to support her category, selling the company's two-day shipping tools to hardware stores in the Northeast. I pulled up the company website, found the sales rep application portal, and answered every question in thoughtful, meticulous detail.

Two days later, she emailed me. I was being summoned for an interview.

I knew I wanted the job by Darcy's third question.

"So, let's cut the bullshit, then. Who are you? Who *is* Alexis Ecker?" she asked, one manicured brow arched.

"I'm whoever you need me to be," I said—and I meant it.

Even though it felt like a bit of a downgrade—going from a notable magazine to cold-calling hardware stores—I was enamored by her. She was kind, competent, and effortlessly stylish, her head-to-toe black ensemble and glossy military boots giving Victoria Beckham sophistication with a sprinkle of Hot Topic. Classy, but with a hint of grit. As she shook my hand goodbye and told me to look out for an email with next steps, there was something in those grayish blue eyes, some current that ran between us. It felt like she had found something in me. A missing piece.

She was beautiful, poised, and self-assured. What could she possibly have been missing? What was she looking for?

I didn't know, and it didn't matter. Not yet.

Because I had this pulsing intuition that we were meant to find each other, that I would reach my maximum potential if Darcy was leading the way.

Jetto's Human Resources Department sent me their offer that Friday. I didn't negotiate. I didn't hesitate. I signed right then and there, eager for my first day on the job, ready to make Darcy proud.

It felt so good to finally be chosen. Especially by her.

Soon enough, she made me a soldier. *Her* soldier. She and the other sales executives were given aggressive, nearly unattainable goals and little to no guidance on how to achieve them. Our real-time stats were projected onto the office TV. You could see who had sent the most emails, booked the most meetings, closed the most deals and, therefore, made the most money. I think this is when Darcy realized I could work well under pressure and keep her organized. *Optimized.* She treated me more like an equal than an underling, which often meant finding my own solutions to problems I didn't want to bother her with or working weekends solo to hit our early Monday deadlines so she could stroll in at 10 a.m., well-rested and ready for the week.

But while we banged out email after email and took call after call, making our boss look good *and* carrying our team's dead weight, the cofounders of the company played Call of Duty all day. Our department chief obsessively organized a company karaoke league. The Head of Finance impulse ordered a mariachi band to soundtrack our free lunch. We weren't sure if everyone in the C-suite had extremely tiny dicks or too much money to spend. Or both.

We'd touch up our makeup in the all-gender bathroom after lunch and shit-talk the account execs who hadn't closed a deal yet. We'd stay late drinking the office wine and bitch about the legality of compulsory company karaoke. *Could we sue?*

Getting to know Darcy like this, not from her LinkedIn details or her press coverage, but through working with her so intimately every day, was like peeling an onion. I know it sounds cheesy, but it's true.

In many cases, she didn't speak unless spoken to. She would only use as many words or sentences as necessary to ask a question or relay a point. I learned to infer who she was from her actions, and from how she made me feel about the world, and about myself.

Darcy used to visit a local high school to do monthly mentoring sessions with young girls. She gave her clothes to battered women shelters instead of selling them, despite the obviously lucrative resale prices of most of her items. She didn't buy in high volume. Instead, she shopped smart. She would pluck five or so pieces from industry obscurity every quarter, wear them relentlessly to the office or networking events, and brandish a new "it brand" without even knowing it. And all this without an Instagram account, which she labeled a "distraction." She monitored me when I put myself down aloud, lightly slapping my hand or making a silent throat-slitting gesture from across the room. Her companionship simply felt too good, her partnership too essential. Sometimes I'd lay awake at night, gaming out what I would do or who

I would be if she ever abandoned me. It would make me so anxious, so overwhelmed, that I'd get physically hot, like catching some spiritual fever.

But as my one-year anniversary at Jetto approached, my worst fear almost came true. Darcy started leaving the office earlier, sending fewer and fewer emails, booking fewer meetings. She was dethroned on our team's public tracker, her sales metrics slipping more each day. It made her apathy quantifiable.

But even if I hadn't peeped her metrics in the sales dashboard, we were at the point in our friendship where if something was going on with her, *I just knew*. But I couldn't quite figure out why she stopped trying. Did she know something about Jetto's prospects that I didn't? Was she interviewing somewhere else? Was she going to leave me?

One day in early summer, Darcy and I were at Jetto sitting crosslegged in our favorite bathroom stall, puffing on her Juul.

"I have to get out of here," she said. Her long, coral nails curled around the vape. She took a hit and put it on the tile floor in between us.

I picked it up, inhaled, and handed it to Darcy. I looked at her but didn't respond.

"If these stupid fucks can raise all this money and build a company, then so can I." She took a hit from the vape. "So can *we*."

My heart swelled in my chest. I could feel it throbbing. She met my gaze but didn't blink. I understood now. She wasn't apathetic.

She was ready.

Darcy was nearing thirty, and she was done "getting by." She always had a business book cracked open on her desk, or a motivational TED talk queued up on her laptop. She had just lent me her copy of *Boss B*tch*, the best-selling memoir-meets-handbook by Jamie Frisco, who raised one hundred fifty million for her vintage e-commerce startup.

She was always G-chatting me LinkedIn profiles of different investors, with little memos on what and who they'd been throwing money at.

All along, she was memorizing the steps, studying the players, and learning the game from afar.

"I've had this idea since high school," she continued, as she pulled back her freckled shoulders and straightened her spine against the cold bathroom tile. "It's partially inspired by *Clueless*. Do you know what I'm talking about? Every item in Cher's closet is like, catalogued on her computer. And she uses all the digital clothes to plan her outfits and stuff, and she has her measurements built-in so she can see how they'll look on her actual body, and—"

"I remember that!" I said, feeling impatient and elated, like an invitation I both longed for and never knew was coming was just around the corner. "I was like *oh my god. This is the future.*"

"Right? Same. So, it's not that, really," she clarified. "But ever since I started shopping online the last few years, I realized how insane it is that there isn't, like, a personalized mall. A platform where you can share your style preferences and influences, plug in your exact measurements and get, like, recommendations basically, for your body shape and color season and maybe even based on pieces you've already purchased. Stuff that's already in your closet. And I want it to feel like magic, like really mind-blowing. Like how that scene in *Clueless* made us feel."

By now she was in full "pitch" mode—her eyes wide and hopeful, her voice loud and bright.

"I mean, it makes a lot of sense." The words rushed out of me. And I believed them. "So, are you just going to leave, then?" I put the Juul to my lips and looked down at the floor. Maybe I had gotten ahead of myself. She said "we," and she said "us," but maybe she was just used to talking like that because I'd been her admin for a year. I thought, *Maybe she wants to do this alone and that would be fine.* I'd be *fine.*

"Well not until I find some help," she replied, crossing her arms over her chest. "Which . . . is why I'm telling you. I think we work pretty well together, and I thought maybe you'd want to?"

Confetti exploded and ricocheted through my ribcage.

"It's obviously a big change, a big risk," she continued, tossing her red curls behind her shoulder. "But I think you're really talented. You can project manage, see stuff through, and you're good at learning shit you don't understand. I have this idea that I can execute on the vision, if you're game to do more of the operational, nitty gritty stuff. It's like a five-to-ten-year commitment, though. I overheard that the Jetto guys didn't draw a real salary until year three, and it took Jamie Frisco nearly two years to get any outside investment. It's a pretty massive decision, so like, take your time if you need it and we can always discu—"

"I'm in," I blurted. "I definitely want to help."

She raised her eyebrows and cocked her head.

"Really?" she asked. "You don't want . . . I don't know. You don't want some time to think it over? It's like no salary, bad healthcare probably, and a really bad grind, at least for a while."

"If working on this *Clueless* closet thing means an end to our karaoke nightmares and a chance to build something with you," I shrugged, "I think I can give it a shot." I smiled and passed her the vape. "Besides, those hardware store owners are creepy as fuck."

"You're not wrong," she replied. Her lips curled around the Juul, then she released a puff of smoke.

After signing our articles of incorporation, Darcy made a reservation at Eleven Madison Park, a three-Michelin star restaurant in Gramercy, one of the most manicured, affluent neighborhoods in the city. But how would I know? I showed up to my desk in high-waisted black short shorts and my favorite tank top, a go-to set I'd purchased in college at the local Urban Outfitters. She promptly advised I go and buy some pants. "Rich people prefer you dress *modestly*," she said. "They don't want a side of your pasty legs with their dry-aged duck breast. You need to change. I don't make the rules."

I wasn't offended. I felt relieved. Darcy was always doing that, sharing the unspoken do's and dont's of the adult world, making sure the faux pas couldn't catch me. I rushed to Zara to find some wide-legged trousers, like the ones Darcy wore to client pitches.

That dinner felt blurry and surreal, like pure magic. It was my first time trying caviar, or drinking vintage champagne, or celebrating myself . . . at all. At the time, I didn't know what was sweeter: this new friend believing in me and choosing me as her partner, or the fact that slowly but surely, I was starting to believe in myself.

On our chilly walk from dinner to the subway, Darcy, tipsy and cheerful, credited her newfound ambition to her "Saturn Return," an astrological event that happens every twenty-seven to thirty years when the planet orbits back to exactly where it was when you were born.

"It's like . . . this slow realization where you remember your childhood desires. You're ready to become your purest self. But it feels very urgent. Very ruthless. Like, it's going to kick your ass—but you come out the other side even stronger. More *you*. And more aware of what you really want," she told me, her arm linked in mine. I felt honored to have a front row seat to her chrysalis, even if I found the whole "Saturn Return" thing pretty "woo woo" at the time.

But I've been thinking about what she said, about entering your thirties, and becoming your purest self.

Because I always felt most myself with her, in her glow.

I don't know who to be, or how to be, now that she's gone.

The Raise

My cab from Syosset Station pulls up to a massive white colonial with quaint blue shutters and a rolling, immaculate garden dotted with daffodils and light pink roses. This funeral home looks way more like a luxury bed and breakfast than a loading dock for dead bodies. I'd definitely earmark this place for a suburban getaway if I saw it on Airbnb.

This is my first time in Darcy's hometown. Whenever she prepared her weekend trips to visit her family, she'd suggest I come with. But then she'd never follow up, and go alone again, so I've only seen slivers of her childhood bedroom, her backyard, and her front porch, all from Zoom calls or on FaceTime. We had a habit of sending each other baby pictures whenever either of us went home: me in a French maid costume and bright red lip for my first-grade dance recital; her and her brother in matching hat-and-glove sets, throwing snow in Central Park.

I'm here by 3 p.m., as promised.

I walk past the staircase and read the signs on the wall. Chapel to the left, Family Room to the right. If the outside looks like a bed and breakfast, the inside looks like the business lounge of some stuffy country club, filled with jewel-toned carpets and all-mahogany furnishings.

I knock on the door of the Family Room and remove the wig from its sleeve.

Darcy's grandmother, Doretta, opens the door. I recognize her crisp white bob and preppy Tory Burch aesthetic from Darcy's family photos.

"Oh, thank heavens! Ceci—the wig is here. Thank you, dear." She grabs the wig from my grip and hobbles back toward the vanity where Cecilia is seated and staring blankly at the empty couch across the room. It's just the three of us. I'm not sure if I'm supposed to leave or stay, but I feel compelled to explain myself before Cecilia paws the cheap spandex cap or sees the eleven-dollar price tag.

I sit on the couch.

"Cecilia, I just wanted to say that I'm sorry for—"

"For what, honey?" Cecilia brings her eyes to meet mine, completely numb. To my relief, a woman in hot pink scrubs cracks the door open and takes the wig from Doretta.

"I'm glad you're here. I'm glad you wrote something. I'm not good at this stuff." Cecilia's hand shakes as she reaches for her lipstick. I never heard her talk for long enough to notice the edges of her Long Island accent. It's melodic, but crass.

"You're so tiny. You look good, though. Lost your appetite?" She shakes her head. "Not me. This whole thing has me eating *more*, not less. Such a shame."

"Oh," I reply. "Yeah . . . between this and planning for the fundraise, I think I just forget to eat most days."

Darcy started planning for our Series C right before she left for Burning Man, but now that she's gone, it's on me to sell investors, new and old, on Savvy's next big move. On why they need to give us seventy-five million dollars to keep going. On how we turn our fifty-million-dollar company into a *billion*-dollar business.

It's been fourteen days since I took over the company, and I've already lost six pounds. I used to indulge in the "distraction" of Instagram from time to time, posting my Sunday brunches: jammy eggs with charred greens and artisanal pâté from the farmer's market, each item meticulously merchandised on my luxe wooden dining table. Now all I can stomach are poorly rolled spliffs and pad Thai on the couch, and I haven't posted to my story in weeks. If I do eat dinner, I prefer to eat alone after my boyfriend is already asleep, accompanied by any show that can obliterate my brain cells. The days since Darcy's death have been nothing but endless spreadsheets, legal documents, and meetings, and by the time I get home from the office at ten or eleven, I need to sedate myself. Most mornings, I wake up at 6 a.m. to some fish-lipped Brit on Love Island crying in her confessional with crusty, shriveled noodles and tobacco crumbs strewn across my chest. I crawl into bed with Ethan for a quick morning cuddle, unsure if he knows we've spent the night apart or is completely oblivious, because he's never said a thing.

Cecilia starts coating her lips with a matte Chanel rouge, looking at me through the mirror. She's the spitting image of an Older Darcy, her cheeks a bit more defined, her beauty undeniable.

"Of everyone on the list you sent me, most people are coming. But I don't know most of them. Only Gordon," Cecilia says.

A flicker of adrenaline burns through my chest.

"Darcy would read me his texts," she continues. "But how bad could he be if he gave you girls all that money? And you won't even have to pay it back? I never got how that worked."

Last week, I texted Cecilia a list of all the Savvy investors who might come to Darcy's funeral. Some were angel investors who wrote a ten-thousand-dollar check ages ago and forgot. Others, like Gordon, had handed us millions. And they remembered.

"Yeah, well . . . it's venture capital. My mom says the same thing," I reply. I've spent countless FaceTimes explaining the nuances of Silicon Valley to my mother, who, like Cecilia and her husband, runs her own small business. "You never pay the money back, but investors hold you hostage in other ways. Like texting you at 10:30 p.m. on a Friday, asking for weekly sales numbers. This or that. I don't think I hate Gordon as much as Darcy did, but to be honest, I dealt with him much less."

I've been waiting for my tête-à-tête with Gordon all week. Of all our investors, he's the most important. And as of our last fundraise, he's now on our board. He has the power to oust me if he wanted to, so I need his support as the new CEO of Savvy, but more specifically, I need him to re-up his investment for this next round of financing, because if he doesn't, other investors will question Savvy's health and potential.

Without Gordon, there's no Series C.

Without Gordon, *it's all over.*

I notice Cecilia's hands are still shaking, though the rest of her seems so sedated.

"Well, he'll be here, apparently. I'm sure you'll have a lot to talk about," she sighs, and gets up from her seat. "I'm gonna go see how the wig's moving along. It's good to see you, Alexis. Feel free to use the Family Room today, if you need."

I make my way toward the Chapel and feel my phone vibrate in my pocket. As I open the door to take my seat, I skim back-to-back messages. They keep rolling in. And they're all from Gordon. He has his default settings locked to All Caps, which I've never understood, but I assume he's just too busy to undo it.

Gordon:
HEY. HOPE UR HANGIN' IN THR.
SORRY I HVNT CHECKED IN.
NECK + NECK W A16Z FOR THIS SEED ROUND.
OVERPRICED
BUT WE WILL SEE.

Gordon:
RUNNING A BIT LATE…
CAN U SAVE ME A SPOT?

The Raise

As I open the chapel doors, I spot Victoria, our Head of Growth, standing and chatting in the third row behind the Lyons and Darcy's college friends. She's with other members of our executive team, and I spot dozens more of my employees mulling around, swapping careful whispers. It feels weird to call them "my employees," even though I started Savvy with Darcy all those years ago. I used to think of them as hers, and me as one of them.

Victoria is wearing what I can only describe as a funeral muumuu. Even though it looks better suited for a sixty-year-old and does her delicate frame no favors, it likely cost upwards of four hundred dollars at some "shabby chic" boutique in Southampton, where her family vacations in the summer, and where Victoria has retreated for a string of mental health days since the accident. *Lucky bitch.*

She turns her head toward the door and waves me over. I quickly text Gordon back before taking my seat with the team.

> **Alexis:**
> I'm sitting toward the front...
> Put my bag down to save ur spot
> It's on a seat in the back
> Look to the left of the main door

I retrieve the eulogy from my purse and then rest the bag on Gordon's chair. He replies:

> **Gordon:**
> TY 4 THE HEADS UP. THE BACK IS GOOD.
> OH
> I CAN DO SUSHI AFTER
> U HUNGRY?

I put my phone on silent and click my screen to black.

I know exactly what this is. Whether it's divorced dads, shitty boyfriends, or detached investors, men always think a nice meal can override bad behavior.

And Gordon is no exception. In the absence of being helpful, like making intros we ask for or vetting our most senior hires, he just feeds us—*constantly*. We go on full-blown food tours every time he flies in from Mountain View. He takes us to breakfast. He buys us lunch. His admin makes dinner reservations at the most garish, bush-league places in the city. He tells us to order whatever we want, gets tipsy off one too many cocktails, and spends the rest of the night recounting his near-death experience in Bali, a story we've heard so many times I could parody it to a tee. After cashing out at Etoys.com right before the dot-com bubble burst, Gordon flew there on a whim. He hoped to stake his claim to some seventeen-year-old coding genius and was living ten miles away from an infamous bombing site.

After that harrowing night, he said, he made a promise to "help as many people as he could, for as long as he lived." A venture capitalist doing God's work. Every time he meandered into the Bali stuff, Darcy and I would grip each other under the table to suppress our disgusted amusement. His eyes were clearly looking for validation, but all we could muster were some "mmm"s and half-hearted "wow"s. According to us, "ten miles away" and "near-death" were far from synonymous, but by then, we understood reality distortion was par-for-the-course in Silicon Valley.

I scoot into the third pew to find my seat next to Victoria, who smells clean, but spicy, like a coastal heiress. She pinches the skin of my forearm. I'm never not struck by her beauty, which stands in stark contrast to mine, whatever little I've got. Where I'm cute and soft, she's foxy and sharp, with her dark brown almond eyes and glowing caramel skin. Whenever she comes back from seasonal trips to Santiago, where her family's from and where her dad still lives part-time, she returns even more golden and iridescent. She always looks chic and tidy, her hair pulled back in a tight, gelled bun. It's not hard to guess that she's meticulous, a perfectionist. I sense, like me, she has something to prove. But my buns have flyaways, and my skin is just oily. It doesn't really "glow."

"You're clammy as fuck," Victoria whispers in my ear.

"I'm aware," I reply. "I'm giving a five-minute eulogy, but I can barely string a sentence together right now."

"What's up? What do you need?"

"Ummmm to go back in time, convince Darcy to stay in the city or at the very least hog-tie her so she can't board the plane to Nevada. I just can't believe this happened," I continue. "I can't believe this is *happening*." I tighten my lips and cross my arms to physically restrict myself from saying more. I'm technically Victoria's boss, after all, and I can't unravel in front of her. Or Gordon. Or literally anyone.

"Okay, well, we both know it's too late for that. But it's not too late for *this*." She discreetly opens her Bottega bag and palms a few peachy-cream pills.

"What are those?" I quickly scan the room to make sure no one's watching.

"Xanax," Victoria replies. "If you took even half of one, you'd feel way less anxious in like, ten minutes. They work quick if you're just starting. I just . . . I don't know if you should go up there like this. You look noticeably damp."

Four words no one ever wants to hear.

On the one hand, Victoria's right. I descend into a sharp, sweaty panic anytime I have to chime in during our Savvy town halls. What'll happen once I'm up at the podium, speaking to everyone Darcy's ever known? On the other hand, I've never taken Xanax before. I'm comfortable with the all-natural stuff—tobacco, weed. They've gotten me through these last few weeks. But prescription pills have always spooked me. I don't like feeling out of control.

I feel both a tinge of hesitation and the promise of relief. Relief wins.

"*Fine*," I blurt under my breath, slipping my hand into her purse. Victoria smiles, and her plump, rosy cheeks hike up to meet her razor-sharp cheekbones.

As I bring the single pill to my tongue, using my teeth to bite it in half, the entire pill crumbles into a zillion pieces that melt into a chalky powder. *Shit.*

Just then, the priest mounts the podium and taps the microphone, asking everyone to settle down and take their seats.

"Victoria," I hiss, "I took all of it. I took the whole pill." She turns to me, her immaculate eyebrows raised in amusement.

"You'll be *fine*," she says. "Just enjoy it."

Within minutes, I'm floating face-up in a hot jacuzzi, indulging in a guilt-free, mid-day nap, tanning by the pool on that fifth margarita.

The funeral hymns sound like a lullaby. My seat feels like a dense, down sofa. Time passes and I can feel my cells yawn and stretch, finding an inner peace I've lacked for weeks now.

As I smooth out my papers, waiting for some cue to approach the podium for my eulogy, I hear a soft creaking noise coming from the back of the room. I turn and see Gordon slip through the chapel door.

He's here. Twenty minutes late.

Just then, Darcy's brother leans back from the second row and finds my line of sight. He tilts his head toward the priest and waits for me to signal back, confirming I know it's time.

I shuffle out of my row and slowly walk toward the front of the chapel. I'm immediately aware that everyone's watching me. *Can they tell I've been tranquilized? Is my gait okay?*

The Raise

Although the Xanax has gifted me an overall calm, it can't undo the fact that Darcy is dead. She's gone. As I get closer to the pulpit with each step, all the adrenaline and the anticipation turn into something more like misery. That feeling when your brain knows you are broken, your sadness is now a fact, but you feel too far gone to worry about it. So you sink deeper.

I let the mixtape of doubt and dread play on—*I can't win Gordon over, I'll never land the plane, I'm nothing without her*—but my body doesn't respond with cortisol. It just listens, like these thoughts are lines in a recipe or assembly instructions for an Ikea nightstand, and stays numb.

I think I like this Xanax stuff. Xanax is good.

As I take my place to speak, I quickly eye Darcy's lifeless body just a few feet away, listening to me from her open casket while cosplaying as Dead Ariel. If Darcy knew she looked like this, she'd be mortified. I wish they never had to shave her head to analyze the impact and injuries of her fall. I wish she never got run over by that moving art bus. I squint my eyes and breathe to shake the image of Darcy's bald, cold corpse on the autopsy table.

"Hello, everyone. And thanks for being here." *Deep breaths. You got this. You are simply sharing straight, factual information.*

"For those of you who do not know me, my name is Alexis Ecker. I started our company Savvy with Darcy nearly seven years ago."

Good job. Nailed it. Keep going. Just read the words on the page and look up sometimes.

"This feels like a very big responsibility. To try to communicate who Darcy was to all of you, and why she mattered so much to me. And I'm not sure I'm in the best condition to do so . . .

"Because like all of you, I am shocked. I am gutted. And I am hurt. I can't believe I have to live every day without her. Without my best friend. My partner. I don't know how to communicate the extent of my pain. Our pain. I am so sorry Cecilia and Rob, and the entire family."

I glance over at the Lyons expecting some sort of nonverbal acknowledgment, maybe a nod or a look we'd all share, but for some reason, no one meets my eyes. I try to shake off my confusion.

"I think all of us here on some level feel the same way. We feel that she was rare. She had that 'it' factor so many chase but can never catch. She was hungry, alive, and persistent, but still so loving and patient. She insisted on having a big life and made her dream a reality, building a fifty-million-dollar business in under a decade, employing nearly two hundred people in four different countries."

If we don't close the Series C, these employees will lose everything. Salary, healthcare. All of it. I look at Gordon, but he isn't even listening. He's texting. Probably back-channeling for his seed deal. *What a prick.*

In an instant, my head starts pounding, and I'm having trouble focusing on the words on the page. My stomach grumbles, and I realize I haven't eaten today or had any water.

My eyes are blurring so badly that I physically can't read. I take a deep breath and turn all my notes face down on the podium. I decide to go for it, raw-dog it, praying my tired, hungry words will still do Darcy justice.

"For those who are LISTENING—" I project into the microphone. Gordon looks up, eyebrows as high as his receding hairline, glancing around to see if anyone saw him texting.

"Darcy wasn't scared," I continue. "And neither am I. She trained me to be fearless. She could look a challenge in the eye and know it was gonna be a nightmare, but she pushed on anyway. She took every 'no' as a 'maybe,' every 'never' as a 'not yet.' Nothing, and no one, got in her way. Once she set her mind to something, it had to happen."

I stare straight at Gordon, my mind racing but my heartbeat steady. The Xanax calm feels like a new superpower.

"To preserve Darcy's legacy, we must keep building. Keep fighting." I look to Victoria and notice she's sobbing, almost uncontrollably. I've never seen her so undone. In this moment, I know we're making a silent pact: to protect Savvy. To grow it. To get this raise done. *Together.*

"She taught me to want more for myself—to want the *most* for myself. And to think big. So, I guess you could say, for many of us probably, we loved her because she was so brilliant and wild, so unstoppable . . ." Stunned by how true those words feel, even with the Xanax weighing me down, my throat tightens.

"The best way we can honor her, how I want us to all honor her, is by taking on some of those qualities ourselves. That way, the best of Darcy can live on. We can look at her resilience and become a bit more fearless in our own lives. And while some of us may never have that 'it' factor, that thing in Darcy that made her so special, we can still channel her persistence and her confidence and live every day like our dreams can come true, too. Just like hers did. And we should all want more for ourselves. We all have the power to look at where we are today, and where we want to be, and do something about it. Darcy stretched my sense of self and what I thought I was capable of, and when someone does that, it's a gift. Darcy—my friend, my big sister, my partner in life and at work," I eke out, with finality, "*you* were a gift. Thank you for everything."

As I dismount the chapel podium and make my blurry-eyed return to my seat, I glance at Gordon again to get a read on how the eulogy landed, but he's back on his phone, engrossed in his private world of deal-making and scrolling Twitter. I shuffle through my row and sit back down next to Victoria, who grabs my hand and squeezes it so hard, it hurts.

2

Everyone has migrated to The Community Room for crudités and tea. I need to recenter for a few minutes before my face-to-face with Gordon. I take every precaution to avoid Cecilia as I make a cup of earl grey and scour for a seat by the window. She couldn't make eye contact with me during the eulogy, which can only mean she finally saw the mermaid wig and suffered greatly.

I wander past a cluster of bodies and feel a tug on the back of my blazer.

It's Gordon.

"Hey kiddo!" he says a bit too loud, a bit too cheerfully. His wispy, barely-there hair looks thinner than usual, and his six-foot-five frame is drowning in his Men's Wearhouse suit. He's either one of those venture capitalists that likes to look like they're not rich, or he simply has no taste, and neither does his wife.

He pulls me in for a hug. His familiar smell of dirty soil and vetiver shocks my system, and my adrenaline surges, challenging the calm of Victoria's tiny sedatives. In my heels, we're almost chest to chest, and I can feel my heart pounding. I pray with all my might that he can't.

"I mean—*wow*. What a eulogy," he says as we break our embrace. "Darcy would've loved it. Really glad I got in on time to listen."

He's glad he "got in on time," like this was a Broadway show, or a Bruce Springsteen concert.

Honestly, it's all pretty on-brand. Nearly two years into working with Gordon, he'd still mix up our names, or completely mispronounce them. One time, during a board meeting, he called Darcy "Daresee" over and over again. Darcy and I Slacked each other furiously, wondering if he was stroking out, or playing some Silicon Valley mindgame he heard about on a podcast.

"It's nice to see you, Gordon," I say assertively, trying to take control of the conversation. "Now is obviously not the setting, but I think we should find some time this week to game out the Series C? I'm new to all of this, and I just want to make sure I'm on track? Isabella suggested an early press push, something signaling that both your funds are happy with our growth, excited for the future . . ."

"Well—*are we*?" he cuts in, eyes squinting.

"Are we *what*?"

"Happy with the growth, and excited for the future," he responds. A server glides by with tiny tea sandwiches on a tray. Gordon picks one up, lifts it to his mouth, and then pauses.

"Are there peanuts in this?" he interrogates in that all-too-familiar tone, like he's poking a hole in the server's business plan.

The server shoots me a blank stare. She glares down at the tiny sandwiches, and then back at Gordon.

"I . . . I don't think so," she replies nervously. "It's just cucumbers and cream cheese. I've never had that with peanuts before, so I think you're—"

He drops it back on the platter, and the server scurries off. I clear my throat, determined to take the reins.

"Our growth is undeniable, Gordon. We're about to break five hundred thousand customers and I thought that—"

"Get to a million customers and we should be in good shape," he says flippantly, like he's telling me to order a pizza, or make a phone call.

He registers the stunned look on my face, then continues. "Look, I got word that Crafted is doing over a *billion* in revenue this year." He leans in closer. "Some analyst at Alliance worked at Shopify with Marz and he says they just hit two million customers."

Marz is the thirty-three-year-old founder and CEO at our competitor, Crafted. His résumé reads like a VC's wet dream: affable Texas kid, Stanford engineer, commerce veteran, and self-proclaimed "thought leader." But that's just a euphemism for "Tweets a lot."

"Marz scooped up all the best ecomm people at Amazon and Etsy," Gordon stresses. "The story's just gotta be super defensible, indestructible frankly, if you girls are gonna keep this going."

He puts his hand on my shoulder and gives it a quick squeeze before turning and disappearing into the crowd. I feel like running. Screaming. My thoughts flit from Darcy's casket to her cracked, barren skull, her body laying helpless in the sand.

You girls. I hear my heartbeat grow louder and feel it throbbing inside my chest as the soles of my feet begin to tingle and my vision starts to blur again. As the tingling spreads through my toes and my ankles, I feel light and nauseous, like I'm hanging upside down with my hands behind my back. Blind and alone.

Double our customer base? In less than two months? Alone? Without Darcy? This can't be happening.

This isn't happening.

I suck in a bit of air. In the last two weeks, when I've felt like I'm on the verge of a full-blown panic attack, I pull up our Slack messages, which calm me down immediately. Because she comes back to life. It's like she's still here.

But I'm stranded at her funeral, and she's not here, and I can't have Gordon see me like this. As bodies shift and move and mingle, I spot a door. It's the one we came in from. I push my way through the conversations and controlled crying and make a beeline for the exit. I grip the door handle and suck in more air as I pull myself through to the other side.

It's quiet. I lean on the door to steady myself and take four deep breaths in and out, in and out, while biting the meat of my left hand, the skin right below my knuckles. My teeth know just where to grip. I used to bite the top of my hands as a kid to quiet my cries every time my parents would fight, their screams echoing in the hallway and slipping through the cracks in my bedroom door. I would listen to Simon gaslight my mom, telling her she was crazy, that she had nothing to worry about. I wanted to sprint through the hallway and burst into their room to call him a liar. But we needed him, and I knew that, so I bit my skin raw instead.

I clench as hard as I can, grinding from left to right. The mouthfeel of my own flesh slows down my breathing and calms me down. I close my eyes and release my grip, quickly wiping the saliva off my face and hand. I perk up, remembering my conversation with Cecilia. She told me I could use The Family Room today. If I needed.

I need it.

I collect myself and walk toward The Family Room, tucking my hand inside my sleeve to hide the raw bite marks and irritation.

I get to the door.

It's locked.

I knock three times and wait. Within a few seconds, Doretta opens the door a crack and peeks her head out to greet me.

"Oh, hello dear," she says sweetly. "Did you leave something in the room? I can find it for you."

"No," I reply. "I'm just . . . I think I could sit. Alone. I mean—I think I need to sit down somewhere, alone. Away from everybody. If that's . . . if that's okay. Just for a little bit." The bites on my hand start to burn and flare out, my whole hand on fire.

"Oh . . . I . . ." she trails off. "One second, dear."

Doretta shuts the door and reemerges seconds later.

"I'm sorry, honey. It's family only right now," she says, slowly shutting the door to leave me here outside, by myself.

"But Cecilia . . . Cecilia said I could use the room. She said I could use it. If I needed it." The words rush out of me.

Doretta pulls the door back open, her eyes boring into mine now, her voice level.

"That was before she saw the wig."

She shuts the door and turns the lock.

I feel my phone vibrate against my thigh. Stunned, I slip my hand into my pocket and click my screen awake.

> **Gordon:**
> TNX 4 WORKING SO HARD
> HAD TO JUMP
> GET THE #S AND YOU GOT THE $$
> ILL GET MORE DEETS ON THE MARZ STUFF

Get the numbers. Get the money.

My body tenses and my feet go light again. My head is spinning. I start walking, unsure of why, or where I'm going.

I find myself back in the chapel. It's empty, but she's still here.

I rush toward Darcy's casket and throw my arms over her chest. I bury my head in her lap and stare up at her freckled face and fake hairline.

She looks so peaceful. So free. No more hourly texts from Gordon. No more trudging from fundraise to fundraise. No more blinking at the screen, eyes weary from endless documents and expense reports.

Nothing left to fight for. Nothing left to prove.

"Wake up," I beg, hot tears and snot pooling toward my lips. *"Wake up, wake up, wake up."*

March 31, 2019

> **Darcy Lyons 7:46PM**
> samira just quit

> **Alexis Ecker 7:47PM**
> NO

> **Darcy Lyons 7:47PM**
> ya

> **Alexis Ecker 7:47PM**
> fuuuckkk r u ok

> **Darcy Lyons 7:47PM**
> ya im just annoyed
> like

> **Alexis Ecker 7:48PM**
> how did she do it
> what happened

> **Darcy Lyons 7:48PM**
> we kicked off our 1:1 and before I could rly go into stuff she handed me her letter of resignation and she walked me through her plans for the next 2 weeks to offboard

Alexis Ecker 7:49PM
oof

Darcy Lyons 7:57PM
im kind of like
whatever abt it honestly

Alexis Ecker 7:57PM
?

Darcy Lyons 7:57PM
i mean she was GOOD but she wasn't GREAT

Alexis Ecker 7:58PM
idk I thought she was a great hire
both a good manager and operator
and culturally brought a lot, like
was very ra-ra about us and the company

Darcy Lyons 7:59PM
yah but u didn't manage her
idk
she was fine I guess

Alexis Ecker 7:59PM
do u know where she's going

Darcy Lyons 8:04PM
no
I didn't ask tho

Alexis Ecker 8:04PM
hmm

Darcy Lyons 8:05PM
she strikes me as the type who will just like
get this next job but then rly hunt for a husband and
eventually
just settle down and do that
like she's not a killer
or that ambitious

The Raise

Alexis Ecker 8:05PM
yah I can see that

Alexis Ecker 8:15PM
r u ok tho

                    Darcy Lyons 8:16PM
          yah idk what I could've done differently
        she said she was looking for more "structure"
             like bitch y r u at a startup then lol

Alexis Ecker 8:16PM
ya im sure it was just a fit thing
like within a year you know if a job makes sense long term
its ok for her to want less chaos

Alexis Ecker 8:18PM
not that ur chaotic I just mean
what u said about being at a startup but wanting structure

                    Darcy Lyons 8:30PM
                                ya
                             well
            maybe I am a bit chaotic
                      who knows

Alexis Ecker 8:30PM
well that's why u have me
ur chaos wrangler
ur systems fairy

                    Darcy Lyons 8:36PM
                               ☺

Alexis Ecker 8:38PM
r u gonna backfill the role or nah

Darcy Lyons 8:39PM
i haven't decided yet
i def need it
but we could maybe put the work on Oren
and see if he flinches
or asks for more money
lol

Alexis Ecker 8:39PM
he loves you
he'll do it fo free

Darcy Lyons 8:40PM
idk
maybe im too chaotic

Alexis Ecker 8:40PM
stfu
ur literally an icon

Darcy Lyons 8:40PM
a chaotic icon

Alexis Ecker 8:40PM
im gonna storm in there and smack u I swear

3

"You're home!" Ethan roars from the bedroom, like a zealous golden retriever puppy. There's no denying that he's always, *always* happy to see me.

I throw my backpack on the floor and let out a loud grunt, tripping over an overflowing cluster of white orchids, lilies and roses. Dozens of identical condolence arrangements line our living room, all clearly ordered from the same flower delivery startup with ten dollars off and free shipping. I beeline for the fridge and pour myself a glass of crisp Sancerre.

Ethan couldn't come to Darcy's funeral today because he was on a fundraising trip for his new non-profit, ALLMENMATR, a community and platform that offers "online resources, real-time text support and in-person retreats for men committed to their emotional and physical wellness." I was sad to go alone, but he's never not there for me, and I know the trip was important to him. Besides, I fear doing the eulogy in front of him would've made me even more anxious, Xanax be damned.

He's been an Associate at the law firm Randall, Strawn and Sterling LLP and pushing paper on behalf of big corporations for nearly ten years. His mom, Janine, is a waspy, New York Lisa Bloom. She's a legendary women's rights warrior who's somehow chummy with both Malala and Woody Allen. I'm sure she helped him get into Columbia Law School way back when, and I'm sure she helped him land his gig at RSS, so it tracks that he's worried she'll blow up when she hears his big news: he's not on the "partner track" there anymore. He found out during a performance review a few weeks ago, and ALLMENMATR is Ethan's anxious but well-meaning attempt to get back in her good graces.

It's always like that with them. She sees him as a reflection of her—of her worth, of her talent—and if he falls short, she implodes. On the phone. Out to dinner. When he's helping her in the kitchen. Regardless of whether it's just the three of us, or a whole room of New York somebodies. And every time it happens, my heart breaks for him. Her voice—that low, vicious crackle—feels both triggering and familiar. It reminds me so much of how my dad would talk to my mom growing up. The carelessness. The venom.

That's why I haven't seen him in over fifteen years. I have to protect myself. And sometimes, the wounded girl in me so deeply wishes Ethan could muster up the courage to do the same with his mom. But until then, I bend a little. I let him risk missing the funeral for the benefit of the non-profit, if that's what it takes to keep Janine sated and even keeled.

"I got you your favorite!" he exclaims, fleeing the bedroom and bringing me in for a tight hug and back rub, my face buried in his lean, hard chest. "Crispy sesame chicken and brown rice. And some bok choy for my *tinylittlebaby*." Wearing cashmere joggers and a long-sleeve waffle henley, he settles in by the kitchen counter and starts prying open the plastic lids. "I figured you wanted to keep things clean, but I went fun n' fried on the protein, given the day you've had. I'll probably just have some veggies and rice, so the chicken's all you."

I met Ethan when he was fat, and he met me when I was poor. And we both moved from an inferior city to the best city in the world. We're both "coastal elites"—he's originally from Boca Raton, Florida, though he always says he's "from Miami" when people ask. Ethan's mom moved the family from "Miami" to Manhattan at some point in the late nineties to get re-licensed and launch her own practice, while mine impulsively moved the two of us from our three-story house in Orange County, California to a small studio in Chinatown after I ruined my parents' marriage.

Ethan and I went to the University of Michigan together, and he was one year my senior. After bingeing *Mad Men* the summer before junior year, I eagerly signed up for an advertising and marketing course in the business school. Ethan and I were put in the same group for our big end-of-semester project: we had to create a comprehensive positioning, go-to-market and media plan for a fake sports drink. The other students in our group were a bit too *Middle America* for us—they wore Old Navy unironically and said "pop" instead of "soda"—so we clung to each other and became fast friends. Ethan invited me on a "research trip" to a football game at The Big House. He snuck in some spiked Gatorade and we got wasted rating all the flavors and shit-talking everyone else in the class, because neither of us knew the first thing about touchdowns or end zones or muff scrambles and all that.

Our friendship didn't bloom into a full-fledged romance until three years later—after I graduated, and he lost about forty pounds. It was the night I got rejected from the full-time job at *The Magazine*, sobering up after hours of pickleback shots with a friend in Union Square. We ran into each other at the diner near my old East Village apartment. He was alone, shoveling down a tuna melt when I walked in, hammered. He called me over to his booth and murmured that his nutritionist says he shouldn't be eating all those carbs—"not even the wheat bread." I didn't recognize him at first. But as I neared, I saw his Bambi-brown eyes soften, and I realized it was Ethan. Ethan from class. He gave me half his sandwich, and we caught up for hours. Suddenly it was 5 a.m., and we were stumbling into his two-thousand-square-foot apartment on Park Avenue. Six months later, I moved in. I had been living with my mom downtown before, so all I had to do was Uber uptown with my suitcase.

Within just two weeks, he posted me to his Instagram grid and started sprinkling scenes from our quaint little life on his Instagram stories—us making breakfast, or a trip upstate with his work friends. No one had claimed me like that before. No boyfriend had ever wanted to show me off or called me his "queen." That's the first caption he ever wrote: "My Storm Queen." It was the day we went to Brooklyn Botanical Garden and got caught in torrential rain. He had me meet his mom only a month into dating. It felt more high-pressure than interviewing for a job with Darcy at Jetto—more intense than giving her eulogy, even. But the idea of Ethan—the security he represented, his status, his stability—was worth any challenge.

"Babe," Ethan says as I dump heaps of chicken onto my plate, "the helicopter is the move. I can't believe I've never done it before. The trip there was like—I wanna say it was under forty-five minutes or something. And Montauk is so much nicer off-season. No bridge-and-tunnel bullshit," he quips as he chews. "Sorry again I didn't make it back. I was on the pilot's ass to make it out by nine. The maintenance delay was insane."

Ethan can rent a helicopter to Montauk because he is rich. New money rich. Beyond Janine's seven-to-eight-figure income, Ethan's father is a quiet albeit powerful real estate developer in Florida, which means Ethan doesn't have to work to live. But I love that he's a striver, anyway. Maybe the average liberal girlie wouldn't *love* that his firm represents the likes of Walmart and Chick-fil-A—massive corporations with questionable politics—but it's a high-paying gig he got on his own merit, even if Janine likely nabbed him the interview, and it's a job he's been deeply committed to for as long as we've been together. That's why we were both devastated when we learned he wasn't in-line to make Partner. I've seen him work too many grueling cases and pull too many all-nighters for there to be no payoff. It would be akin to Savvy collapsing after years of hustling and hiring and growing—of checking every box, but with no gold star in sight. I couldn't imagine being with someone who couldn't empathize with my ambition or my workload, especially now, when I feel like I'm drowning in more to-do's than ever. I find his commitment not only sexy, but essential in how we understand each other.

I still don't know why Ethan was overlooked for Partner, though. It seemed like things had been going so well. But he told me the day before Darcy died, so we haven't been able to revisit it. He hasn't said anything, and I haven't brought it up again.

"So, how'd it all go, then?" he asks between bites of bok choy. "I want the highlight reel. I mean, not that there are 'highlights' to a funeral, but I—"

"I mean, I kind of blacked it all out anyway, so it's fine," I reply, forking my mound of chicken. "But guess who showed up twenty minutes late? And almost missed my eulogy?"

"Gordon?" he asks, a wad of black bean sauce dripping down his chin. He wipes it away and pops another piece of bok choy into his mouth.

I nod. "I think I did okay. I went off script a bit. But Gordon wasn't listening, and I felt like—"

"*You* went off script?! Overcoming your fear of public speaking *and* ad-libbing in one fell swoop? Jesus." He smiles, proud of me.

"Yeah, well, it just kind of happened." I have no intention of getting Ethan up-to-speed on my rendezvous with Victoria's magic pills.

"I'm sure you crushed it," he says, giving me a quick kiss on the head before spooning more veggies. "It's all good with Gordon, then?"

Get the numbers. Get the money.

"Kind of," I reply. I pulled an Irish exit at the funeral, but on the train ride home I made sure to text Victoria about Gordon's newest mandate.

"Kind of? What does that mean?" Ethan asks.

"Crafted is doing even better than we thought," I explain. I fill my frail, hollow body with more food and my phone buzzes. I pick it up and read Victoria's reply.

> **Victoria:**
> We just have 2 regroup + crunch the numbers!
> Throw cash at some trusted channels
> All good, I promise
> And beautiful job today <3

I notice another unread text, this time from Hazel, a freelance HR executive we hired to help us do layoffs last year. She works with startups to hire people, fire people, and do internal investigations.

> **Hazel:**
> Couldnt make it today but want you to know Im thinking of you
> Let's chat when you have a bit more breathing room
> But very soon

"How much better than you thought?" Ethan pries, using his spoon to scrape the last of the sauce from the bok choy container, then licking it like it's ice cream. He's doing the head tilt thing he does when he wants me to get off my phone but doesn't outright say it, so I click my screen to black, ignoring Victoria and Hazel, and try to focus on our conversation.

"Um...they're doing a billion in revenue—maybe more—and they have, like, two million customers?" I shift in my seat. "Gordon wants us to double our customers now. Finally hit a million."

"Alexis, that's . . ."

"I know. But we have two months to do it, and I think Victoria and I can—"

"Two months, though? Couldn't he have told you earlier? He's putting all this on you at her funeral?" Ethan fumes as he snaps plastic takeout lids into place, loose juices and condensation spattering across the kitchen counter. "You should replace this guy."

"It doesn't work that way," I say.

"Well, let's call my mom," he continues, pacing the apartment. "You could buy him out. You could use this, you know, to turn the rest of the board against him and push him out." He goes quiet and starts biting his cheek, likely recounting his favorite episodes of *Billions* and *Succession*, which are his primary and only references for what happens on startup boards, or in board rooms period. He works for storied institutions, not scrappy little tech companies, and as an Associate, he doesn't have massive exposure to crazy corporate drama quite yet. But soon. He'll probably switch firms in the coming months. Find a firm that's more aligned to his values—to *our* values. Or maybe ALLMENMATR will take off and grow into something more than just a side project.

What Ethan may never fully get, though, is that for founders, but especially women, legally removing someone from your board is just as unlikely as securing enough investors to form one in the first place.

But more than that—Gordon deserves his seat and his ownership stake in Savvy. It makes me sick because he's so obnoxious and insensitive sometimes, but it's true.

Two years ago, running out of cash from the Series A financing and on the brink of bankruptcy, Gordon and Alliance Capital gave us our big break. Alliance was a blue-chip legacy firm with a sound reputation and three decades of experience building billion-dollar companies. They were one of the firms behind Apple, Netflix and Uber, and we knew that their seal of approval would matter more to potential investors than any data point or story arc. They confirmed our meeting on a Tuesday, and we booked a flight to San Francisco that night to meet with their team first-thing Wednesday morning.

As I clicked to the last slide of our pitch deck, eyes glazed over from no sleep and burnt JetBlue coffee, Darcy's voice was straight and steady on the closing line I'd composed: "Because we know that the future of retail is online, personal, and programmatic." Gordon interrupted with four words that would save Savvy and usher in a new era of legitimacy.

"Do I know you?" he asked, eyes on Darcy.

Darcy looked at me, then at Gordon.

"Um . . . I . . . I'm not sure!" She laughed, sensing an opportunity. "I was named Salesperson of the Year at Ramper, which I know you invested in, and I was featured in a big Forbes piece a few years ago. So maybe from that?"

"Not that," Gordon cut in, shaking his head. "But I know now. Now I remember." We all waited in silence for the big reveal.

"Darcy Lyons," Gordon said, punctuating each consonant. "I knew this pitch sounded familiar. And I *knew* I knew you from somewhere. G Calibrator. God knows how long ago. You must've been barely legal." He chuckled and bit his lip.

Darcy winced, but quickly plastered on her poker face. She was used to this by now, being remembered for her looks, identified by her pristine, model-esque vessel.

But he was right. In between her freshman and sophomore year at Duke, Darcy attended a month-long bootcamp in Mountain View called "G Calibrator" which brought together young startup hopefuls for four weeks of education, hack-a-thons, and networking, all culminating in a final mock pitch to real investors. Darcy presented a clunky, nascent version of Savvy, the deck chock-full of *Clueless* references and screengrabs from the film. At the time, the all-male judges, Gordon included, said the concept was "too niche."

But this time, Gordon said he was impressed with Darcy's foresight and consistency. Within weeks, we had a term sheet from Alliance and money in the bank. The firm became Savvy's majority stakeholder, Gordon joined our board, and his reign of terror began. Gordon was grating and incompetent, but Darcy and I kept our eyes on the prize. If we nabbed a new lead investor in our Series C, we could potentially cut Gordon loose, but in the meantime, we needed his approval, which meant kowtowing to his ego and doing whatever he said.

I've explained this to Ethan a thousand times, but for some reason, it's hard for him to comprehend why Gordon has so much power over us and what we do with Savvy.

"I've said it before and I'll say it again, but I'd *really* like to stop saying it," I tell Ethan. "I love that you want to help, and I know your mom would love to help, but there's really nothing we can do, here. Trust me." I kiss him with salty, black-bean-sauced lips.

"Look, if anyone can make all this happen, it's you," Ethan says, coming up behind me and wrapping his arms around my chest.

"We're fucked on cash though," I murmur into his bicep. "I gotta grow this thing on a shoestring budget."

"You got two months," he says, squeezing my shoulders, "and you'll do it, and it'll all calm down after that."

"I don't know about that."

"About what? It calming down?"

"Yeah."

"I mean, how much different can the CEO gig be from the COO gig after the raise, right? Why would it be more work?"

"Well, it's more public-facing. That was all Darcy. I never did the podcasts or town hall speeches or press and all that stuff." I think back on how excited I would feel watching Darcy mount a microphone or flirt with a journalist. She was effortlessly extroverted, and she perfectly embodied the Savvy brand and its mix of elegance, joy, and spunk.

"Yah but if you crush it, you get all the credit." He kisses my neck and retreats to the fridge.

I would rather have Darcy back, doing the press, running the pitches, leading our all-team town halls, and stay behind the curtain where I belong. I never wanted or needed the exposure of a "CEO," but I guess Ethan sees the exposure as currency in a way I never have. I've always seen it as a liability and still do.

"If I crush it then yah, sure. But if I screw up or if I don't raise the money, it's like, very squarely on me . . ."

"You won't screw up," Ethan says, playfully rolling his beautiful doe eyes, and smacking me on the butt.

4

September 18, 2019.

I wake up in bed, my eyes crusted closed as I paw around for my phone. My alarm sounds louder, more grating than usual. I finally find it and lurch forward, nearly knocking over a full lukewarm glass of water that's conveniently stationed on my bedside table.

The bedroom door is open. Ethan's not here. I feel disoriented and confused, unsure as to how or when I went to sleep.

I do my usual morning scroll—emails, Twitter, iMessage—and catch a text from Ethan.

> **Ethan:**
> You passed out during Colbert again.
> There's cold brew and parfait for u in the fridge.
> Good luck today

After slathering my under eyes in color corrector and concealer and dabbing on some ruby ChapStick, I slip on my trusted wide-legged trousers, oversized black blazer, and gilded loafers. The outfit says dutiful and methodical, while the gold-studded loafers promise spunk. The goal, Darcy would say, is to look polished but approachable, like you can pound a beer with the sales team, then playfully demand that they get back to work. "No one wants to work for a stiff cunt in a sheath dress."

Which is just my luck because I'm not physically built for a sheath dress. My boobs are too big, and my hips are too narrow, so I just end up looking like SpongeBob SquarePants in drag.

I top off my look with my thick-rimmed, oversized frames. They are my armor. Right before graduating high school, my college counselor—who I loved—asked me to hang back in her office for a few minutes before swapping goodbyes. "You're smart," she said, "but between the blond hair and your baby face, folks may not see that right away." I bought these Oliver Peoples on sale right after closing our seed round, as soon as I knew I'd be managing other people. They add some chisel to my otherwise soft, pasty appearance. Where Darcy was tight, petite, and lean, like an athlete, I've always been a little round. Not heavyset, per se, but cherubic and pale, like the Pillsbury Dough Boy is somewhere in my 23andMe.

Waiting for the elevator down to the lobby, I hear my phone ping. I wonder if it's Gordon, terrorizing me with requests for our latest customer count or revenue targets.

But it isn't. It's some unknown number I don't have saved.

Dr. Wes:
Hey friend. Its Wes. Gordon gave me your number at the funeral. Your eulogy was beautiful. I know you need some space right now, but I got resources if you need 'em. Watched one of my best friends go recently too. Its brutal. Take care. You got this.

By the time I get to the pizzeria behind our office, I've nearly committed his text to memory. I pull out a cigarette and lighter as I watch the morning rats dart around eating scraps from last night, the "take care, you got this" swimming inside my belly against my will.

I feel lighter somehow, hearing from him. Wesley Atkins was the only investor who sent us a thoughtful, honest rejection after our pitch. So many investors, and especially all the guys at his firm, FifteenFive, write you back some soft bullshit like they "don't know enough about the space to cut a meaningful check" or they "don't think it's a fit with their investment thesis" or they "worry about the market and how it scales," when what they really mean is, "we don't trust you," "we don't think you'll make us any money," and "we don't think you'll make it big enough."

Wesley said he was skeptical of the business model and how we'd reach profitability. He said Crafted was a real concern. They had more money, and a bigger and arguably better team. But he also said the numbers proved we were determined and effective founders, and that he'd like us to stay in touch.

So we did.

We started calling him Dr. Wes after he took a break from venture to get his PhD in computer science from MIT, where he teaches now. He's been generous with his time when we've really needed him, which is twice a year or so, and openly shares his wisdom on everything from our fundraising strategy to what to look for in a Head of Finance to how to compete with Crafted.

I stomp out my cigarette and draft a quick, tame response before heading up to my desk.

The Raise

> **Alexis:**
> You were at the funeral? Had no idea.
> Thanks so much for coming and the kind words
> I'm in "oh no I'm CEO now" mode
> but hoping things settle soon
> And sry about ur friend! That sucks.

I always get to the office at 7 a.m., nearly two hours before everyone else starts trickling in with their minimalist leather totes in one hand and matcha latte in the other.

The space reflects Darcy's taste to a tee: the mix of soft and sharp edges, the muted tones with thoughtful pops of color, the faint candle smell laced with black currant, wood, and fig. It's pure comfort. Womb-like.

This has always been my favorite time of day, no thundering knocks on my office door, no meetings to run, no egos to manage. Running a company is kind of like getting shoved into a blender, ground to a pulp, then boiled into Jell-O. People bum-rush you with their problems all day; they fling unsolicited "feedback" around while begging for some grateful acknowledgment; they incessantly Slack questions that ping every device on or near your person, then cling to you for answers only you can give. It feels like a constant crushing; you can feel it in every meeting, every interaction, but like Jell-O, you must stay firm. You must keep shape.

Every morning here alone, I slip into a new skin. I become the version of me that can keep shape, or at least try. In these flesh-tones hallways and endless Nespresso pods, I convince myself that I deserve to be here. That I deserve to lead.

Sometimes it feels like I'm only able get dressed, show up and put on this daily charade because I watched Darcy do it for so many years, like I was her understudy, and we were in some drawn-out dress rehearsal. And in everything she did, she operated with so much empathy, which makes the weight of replacing her feel even more daunting.

I watched her give job offers and take jobs away. I watched her share constructive feedback on parts of the business she struggled to understand. I heard her calm down and motivate overworked employees she still needed more from. I helped her vet ideas and navigate mistakes. And every trial, every tribulation, taught me something new and reassuring about Darcy: that she was patient, that she was reasonable, that she was wise. A part of my brain was always lightly suspicious—because she was so beautiful and talented, and such a strong leader. She seemed too good to be true.

One time, we received a series of complaints that Bianca, one of our senior sales executives, was bullying the junior talent on her team. Bianca was a top performer. Most of the brands who sold with Savvy signed with her more than anything else. Darcy used to say that "good salespeople don't sell you a product, they sell you a coke bump of their friendship." And she was right. Brands wanted to be affiliated with Bianca. She was a micro-influencer with amazing taste, knew all the coolest spots in the city, and made everyone feel like the most special person alive. She was Victoria's golden goose: the cog in her growth wheel that spun faster and harder than everyone else. The public sales tracker meant everyone knew how effective and powerful Bianca was, so when the complaints about her trickled in, I knew Darcy was incentivized to look away. To bury it.

But that's not what happened.

The Raise

"We have to find out what's going on," she told me in her office after the third complaint popped up in the anonymous employee feedback widget. "I feel like I need to talk to all the girls or something."

Darcy called the more junior, female members of the team "girls," not because she wanted to infantilize them or felt any explicit ageism, but because on some intrinsic level, she loved them all like the little sisters she never had. Like how she loved me. But while I welcomed her moments of tough love, her high bar, and her critical feedback, many of the more junior women on the team were simply more fragile and sensitive.

"I don't think they'll talk to you openly," I said, always more aware than she was of the effect she had on people, her tendency to intimidate without trying. "But I agree that it's no bueno."

Weighing my words, Darcy emailed Isabella, one of our investors, to see if she knew a freelance Human Resources Investigator, someone skilled in navigating these types of complaints and sussing out the severity and legitimacy of various allegations. At this point, we were only fifty people, and we didn't have a human resources department. Our investors said companies typically hired those teams after their Series B, and we never had one at Jetto, either. It was usually fine, but when stuff like this flared up, the scramble to fix it could easily become all-consuming.

That's how we met Hazel. Hazel was a Southern child psychologist turned Workplace Culture Specialist. She never said it out loud, but I could glean that there weren't many Southern kids going to therapy, and she had a sixth sense that the tech sector could net her more money and more status than coaching seventh graders through the misery of middle school.

Hazel performed a quiet, internal investigation, meeting with each of the "girls" and scanning communications between Bianca and her direct reports. Hazel proposed that Darcy let Bianca go despite her stellar performance, and she did, without second thought.

Darcy was always cool, calm, and collected like that, and that's why it hurt so bad when she snapped at me right before she left for Reno. I can't get it out of my head. It was so unexpected and out of character, possessed by a pulsing anxiety I didn't think she was capable of feeling.

I was always in the background, plugging holes in the Savvy ship and making sure things went off without a hitch, whether I was troubleshooting issues with our logistics partners and renegotiating our contracts or vetting better software for our customer success teams. Any time something wasn't working right, working perfectly, in how the business functioned or how our systems flowed, I'd drop in with an invisible parachute and clean the mess. That was my value. That was my purpose.

A few months ago, we were supposed to launch a program that would remove our need to hold any inventory. Our brand partners— the ones we promoted to customers on the platform—would start fulfilling the orders instead. The only thing we'd keep sending were the fifteen-dollar welcome boxes we offer first-time customers. Internally, the project was called "Stop The Bleed," because we were spending so much of our funding and our sales on inventory, and by successfully launching, we'd save us tons of money, and lots of headache. We hired a dozen new engineers, because we had to build tons of special software and tools to make it work, and I was the sole owner of the entire project. I was more underwater and overwhelmed than I had ever been before.

I was worried that the timeline of the launch was way too tight. The engineers were working as quickly as they could, but we didn't have a stable system for testing the new tools internally, or with our brand partners. I told Darcy I felt like I was accountable for too many disconnected projects, and that organizing and overseeing every detail of "Stop The Bleed" was edging me toward the brink of a breakdown. I came to her office to ask for help, for us to hire an air-traffic-controller-type to come in and do the project management, so I could brainstorm and implement a testing protocol.

I got a hard "no."

"We're tight on cash as it is," she said from behind her cluttered desk, empathetic but still firm. "That's why we need this to launch on time. After the Series C, we'll have the cash to hire whoever you want and get you some support. But I need to know you're cut out for this—for the future. Because things will only get harder and messier from here." I can still hear her in my head, like she's sitting right next to me, instead of laying lifeless underground in Syosset with a Mermaid wig glued to her head.

So, I charged forward, as instructed, and things continued to spin out of control. There were endless bugs and glitches in the new tools. The marketing team was behind on getting "how-to" instructions to our brand partners so they could learn the new process and system for sending orders out to customers. Darcy was slammed networking with investors and strategizing the raise with Gordon and the rest of the board, which had her more tense than ever. I didn't want to stress her out, so I kept my concerns to myself as we barreled toward the deadline.

We launched on time. But the program imploded.

The tools froze mere minutes after going live. Our brand partners were calling our customer success reps at all hours of the day, confused as to how to fulfill orders and use the new system. And for some reason, whatever the engineers had built into our code broke another part of the codebase that impacted customer checkout, so customers trying to buy welcome boxes were having trouble placing orders, and our sales dipped significantly for nearly a week. Victoria, who lives and dies by our revenue as Head of Growth, was understandably agitated.

And so was Darcy.

"This is unacceptable!" Darcy snapped at me in my office, towering over my desk as I sat feeling small and stupid. "I don't understand how this happened. There has to be no room for error. This is really bad, Alexis."

I debated bringing up our past conversation, the one where I flagged my concerns, the one where I asked for help. But she looked so distraught, so completely on the fritz, I couldn't muster the courage to defend myself. She continued to chastise me, and I just swallowed it down, her restless, panicked energy radiating from her tiny frame and filling the whole room. I had never seen her like that before—so noticeably angry and on edge. I wanted to give her calm. I wanted to make her happy. Because her pain was my pain. When she was disappointed in me, I felt disappointed in myself. Without thinking, I absorbed her emotions like a sponge. It wasn't a conscious choice; it was just something that always happened with us.

I apologized over and over again and promised I'd handle it—I'd fix everything—before she stormed out of the office and said something like, "I need to know you can handle what's coming. We'll pick this up when I'm back from The Burn."

But of course, we never did.

Her tense, tight voice still ringing in my ear from that fated conversation last month, I continue pawing through our office and grab a pack of branded matches. They're gold and say "Stay Savvy" on the back. I start lighting candles in the lobby, then pause to open my phone.

Right before we lost connection, before Darcy entered the spiritual abyss of the Playa, she sent me a smiling selfie from the back of her camp's minivan. I stare into her eyes and sit with her dimpled smile, a bedazzled Juul pressed to her lips.

I knew then, and I know now, that this was her apology for lashing out at me. It was two days after our big fight. Like her family, she wasn't great with words, and she was far from vulnerable. But she had her own ways of saying "thank you," "I love you," and "I fucked up."

I wish I'd gotten more, but I've come to accept that this picture, this image, was the last thing she ever told me. Maybe if she'd said something, maybe if she'd explained herself a little or taken it all back, I wouldn't be here second-guessing myself, worried that she was right: maybe I'm not cut out for this, after all.

As I light the last lobby candle and blow out the match, Victoria appears unexpectedly with a big takeout bag and two coffees. She's traded her black funeral moo-moo for head-to-toe cream in an oversized tunic from The Row and billowy palazzo pant.

"I've got the two-month 'Let's Fucking Grow' plan queued up in Tai Frasier!" she squeaks, waving toward one of our many *Clueless*-themed conference rooms. "Just give me your sign-off and I'll share with my team. Oh! And I grabbed you the yummiest goji berry acai bowl on the way in, to carry on me and Darcy's tradition."

"Of eating goji berry acai bowls in the morning?"

I didn't know about this. Acai bowls are frozen, mashed fruit with toppings. Like breakfast ice cream. I've never seen Darcy down a bowl of sugar like that. She was strict with her diet, at least around me.

"Not every morning. We did a quick growth standup every other week, and sometimes we'd do a dollop of almond butter instead of the goji. You know, to switch it up. Darcy preferred the goji, though." She organizes the plastic containers on the table and carefully places a paper napkin and spoon at each seat. She grabs the remote and clicks three times, and the screen lights up with our signature brand colors: marigold and pale pink. They scream spring. They feel joyous. They are, unlike me, wholly optimistic.

She prepared a full-fledged PowerPoint for this. This is so typical. I better say goodbye to my entire morning.

"Ready?" she says, blinking her long, luscious lashes.

"Yes," I say, annoyed, but desperate for some silver bullet to get us to that million. Anything to keep Gordon at the table for this raise. "Let's fucking go. Sorry. Let's fucking grow."

Victoria has been perfecting our growth engine since she joined Savvy as our first hire. She is hyper-competent, a "unicorn," as Darcy would put it, and she's never required much handholding or oversight, much to our relief.

Darcy met Victoria when she was working the sales floor at the Anthropologie in Chelsea Market. Darcy was guarded and aloof at first blush. She'd float into a room and quietly command everyone's attention while giving not a single fuck that you existed. When she asked you a question, you felt like you'd won a prize.

You wanted to impress her. You wanted to give her information.

So, while filling Darcy's fitting room, Victoria confided in Darcy that she was great at math and a fast learner, but that she didn't know what she wanted to do with her life. Darcy learned that Victoria came from wealth, but was on the outs with her dad because she didn't want to follow in his footsteps and become a doctor. She took the job at Anthropologie to "get some real-world retail experience" because she loved clothes and fashion and found the monotonous folding "therapeutic." In Victoria's meandering path, Darcy saw an opportunity.

Two years into building Savvy, Darcy and I both hated Excel.

Was Victoria comfortable with Excel?

She was. And she could start immediately.

As Victoria clicks to advance each slide of her presentation, she recites the words aloud.

HERE ARE OUR OPTIONS

Her demeanor is that of a CIA operative sharing national security intel.

FIRST OPTION: LAUNCH EARLY IN CANADA (crazy but doable)

She clicks.

2ND OPTION: 4X ADVERTISING SPEND (AKA light money on fire)

Click.

OUR FINAL OPTION: PAY CUSTOMERS 3X MORE TO REFER OTHER CUSTOMERS (AKA light money on fire)

"Couldn't you have put all of these on one slide?"

"Darcy and I like to look at all of our options upfront, in isolation, before we unpack them in more detail," Victoria says, flipping her chocolate hair. "Then at the end, we look at them all on one slide to compare. You'll see. You'll like it."

Victoria has always been the third Powerpuff Girl—Buttercup, the brunette—but it's like she came from a different lab because she never had to worry about money. Darcy and I used to wonder why anyone with a trust fund would elect to work as a salesgirl at Anthropologie. It's wild to look at her now in her corporate ensemble and crisp, clean makeup and remember how it all started, her in some boho dress stacking candles and untangling cheap necklaces. But Victoria was one of "those" girls, the rich kind who can afford to get lost for a little while.

I've known what it's like to have everything, and I've known what it's like to lose everything. And it's just different, really, when you're dealing with someone who hasn't. You feel like they'll never really understand you.

But she's all I've got left. And I can't do this alone.

"So," she continues, "If we launch early in Canada, I'll need a General Manager to help oversee the entire region. Katie is slammed staffing the UK launch so she's def off the table. I can call the other recruiter, though." Wait, who's Katie?

"I'll need another analyst or two to track demand so we can quickly throw ads against the best-performing cities. And you may need to move some budget around—away from domestic holiday and into this. Our CPCs are low to begin with and we could use the extra muscle." CPC is . . . cost per click? Right. But muscle for what channel? Okay—just nod. You can Google all of this later.

"Alexis?"

"Yes?"

Victoria furrows her brow.

"Do you need me to slow down?"

"No," I reply, a bit too loud. "This . . . this is great."

"I totaled the cost for all the hires and the rush recruiting fee. I also threw in budget for bonuses, for everyone who works on it, because launching early will likely 'burn out' the team. You know how they can get." She rolls her eyes to say, *Those fragile fucks.*

"I marked it as discretionary, though," she adds, "In the event it goes well and times nicely with the Series C. Once we close the raise, I'm pretty sure the Canada team won't give two shits about those thirteen-hour workdays."

"So your recommendation is that launching early in Canada is the cheapest way to get to a million customers?"

"No," she replies curtly, her thick eyebrows bunching to form delicate wrinkles above her nose. "That's not where I'm going. I haven't even walked you through the ad spend or referral options. This is why Darcy had me present each option before asking any—"

"But we'd have to burn through more cash. And we're bleeding money as it is."

"You have to burn money to make money," Victoria replies with her arms crossed, her tone confused. "If you look at our second option—"

She clicks.

"The potential ROAS on scaling Adwords and social looks really good. It may be a more fool-proof plan than an early GTM in Canada. We'd be betting on a brand new region to double our customer base in just one quarter. It's just risky."

My anxiety catches me off guard. GTM? ROAS? Was there some growth jargon dictionary I was supposed to read?

I breathe, composing myself. "We should do the cheapest and quickest option. You clearly did the research and know all this stuff."

"No matter what, we're spending money. Lots of it. I assumed you want to feel part of that decision? If we don't hit the million mark, the board might ask why, or what happened; did we have alternatives?"

I purse my lips and sink deeper, my confidence crumbling all over the chair. I am losing shape. I don't like decision trees. I don't like calling the shots. Darcy always determined the "what," and I designed the "how."

"Well, what would you do?" I ask Victoria, feeling like a child, and despising it.

Victoria's eyes widen.

"I would do some hybrid of option two and option three. Putting more money into ads and referral incentives might be pricey, sure, but we'd be pouring fuel into a well-oiled machine. It's just math, basically. With our ad spend right now we're bringing in like, thirty thousand new customers a month? And that's held pretty steady. So if we pour more into the channels that are working best—"

"Then we can get to a hundred thousand new customers a month and prove we can close the gap."

"Exactly," she replies, satisfied. "It's not the cheapest option, but it is the quickest and most reliable."

I sit in silence and stare at the screen, the glow of the marigold gently burning my retinas. I let my vision fog and try to slow my racing thoughts. I'll have to sync up with finance on this. I'll have to check our burn rate again, and our balance, to make sure we can actually afford it. But if we time this right, and we close the Series C come early November, we'll get that massive infusion of new cash before hitting the brink of bankruptcy.

"Fine," I say, reluctantly. "Get me the plan in writing and let's bring it to finance later today."

Victoria clicks the screen to black.

"Great!" She chirps, just as a young employee trots in and knocks on the slightly open door.

"Ladies," says the pint-sized twenty-something, "The resilience workshop lady just got here. Should I help her settle in or will you be done soon?"

"Resilience workshop?" I ask, confused.

"Yeah, today at lunch. With Amani Williams," says the employee.

"Who?"

"Amani Williams!" Victoria replies, "She's everywhere right now. She killed her abuser a few decades ago. It's such a crazy story. He was beating her up and I think, like, messing around with her younger daughter maybe? She got out of prison and started a catering company. It's blowing up."

How did I miss this? Who approved this?

I straighten up in my chair. She clocks my concern.

"I thought it would be good for the team to hear from her, you know?" Victoria continues, "She's a resource. She has a whole resilience bit. I think the team really needs that right now."

She folds up her laptop and trails behind the anonymous employee, tossing her barely eaten acai bowl in the trash.

> **Ethan:**
> Can you do din with my fam in the next few days?
> I know it's nuts rn

> **Alexis:**
> I can make it work
> And ty for my parfait this AM baby
> Love me some gloopy yogurt

> **Ethan:**
> I kno u do :)

5

About sixty employees have gathered in our massive, open-air kitchen to hear Amani speak. The seven men who work here have dumped heaps of charred chicken, brown rice and slaw onto their plates, courtesy of Amani's catering company. They pillage and shovel as though they're never going to eat again. The women are more skeptical, taking the try-before-you-buy approach. They pluck tiny morsels from each dish and nibble in curiosity.

"Resilience isn't about knowing what's on the other side of your struggle," Amani continues, floating across the kitchen in her maroon pantsuit and graphic MAKE IT HAPPEN T-shirt. "It's about developing techniques that not only get you *through* to the other side, but that help you *define* what's on the other side. So that even in the worst situations, you persist. You take control of your outcomes."

I see simultaneous nods ripple through the crowd. Female employees rush to write down every word Amani says in their Savvy-branded journals, as though now, armed with her perspective from surviving domestic abuse, prison, and murdering someone, they're better equipped to take on life than ever before.

As I peek over at the nearest journal entry, "RESILIENCE = TAKE CONTROL, EVEN WHEN SHIT IS BAD," my phone vibrates in my blazer.

> **Dr. Wes:**
> All good, he died suddenly too
> So I know how overwhelming it all can be...
> Lets grab a bite when things settle then ya?
> You in the office today?

It's him. Dr. Wes. In the throes of trying to comprehend and approve Victoria's growth plan, I had completely forgotten about our morning text exchange. And even if I'd remembered, I wouldn't expect him to continue our conversation. I assumed I got a one-and-done condolence text.

Seeing his name feels like a reward of some kind, the rainbow marshmallow in a handful of Lucky Charms. I can feel my tummy turn again—but lower this time. The pressure's building near my groin.

> **Alexis:**
> Sounds good!
> And yes Im here today
> But sitting in a 'resilience' workshop that
> one of my employees planned
> I'm p sure this Tony robbins stuff is a hoax lol

As I hit "send," I feel a flutter of anxiety. Did I say too much? Was that TMI? I should've just said "Yes, sounds good thanks" and "yes, I'm at the office," and let him go on with his day. I shove my phone under my ass and sink deeper into my spiral.

"Your CEO has passed on," Amani continues, as my phone buzzes and everyone turns to look at me. All I want to do is quell my anxiety and guzzle the serotonin promised by Dr. Wes's reply. Instead, I hold my head high and try to look somber for my team.

"But use that sadness and shock to fuel you. Not deter you. You can live in that choice. Only you decide how you emerge from hardship." I see over a dozen employees tear up and look at me with soft wonder, reverence even. They must think, "Wow, here she is. Emerging from hardship, a phoenix rising from the ashes. A leader we can count on. Someone to follow." I squirm in my seat.

Amani, sensing my discomfort, brings the room's attention back to the front of the kitchen, and I immediately grab my phone from under my butt cheek.

> **Dr. Wes:**
> Dont knock tony too hard
> He's a legend

I'm fixated as tentative text bubbles with "..." form below his last message. They appear, disappear, and reappear again.

> **Dr. Wes:**
> Glad to hear youre back in action already though
> Take care.

My vagina tenses. I glance around to make sure no one can tell. I'm not one for witty text banter with someone who isn't Ethan. Not that we flirt text a ton these days, anyway. But I admit that I do enjoy the distraction. Future Me can't afford distractions, though. She has money to raise and customers to acquire.

I put my phone on silent and drop it in my blazer pocket.

Suddenly, a flurry of chairs move, float, and scrape against the floor to form new shapes. Savvy notebooks whiz by as employees rush to grab pens and highlighters from their desks. Breakout sessions bloom all around me. Amani shoots me a glance and a shallow bow, relieving me from workshop duty for the day.

I extend a smile and saunter toward the kitchen, finding a little nook that keeps me "in the mix" visually, but offers enough distance to promise privacy.

I immediately click my phone to get more Dr. Wes, like pulling a slot machine over and over until all the symbols line up and it shits silver.

But there's nothing.

And honestly, it's for the best. I'm entering dangerous territory. And I know it.

Starving, I sneak over to the catered leftovers and use my fingers to pluck a piece of blackened chicken from its leaky aluminum tray and pop it in my mouth. I scroll through the notifications that have poured in over the last few minutes and find a single email subject line that sends my stomach into a sharp, curdling panic.

Subject: Confirming Tomorrow 9AM - Savvy x Crafted @ The Battery House

The chicken gets stuck in my throat as wretched, loud hacking sounds escape my mouth.

I can't breathe.

I get ahold of myself and grip the table, making a point to breathe in and out through my nose while staring into a vat of wilted salad. Victoria and Amani rush toward me, their heels click-clacking from behind.

"Alexis?" Amani says tentatively.

I don't reply.

Victoria runs to the other side of the long kitchen table, so we're face to face. I wave my hand erratically for her to bring me a napkin, afraid that if I move, I'll lose control of the morsel in my throat and choke even harder.

Victoria runs to grab a napkin, then shoves it in my hand. She starts pounding on my back with an open palm, like she's freeing some trapped pack of M&Ms from a vending machine. I'm mortified, but it's working.

By her fifth slap, the chicken dislodges from my throat, and I cough it up into the napkin. I immediately scan the room to see who saw me. "Leadership is exhausting," Darcy used to complain. "We're under this constant microscope. We must manage people and their perception of us all at the same time. No room for gaffes or mistakes."

Welp.

"Jesus Christ. Are you okay?" Victoria is genuinely concerned.

"Yah . . . I'm . . . I'm good. Thanks. I'm gonna chill for a few before the finance meeting. I'll be fine."

Victoria rubs my back gently and struts off.

Finally alone, I pull up the email that almost killed me and read it slowly, in full.

Subject: Confirming Tomorrow 9AM - Savvy x Crafted @ The Battery House
From: Jillian McCord <*Jillian@crafted.com*>
To: Alexis Ecker <*Alexis.ecker@besavvy.com*>
September 18, 2:02PM

    Alexis,

    Darcy never accepted the invite + I just received her autoreply to this meeting reminder. My greatest condolences. Confirming you will be taking this meeting instead? Plz be aware Marz has a hard stop at 10AM. Thanks.

Best,

Jillian McCord

Office of the CEO
www.Crafted.com
Your Stylist On-Demand.

My mouth goes dry.

Darcy planned a meeting with Marz? Why?

Why would she set up a meeting with the CEO of our biggest competitor without telling me?

I walk as fast as I can to Darcy's office, hitting a pace that gets me there but doesn't raise alarm. I draw the curtains shut. I pull Darcy's old laptop from her desk and pry it open. It's a few years old, but we've known each other's work passwords since the early days, when it was just the two of us. So now, I can easily access any important documents or conversations I wasn't copied on. It's how I set up her "*Sorry, I'm dead, please email Alexis*" auto-reply.

I search her inbox for every keyword I can think of: Crafted, Battery, Marz. Nothing relevant pops up. No exchanges back and forth with Marz or his admin. Nothing to give me context. Just the meeting confirmation, and a mysterious hold on Darcy's work calendar. *What the fuck is going on?*

I know they have history, but they hadn't spoken in over ten years, after graduating from G Calibrator together. It's how he came up with the idea for Crafted.

And by that, I mean he stole it. From *her*.

As I chew on the possibilities—*Were they texting? Maybe they met up in person before this at some point?*—I hear a knock on the door. I shove Darcy's computer back into the desk drawer.

"Come in."

It's Victoria. She looks confused as to why I'm in here.

"I um . . . I didn't find you in your office. Your throat all good? Is everything okay?"

"Yep."

She cocks her head, unconvinced.

"What's going on in here? Are you finally gonna clear out all her stuff, or—"

"No, um. Not yet," I bristle, her suggestion to clear Darcy's office landing like an accusation, but of what—I'm not sure. "But I'll . . . I'll get on that soon."

"Uh, okay. Well, finance is in Cher Horowitz. To sign-off on the growth plan and do the re-forecast."

She isn't blinking, and while I know she's clueless about the Marz meeting, it still feels like she can see right through me.

"I'm joining now, sorry," I reply hastily, grabbing my notebook. "Oh, and I'm gonna be out tomorrow morning. Actually, I'm gonna work from home the whole day. I have an early meeting."

"Oh! With who?"

I brush past her and don't respond. I stride into Cher Horowitz and quickly take shape.

"Hunter! Hannah!" I greet everyone with a smile that says I'm present. I got this.

I'm resilient.

"Let's *Fucking* Grow!"

June 11, 2018

> **Darcy Lyons 9:38AM**
> www.thesituation.com/2018/06/11/crafted-ceo-on-their-latestproduct-improvements-and-the-future-of-shopping

> **Alexis Ecker 9:40AM**
> fluff piece
> fluffy affffff
> i feel like their investors have all the press hookups
> like all the good business journos just on their knees
> suckin' dick

The Raise

Darcy Lyons 9:40AM
lololol
ya

Alexis Ecker 9:41AM
do u want me to ping the PR peeps and
and get u back on the circuit?

Darcy Lyons 9:44AM
idk
maybe
wdyt

Alexis Ecker 9:44AM
i don't think it would hurt

Darcy Lyons 9:45AM
u know I hate this shit

Alexis Ecker 9:45AM
but ur so good at it

Darcy Lyons 9:45AM
says who

Alexis Ecker 9:45AM
bitch if I tried to form 3 sentences for a
journalist id go full word
salad
like
idk it just comes naturally to u and u don't need
to plan what u say
id have a script committed to memory
and also scrawled on the inside of my arm

Darcy Lyons 9:49AM
lol well im thrilled I have u fooled

Darcy Lyons 9:51AM
but ya
maybe I'll see what Isabella says
bc we don't have any like
news news tho

Alexis Ecker 9:51AM
idk that Marz's shit counted as news lol

Alexis Ecker 9:51AM
"we've expanded our data science team to ensure our recommendations are the most rich and personalized of anyone
in the industry."
like ok ?????
the dude hired 10 new people
big whoop

Darcy Lyons 9:52AM
eh
they do technically have a sharper algorithm than us
and they made some pretty horny hires
but we'll get there

Alexis Ecker 9:53AM
WE WILL
we must
ur doing great sweetie

6

September 19th, 2019.

The Battery House is a place for people who have nowhere else to go, always acting like it's the only place to be. It is unclear what everyone working from here does for a living, or if they work for a living at all. But the sweeping, cinematic backdrop of the Manhattan Bridge and downtown skyline would give anyone delusions of grandeur.

Every house "member" is meticulously dressed to fit some sort of archetype as they perform for the entire room, speaking a bit louder than necessary and sitting noticeably straight. I use the House's concierge text service to order more coffee. I'm counting down the minutes until I can retreat into fetal position to process whatever's about to happen. I spent the entire night racking my brain over what's going on, and why Darcy would schedule this meeting. I feel an overpowering urge to sprint toward the bathroom, lock myself in a stall and suckle the living juice out of my Juul. Despite looking like an assassin sponsored by Ralph Lauren in my crisp cream pantsuit, slicked-back bun, and bold red lip, I'm not ready to confront Marz, who knows more than I do as to why the hell I'm here.

I scan the bold, velvety interior for a waiter who can help me mainline some caffeine. A gaggle of chubby millennial men in leather bomber jackets gesticulate over a pitch deck: "FAKE CHICKEN AND FAKE BEEF ARE MAINSTREAM," one crows. "IT'S TIME TO MEET FAKE SALMON. A THIRTY-BILLION-DOLLAR MARKET OPPORTUNITY SWIMMING IN PLAIN SIGHT." A woman wearing a tan, wide-brimmed hat pensively pets a pile of string bikinis but is particularly drawn to a metallic tube top with a retractable hood.

Suddenly, Marz glides out of the elevator and toward the dining room. He looks like a friendly farmer. Frail, but folksy.

Even though he's dressed like an Old Navy mannequin, the chubby boys and a few others recognize him as the paper billionaire he is and shoot urgent glances to one another, then to Marz, before he takes a seat at my table.

This is really happening. Judas in the fucking flesh.

A forced, sympathetic smile draws my attention to his patchy facial hair. I get the sense that without it, like me without my glasses, he looks a bit too young. It settles my nerves a bit. Brings him down a notch.

"Alexis," he says, eyes boring into mine while his face contorts to convey some sympathy. "Good to finally meet you. I'm so sorry about Darcy." He shakes his head. "What a nightmare." His drawl makes it clear he's not coastal.

He purses his thin lips and leans back in his chair. He takes a deep breath, and we sit in silence for a beat too long. I'm impatient. Crabby. Ravenous for an answer as to why I'm even here. Why this secret meeting was scheduled with Darcy in the first place. But I must stay composed at all costs.

"Thanks. It's all pretty tragic."

"Right, right," he replies, nodding. "But you're holding up okay?"

Darcy would tell me to keep my cards close. Suppress any twitch of vulnerability.

"Well yeah, considering the circumstances. It's been difficult. But nothing I can't handle." I hear the words leave my mouth. Sitting calmly across from Marz with my back arched and my chin high, I try my hardest to believe them.

"Oh, I'm sure. The CEO gig is its own thing." His tone is patronizing and faux empathetic. It reminds me so much of Gordon. Simon. Even Ethan, sometimes. "Must be a lot to process. You're not in a supporting role anymore, right? You're the one calling the shots."

"Well, yes. But I have a lot of support. Easier to make decisions when you have the right people around. We're doing just fine." And I mean it. Savvy is *growing*. Our resilience has been *workshopped*.

"I'm glad to hear it." He offers a quick smile, before it dims to a grimace. "So, then. Let's get down to business?"

I nod, hiding my impatience.

"Right, well, we're definitely going to pass. I was curious at first. Darcy brought me the idea at Burning Man, and I sat on it, but no one from your team followed up." Panic and confusion weave through my system, filling every crevice.

"Wait. You were there? You were at Burning Man with her?" The words rush out of me.

"I wasn't 'with' her, no. We saw each other briefly at the airport. But I went with Jack and Brian. Didn't see her text 'til I left camp, though. The service there ranges from shit to non-existent."

"Right, right," I reply, nodding. "And the text was about . . . ?" I quickly sip what's left of my coffee, hiding my ignorance, hoping he'll fill in the blank.

"The acquisition. Crafted buying Savvy." He replies sharply. "She didn't tell you?"

The creeks of my palms fill with sweat.

Darcy was trying to get acquired? Why?

I fidget with my bun in a sad attempt to buy time, not sure if I should admit I was in the dark or pretend I'm in-the-know.

In the silence, Marz taps the faux marble table with the fleshy tips of his fingers, watching me squirm.

"I got a few texts from Darcy," he sighs, "Something like, 'Do you have Wi-Fi? Are you getting this?' And then 'I need to talk acquisition,' or like, 'when can you meet.' Something like that. But I only got service on my way out," Marz continues. "So I don't know when or how she even sent it. You gotta be kind of desperate to send a text, though." He puts his hand through his hair and pulls out his phone. "Do they do to-go orders here?"

"*Desperate?*" The thought of Darcy desperate for anything just doesn't track. Her scrambling for a single bar of service feels wrong. Morbid. It makes me want to cry.

"Yeah. It's ridiculous. I mean you can bring a hot spot, but they're rare. And they die. They glitch. It's wild no one's disrupted this stuff yet. I'm sure Elon or someone else will soon." He scrolls through his phone, tapping mindlessly.

Why would she turn to Marz, of all people? After what he did to her?

"Did you reply to her then? Once you got the text?"

"No," he retorts without looking up. "Well, not right away. I said Jillian would throw something on the cal for the next time I flew to New York to meet with investors. She sent an invite right then, but Darcy never confirmed or anything." He shrugs.

The waiter I text-summoned a lifetime ago finally trots up to our table and pours fresh coffee into my mug. He leaves a Battery House-branded to-go bag on the table and nearly bows for Marz before scurrying off.

"Look. I have no reason to acquire Savvy today because we're doing the same thing, I'm just doing it better. You have a significant customer base. You're growing. But the calculation I have to make is: Do I really need to buy those customers from you right now? You're bound to lose to us. So eventually, I'll get them for free—or close to it."

"That's a rich thing to say about a company you copied."

He laughs. "I worked on an early—no—an *infantile* version of Savvy. When we were *kids*. At some bullshit program we *paid* to get into." He recoils at the memory, disgusted that in a past life, he coughed up money for access to a kingdom he's finally earned the keys to.

Marz paid fifteen thousand dollars to go to G Calibrator, which promised four weeks of hack-a-thons, networking, and a mock pitch to real investors. That's where he met Darcy, the summer in between their freshman and sophomore year of college—him at Stanford, and her at Duke. She, an aspiring tech executive burnt out on barbecue and basketball, and he, a talented engineer with a newfound love of Latin, were paired up for lunch at cohort orientation. She told him about her dream business, and he listened, enchanted.

According to Darcy, later that night over cheap beers and taco takeout, Marz helped her map out the technical side of Savvy.

And he was captivated. To him, she had it all: she was stunning, brilliant, ambitious, and easy to talk to. I know because he said so. I read it all firsthand. He wooed her with handwritten letters and Latin love notes. He praised her "magnum cerebrum" and talked through his aspirations to become the next Jeff Bezos or Jack Dorsey. But he lamented the fact that he thought more technically than strategically and was still looking for his "big idea," the *sine qua non*—the absolute, necessary component—of entrepreneurship.

The four weeks passed, and Marz never found his big idea. He didn't do a mock pitch. He doled out technical advice to the

Darcys of their cohort, to the dreamers, and spent his summer in a "supporting role."

As the summer sun dimmed and fall's chill crept closer, Darcy and Marz parted ways. They were two rational people who still cared about each other agreeing to live separate and full college lives. They stopped speaking, graduated, and found employment. Darcy nearly forgot about him.

But then, during that first year at Jetto, she caught wind of a *TechCrunch* announcement: Marz had raised a twenty-million-dollar Series A for a company called Crafted—a technology platform that "used data science and self-reported preferences to craft the perfect digital closet for anyone, anywhere."

Darcy was irate. I had never seen her like that before. Marz, forever lacking his *sine qua non*, stole nineteen-year-old-Darcy's 'Big Idea,' dressed it up in some big boy pants and tech-guy buzz words, and took it to market more than ten years later.

After the initial wave of anger, though, she softened and started to reminisce. We stayed at Jetto late into the night, laughing at Crafted leadership and their clinical, cheesy TechCrunch photo. Darcy forwarded the fundraising announcement to Marz with the words, "et tu, Brute?" and then gave me a two-hour tour of her Facebook photos, a glimpse into her past with Marz, G Calibrator, all of it.

Darcy never heard back from him. But four months later, I was on the bathroom floor at Jetto, receiving my invite to abandon gainful employment and start a direct competitor with her.

Behind the veil of his pubic scruff, he still looks like the teenager Darcy knew, but whatever sincerity young Marz once had, whatever drove him to write those earnest, exuberant letters to her, it's all long gone.

"Listen, Alexis," Marz chuckles, numb to my knowledge of his and Darcy's history. "You're not catching me in some sort of 'gotcha.'

No one cares that I copied her. No one in the Valley gives a fuck about what happened. She had vision—sure. But that's not the hard part. She couldn't *execute*." He snarls.

It takes everything in me to suppress a shrill, barbaric scream. I feel like a child again, overhearing my dad shit-talk my mom to the other dads at carpool, overcome with an urge to kick them all in the crotch. I remember feeling so angry and confused. My mom was my everything: she fed me, clothed me, loved me, validated me, motivated me. But he still saw her as some mistake, an embarrassment even. The dissonance plagued me my entire childhood, this inability to tease out who was right—me, or him. It's like I lacked some center of gravity everyone else seemed to have, because I didn't know what was real.

But I clench my jaw and keep my mouth shut.

"And that's the difference between a multi-billion and multi-million-dollar company, right?" he shrugs. "That's why some founders take their companies public and others, you know, frantically text their competitors with an urgent plea to buy them out."

Deep down, I know he's right. He's on track to mint billions, and in this world, that's all that matters. His investors won't care about a "petty" allegation like plagiarism, or cheating.

But I know who will.

"Well, if your customer base looks anything like ours," I say, forcing my voice to stay level. "It's all women. And in this climate, if they knew you stole from a female founder, a *dead* female founder that you *dated*, I think you'd have a problem. I have all her mockups and old documents in her office, you know. All her old pitches from back then. And all those beautiful letters you wrote her. I'm just thinking . . . it wouldn't be hard to connect all the dots."

He sits with this for a second, his mouth tightening into a thin line.

Wait a minute—did I just win?

"I don't think you get it," he says, finally breaking the silence, and leaning in. "Our investors have power. Like, real power. If you pitched this to *any* tech journalist, we'd just get it squashed. They'd send our PR people to kill the story."

"That may be. But if *I* write it, you can't kill it. And last I checked, I'm the one with all the documents."

"If you do that," he says sternly, his eyes widening. "I'll tell every journalist in the valley that Darcy tried to sell Savvy before she died. And good *fucking* luck on your next round if that happens."

"Are you threatening me? Is that a threat?" I hear my voice quivering, like I'm a little girl confronting her father's cruelty, when all I want to be is Sharon Stone in *Basic Instinct*.

"I'd prefer to call it an agreement," he says, before grabbing his to-go bag and jumping from his chair.

He rushes out of the room. People ogle him as he passes, then turn to look at me. They want to know who I am. They want to know why I matter.

I smile. I keep shape. I breathe in and out, and count slowly to sixty, praying that by now, Marz is long gone, dozens of buildings and brick walls in between us.

Hands trembling, I gather my stuff and flee without paying, keeping my head down as I burst through The Battery House exit. In the relief of the crisp fall air, I point my eyes toward the Savvy office and fumble through my purse to find a cigarette.

As I prepare to infiltrate Darcy's laptop, read through every email she's even written and get to the bottom of this acquisition bomb, I remember: I can't go to Savvy today. I told Victoria I'd be gone.

I have to go home.

As I map my way back to my place, I sit with this new information: You only sell your company at this stage if you're in dire straits, which we are *not*. And even if we were, why sell to Marz? Why did she think he'd bail her out after everything he's done? Did she have some sort of leverage over him—something other than his plagiarism? Something bigger? Or was she just that desperate, like he said?

And is it true he never saw her on the Playa?

Ethan:
Do u wanna grab din tn or stay in?
Ill be home in 20ish
Wat u feelin

Alexis:
Stay in
I mean
Idk
Wat do u wanna do

Ethan:
We can stay in babe
Its fine
Its been nuts with the non profit launch
so I'm good to chill
R u ok?

Alexis:
Ya

Ethan:
Okee

The Raise

Subject: Confirming Series C Drop Dead - NOVEMBER 5
From: Hunter Baker <*finance@besavvy.com*>
To: Alexis Ecker <*Alexis.ecker@besavvy.com*>
September 19, 10:03PM

Hi again,

The investors would need to wire us money by the first week of November. Ideally by the 5th. Otherwise, we will have to plan for layoffs asap. 70% of staff or more. 80% would be better. I know we're growing but we will be out of money by January if we don't act quickly with current team size. Headcount by team/salaries attached for your review.

Best,

Hunter Baker

Head of Finance
www.BeSavvy.com
Meet Your Dream Closet

7

September 20, 2019.

The cleaning staff are scurrying out, which means it must be 8 a.m. Standing in the glow of the live sales tracker, I grab a LaCroix from our freshly stocked fridge. I've been here since the crack of dawn, desperate to crack the mystery behind the Marz meeting, incapable of focusing on anything or anyone else. My brain is wired. My sleep is fucked. Ethan took to the couch last night because of my tossing and turning. I'm not ready to tell him about Marz because I'm worried that he'll go lawyer-mode and try to get involved. Which is sweet—it is—but it's not the energy I need right now.

How am I supposed to run this company and raise money with this acquisition bullshit hanging over my head?

I hate this feeling, like I'm trapped in a spider web I can sense on my skin but can't see. I know something's wrong. I'm just not sure what it is yet.

But our user count is *up*. Our sales are *up*. Our sales per user are *up*. Every graph I'm looking at goes up and to the right. So why would Darcy want to sell?

The Raise

It makes no sense.

I remember that as a Jetto salesperson, the live sales tracker felt oppressive. Intrusive. Given my experience, I had some hesitations about broadcasting a single team's productivity to everyone at Savvy. The engineering team didn't have to share their development output, the marketing team didn't have to announce their email open rates. And those teams still did well, so the tracker seemed unnecessary. As salespeople, Darcy and I wanted to win, of course, but it was never *because* of the tracker. It was never because we needed our colleagues to know how well we were doing. When I mentioned this in passing to Darcy—that the tracker felt invasive—she told me "That wasn't the point," and I didn't understand.

But I do now.

The tracker is everyone's daily diagnostic for how well the company is doing. Having no tracker is like having no stethoscope.

More importantly, though, the tracker is the antidote to the voices in my head that tell me we're fucked. That I'm fucked. That without Darcy, this company is a mess and it's all my fault. Whenever the voice starts to crackle, like today, I can look up at the tracker and know what's true. What's *real*.

I glide past the last of the cleaning crew and shut the door to Darcy's office. I scan through her old laptop while Juuling. The tracker is the first thing I see, and it helps calm me down a little, but the spiderweb is still there. I can feel it.

I quickly type the keywords I searched before going to The Battery House—Marz, Crafted—and nothing relevant comes up. Again. I plug in "acquisition," "acquired," "sell company," "selling the company," "selling Savvy," "banker," "looking for banker," "intro to banker," "sale," "sell," "selling." I scan every single email between Darcy and Gordon. I read recent conversations with all our most trusted advisors.

Nothing.

I plug in "scam" "whistleblower" "whistleblowing" "cops" "FBI" "criminal" "allegation" "illegal" "fake" "fraudulent."

More nothing.

I move past Darcy's emails and try the files in her Google Drive.

While searching every keyword I can think of and scanning troves of invoices, Savvy manifestos, creative briefs, and financial models, I find our Investor Outreach List. Darcy kept meticulous notes on each investor she met over the last decade, indicating how she met them, any personal details she recalled, and their fund's average check size:

Henry O'Sullivan - balding. twitter addict. eats raw spinach from the bag. 1 million.

Jennifer Galo - up to 500k. former consultant. acrylic cardigan. Can intro to FJ for more $$$.

Aaron Andrews - just promoted. 24 yrs old? "try *telling* Savvy not *selling* savvy." VIDEO OFF bc you WILL laugh.

Fisher Jing - #1 for consumer ecomm. Amazon vet. Board of Skims, StockX, Rent The Runway. Can do 10M ++ **GOLDEN DADDYYYYYY!!!**

We used to jokingly call our investors "daddies," whether they were on our cap table already or we hoped they might be soon. Gordon was just plain Daddy. Fisher Jing was Golden Daddy, Jürgen, a mediocre investor from Germany who cut us an early check, was Schnitzel Daddy. Reading through Darcy's notes-to-self, I'm overcome with nostalgia. Longing. It's like she's here with me, alive again, making all the bullshit so much more fun.

Then suddenly, in the bottom right corner of the database, I spy a phone number. It's floating in Column V, not tied to any cell, like she needed a place to quickly write it down and used whatever document she had open. I do it, too. It's why a project timeline may feature the name and address of the lady who waxes my pussy, or why a vendor proposal may end with the reservation time for a date with Ethan. I'm meticulous enough to scan and remove these notes-to-self before sharing them with the wider team, but I'm less vigilant with the stuff no one will ever see, like this.

I copy and paste the number into Google and hit search with a sense of both triumph and dread because I finally did it. I found something. But for all I know, this number leads to an investigator auditing us for tax fraud.

I scan through the first few listings and hit the jackpot: the number is a direct hit for the Manhattan Center for Psychotherapy, some doctor named Cheryl Prince who specializes in stress management and anxiety.

Of course.

Darcy didn't really want to sell the company because of tax fraud or some other criminal stunt.

She just wanted to feel free.

She was probably on crazy hallucinogenic drugs at Burning Man, just like everyone else. People subject themselves to nine days in the desert with no running water, no showers, no shelter, for what? To escape.

In a moment of weakness, tasting the bitter jolt of some cocaine-and-ecstasy cocktail and its flickering relief, she found a version of herself unburdened by Savvy. Her hair thrashing in the dusty wind, a crisp beer in hand, Darcy was basking in the promise of an easier life. The drugs told her to relinquish the weight of it all: of this office, of these two hundred people who rely on her to live, of all the investors who give so little but demand so much. That's why she texted Marz. That's why she concocted this whole fantasy of selling the company.

It's all clicking now.

God. What am I doing? What would she think if she saw me like this? Hunched over her computer, chain vaping, looking for proof that she's the Elizabeth Holmes of e-commerce. Is this how I honor and build her legacy, by mistrusting her? By caving to baseless suspicion? By letting Marz Davis, a known cheat, get in my head?

No.

I have the tracker. I have the emails. I have access to every file, and the name and number for Darcy's new therapist. They all tell me there is nothing to worry about, and that if anything, Darcy was hoping to take a brief, commercial break from being Superhuman. She wanted to stop the constant crushing of expectation and make Savvy someone else's problem. And who could blame her?

Get it together, Alexis. The real fire is the raise. And you're behind. I should be emailing Jen and Aaron and Spinach Guy, but there are hundreds of names on this Outreach List and zero guidance as to who to contact first, no instructions on how to play the "game."

And at its core, that's what fundraising is: a game of knowing the right people, talking to them in the right order, generating hype in the right pockets and creating a sense of momentum. For years, I watched from the sidelines as Darcy led our previous rounds of funding, meticulously planning like a general going to war. She'd lock herself in her office and create a timeline of conversations and events, trying to decode who knew who and which people could make what introductions, watching YouTube videos and interviews with each investor to dissect what they cared about and how they carried themselves. I was always just beyond the door, trying to streamline our accounting systems or optimize our delivery times, making sure that the thing we were pitching was adequately glued together, minimal blobs visible to the naked eye.

Darcy would kick off our fundraise and I'd slide in for the third or fourth pitch. As her co-founder, my role in those meetings was, as usual, a supporting one. I backed her up, hyped her up, and mirrored her confidence and excitement. Until now, I was just the fluffer, entering some foreign, intimate set where the plot and its characters were scripted long ago. All I had to do was show up and keep everyone hard. Those earlier beats—timing the meetings, studying the players, building that sense of momentum—they were always, and still are, a mystery to me.

I need help. Now.

I need Isabella.

I search her name in Darcy's inbox and quickly find her cell. It rings twice.

"Alexis!" she oozes in her infamous transatlantic accent. Back in 2004, Isabella raised $75 million for LeBebe, an online children's apparel and accessories company, and then sold it for $215 million—just before the crash in 2008. Her fund, Maia Capital, is now dedicated to supporting underdog founders in overlooked categories.

"Beautiful eulogy last week, my love. Darcy was beaming from the beyond. I'm sure of it. The power. The conviction." I hear loud clanging and shuffling in the background.

"Thanks . . ." I reply, my guilt over the mermaid wig swelling up again, knowing full well that if anything, Darcy was cringing all the way from heaven. "Sorry to bother so early but I was wondering if we could schedule some time to—"

"No sorry needed! Look, I'm rushing to St. Bart's for this retreat," she says, panting now. "I'm told its Davos-esque but for sustainability. Ethical tech. Affordable healthcare. But I'm glad I caught you. I've been thinking about your raise."

Of course she has. As our only woman investor, Isabella is squarely in our corner. Darcy used to ask Isabella questions or favors she never brought to our male investors, like how to comment on our rivalry with Crafted if it came up in interviews, or how to be taken more seriously when pitching a room full of men. One time, when we were low on cash, she even bridged the business, floating us for four weeks before we finally closed our Series B. She believed in us, and it's a big part of how we grew to believe in ourselves.

"That's great," I share eagerly. "Because that's exactly what I wanna talk about. I have Darcy's investor list and everything, but I feel like I don't know where to start. I'd just love your take on, like, who I should reach out to first and if you wanted to make any intros. I think I'm a step or so behind and—"

"No no no no no!" She interrupts. "No intros yet. Don't even look at the list yet, Alexis! What we need to do," she continues, catching her breath, "And what I wanted to talk to you about, is that I'd like to brand you first. Get you out there and make a little splash. Nothing too crazy or anything but we want your name in the right press pieces, with the right tone, hitting the right inboxes, before you even meet with anyone. We have to prime them a little."

Some fluffing. Of course.

"Nobody knows who you are really, right? You were the mechanic; she was the race car driver. And she didn't have to try with this stuff. The story practically wrote itself. 'High school visionary makes good on her decades-old startup idea.'"

She's right. Darcy collected glowing press like corduroy collects lint. That's why we send a complimentary lint roller to every Savvy user who has corduroy in their digital closet. My idea.

"But whenever new leadership comes in, you have to do the whole song and dance. We should schedule a photoshoot, connect you with one of the girls at The Situation," she continues, rambling off a to-do list that seems to bloom with each breath. "And I'm gonna ask Mike if we can get you in for Disrupt this year. It's soon but it's worth it."

"Oh, yeah. I'd love to attend."

"No no no, to speak, my dear. To speak," she responds, amused. "And after your big talk, you let the funds come to you. But don't answer any of their emails for a day or so! Promise! It's a trusted formula: big debut, then busy busy."

"But how does it work with Mike?" I'm taken aback by her influence but know I shouldn't be.

"I have enough. I mean, your co-founder died at Burning Man. It's a headline. You're a headliner. And he owes me. So he'll do it."

I feel lighter. I feel relieved. I am proud of myself for making the call—for asking for help. Darcy built a tight circle of believers, people with good judgment who could help her course-correct or gut-check her decisions. It's about time I built my own circle. Now I have Isabella. Maybe even Dr. Wes.

"Okay, yeah. Thank you so much. I'll get a draft together in the next week," I reply, ready to act on my newest assignment. Ready to follow instructions.

"It's in less than two weeks, darling. Can you send the draft tomorrow?"

Subject: Good seeing you
From: Marz Davis <MarzDavis@gmail.com>
To: Alexis Ecker <Alexis.ecker@besavvy.com>
September 21, 11:27PM

Alexis,

Thanks again for taking the time to meet.

I hope everything we discussed was clear, but if you have any questions, please reach out. I know that neither of us wants to step on the other's toes... I am sorry again for your loss. I know it must be quite difficult to take over so suddenly in addition to mourning a friend.

Darcy was a wonderful girl.

Let's hope she's resting in peace.

M.

8

September 22, 2019.

It's Friday night and everyone's gone. Victoria invited me to happy hour with a few of her direct reports, but I told her I had plans. Which is true, but I would've lied if I had to.

The office merlot is corked, and the tannins burn my insides. I stare in the mirror and notice my under-eyes are sufficiently sunken, praying that this Nars concealer can loan me a brand-new face for the next few hours.

My phone vibrates under the vanity light at my desk. It's Ethan. I put him on speaker so I can keep getting "radiant" and "creamy."

"I'm thirty out," he declares, like he's landing a fighter jet, not riding in the backseat of a forty-five-dollar Uber to Chelsea. "What's your ETA?"

"I'll leave the office in ten," I lie. I need at least fifteen to get presentable. "I'm gonna finish up my makeup and call a car."

We're heading to my investor's fortieth birthday party so I can show face and help Ethan. Theo—short for Theodoros—cut us a one-hundred-fifty-thousand-dollar check a couple years ago, before we had product-market fit, which, in the scheme of things, means I owe him nothing.

Investing that early means you're inherently a bit reckless—a gambler, even. He has generational wealth, but Darcy and I could never quite figure out how or why. Our theories ranged from something quaint, like his great-grandfather was an olive oil magnate, to the shady, like his great-grandfather ran the Greek mafia. Parties like this, though, the kind stuffed with egotistical middle-aged men with gobs of money but little purpose, are the perfect hunting ground for ALLMENMATR investors looking for a write-off, so Ethan's feeling giddy about the prospects of finding money for his new non-profit.

As I zip into a lilac jumpsuit in front of our full-length mirror, I notice how brittle I look. How girlish. There's something about the cut that ages me down a bit too much, and something about the material that's giving clearance TJ Maxx. And the sneakers?

The look is categorically juvenile.

I untie my trainers and remove my statement bracelet. I open my door and tiptoe barefoot toward Darcy's office. I'm 99 percent sure no one's here, but on the off chance there's an analyst who hung back to impress her boss—or a sales executive giving a late-night tour to some brand we're trying to close—I need to be stealthy.

Evading detection, I slip through Darcy's office door and use my cell's flashlight to find her closet. She always had last-minute networking events and soirees to dress up for. If I've guessed right, there may be a shoe, a necklace, a blazer—something—that can save me. That's not why I've kept the entire space intact, per se, even though she's been gone for weeks now. But I guess it's a deranged little plus.

And just like that, the flashlight catches a dark twinkle in the corner of the closet. I paw for the shiny, mysterious garment and pull it out, accidentally knocking over a tiny, glossy gift. Darcy was constantly receiving freebies from the brands that sold with us, or small businesses who aspired to someday. I'd normally be curious, and maybe steal it for myself, but I have no time. I lay the garment down on the floor and return the gift bag to its upright position.

I feast my eyes on her two-piece emerald suit, the Sies Marjan one that Darcy wore to everything. It's been with her since our seed round. She wore it to dinner with Jürgen a few weeks after his money hit our account. To pitches. To panels. She bought it days after seeing Zoe Kravitz in the black one on Instagram.

I shove the suit under my armpit and tiptoe toward the door. I peek down the hallway and hightail it back to my office, the satin flouncing against my thigh. I return safely and breathe a sigh of relief.

In the light now, I can see the suit in all its glory. It's perfectly unstructured but tight enough to flatter. The phthalo green would make anyone look beautiful, but especially redheads. Especially Darcy.

I slip into the blazer and take off my underwear, so my panty line doesn't show. I feel the soft material brush up against my labia. I button the flared bottoms and take a good look in the mirror.

The styling feels rich, yet simple, and the suit looks different on me than it did on her. On Darcy, the look felt baggy and chic, like Mary-Kate Olsen tucked into a loose, flouncing silhouette. Not a curve in sight. In contrast, the suit hugs the thicker parts of my thighs and my plump breasts ever so gently, accentuating the hills and valleys of my body without making them the focus.

It's perfect. Even though this is a quasi-work event, there's no harm in giving Ethan a little something to look at.

I grab my liquid eyeliner and the peachiest blush I own. I walk closer to the mirror and draw a thick, clean cat eye on the right, then the left, and dab my cheeks with dots of coral. I step back to assess.

I'm no Darcy, that's for sure. But her color palette feels right on me, and the suit fits beautifully. But, most importantly, I no longer look like an assistant camp counselor.

I coat my lashes with mascara and hear a knock at the door.

I scan the room quickly, making sure my Juul isn't charging somewhere obvious and that my soddened panties aren't dangling on my desk chair.

"Come in."

"Sorry to bother you?" says our petite recruiter Yardley, sensing my irritation. "I just . . . I didn't want to send anything in writing yet because it's kind of sensitive?" Her up-speak is maddening, but she means well. I always try to remember that, but some days I want to unzip her head, redo her factory settings, and press a little button so she can speak in declarative sentences.

I walk to my desk and ask her to take a seat. She's wearing a pair of knockoff Rothy's and a Free People dress.

"So I don't know what you know? But um . . . Jada? The Chief Data Scientist candidate? Is gonna sue for hiring discrimination. Well, she's threatening it? But I've been here before and think we can fix it."

"We can fix what? When did we interview her? What happened?" My thoughts are clamoring to get out, tripping over each other. I have no idea who Jada is, but this doesn't sound good.

"Legit, like, a few days before Darcy left. It was my fault, but Darcy—"

"But Darcy what? How did you discriminate against her? What happened? What are you saying?"

Yardley goes on to tell me that Darcy had tasked her with finding candidates for our open Chief Data Scientist role. "A-listers only." I knew that part. Ahead of the Series C, it was critical that we beef up our data science team and stack it with incredible talent. Crafted's recommendation algorithm was nearly three years more mature than ours. It had more data to ingest, more customer behavior to analyze, and more engineers fine-tuning its code.

Darcy met with Jada and absolutely loved her. She came with a Masters in Computer Science from MIT, eight formative years at Amazon, and a passion and vision for what Savvy could be. I remember Darcy raving about her, and figured she'd offer her a next round interview at minimum. I never caught her name, though, or what happened next.

According to Yardley, Darcy sent Yardley an email with feedback and next steps. As Yardley pulls up the email, I hold my breath and clench my asshole:

Subject: CDS candidate Jada Greene
From: Darcy Lyons <Darcy.lyons@besavvy.com>
To: Yardley Goffin<Yasmin.goffin@besavvy.com>
August 19, 10:03AM

Yardley -

Jada was perfect. Has the degree, experience. And clearly knows the space. She did her research and pitched me her own 30-60-90. Very impressive.

But let's pass for now. Black/bipoc/womxn etc candidates are great for more junior roles, but we need more men in the C-suite as we go out to raise!!!

Let's do this :-)

D

Darcy Lyons

CEO, Co-founder
www.BeSavvy.com
Meet Your Dream Closet

Okay. *And?* Darcy's obsession with getting more sausage in the C-suite wasn't new to me. "Investors pattern match," Darcy used to tell me. "And they just trust guy founders, guys in general, *way* more than they do women. The boys IPO and bring home the bacon. We just need more guys on the Zooms and in the pitches and stuff. It feels familiar."

"Jada has the email," Yardley says.

Fuck.

"Because I accidentally forwarded it to her?" She continues, my need to unzip her head and redo those factory settings turning me more homicidal. "Or I forgot it was in the same email chain. We were putting her on CC, and then off CC? And then I looped her back into the wrong chain on the thread?"

She's standing up and pacing now, unraveling, like a physical mirror of my hidden distress.

"But what can they even do?" I ask, finding my focus as I watch her dart across the room. "Right? Darcy's dead. There's no one to litigate. Can't we just apologize and say . . . I don't know. Say that it doesn't represent Savvy's values and that I'd be happy to talk. I should definitely talk to her, right?"

"If you're bringing your checkbook, then yeah."

"My checkbook?"

"When she and her lawyer replied to me or whatever? They kind of gestured toward a settlement. I know the lingo. So it's just a budget thing, really. If we can swing it."

We can't. The budget was set before Darcy died. We didn't earmark a settlement payout to a Black candidate we discriminated against. And we're already overspending because of Operation Let's Fucking Gag Me and Bind Me and Shove Me in a Dumpster.

I need answers.

"Who knew about this and why am I just finding out about it now?"

"I thought you knew?" Yardley says, confused. "Darcy knew? So I thought you knew? But that's it. We got Jada's reply, you know, to the email? And we were gonna handle it once Darcy got back? But then she died, and so I think that bought us time? They wanted to be respectful. But then Jada and her lawyer followed up today?"

I wonder if Darcy planned to pay Jada and then immediately fire Yardley. Because that's exactly what I want to do. This up-speak is terrifying.

"So what are they asking for?"

"They didn't get into details yet, Alexis. So—"

"You said you've been here before. So how *'much'* is *'here'*?"

"A couple hundred thousand? Maybe more?"

"No. No no no. We can't do that right now," I reply, trying my hardest to cast a brave face when all I want to do is jump out the ninth-floor window and turn into intestinal spaghetti. "I'll take care of it. Write down their email addresses. Here." I hand her a piece of paper and a pen.

No digital footprint. No trail.

Once Yardley's done pissing me off and giving me what I need, I tell her to leave. But not before I gently urge her to keep her mouth shut. This can't come out. It'll completely blow the raise. It'll taint my public persona before Isabella "soft launches" me to all the investors.

Alone again, I wake up my laptop and start stalking Jada on Google, Instagram, and LinkedIn, stress clicking to vet her clout, who she knows, and how much trouble we're in.

My phone buzzes and breaks my trance.

It's Ethan.

The Raise

Ethan:
Where r u babe?
All good??

Alexis:
Sorry baby
Leaving now.

9

I should have pounded more wine at the office. As I pull up to Theo's penthouse on 22nd street, I'm rattled by the strobe lights pulsing through the top floor windows and fortysomethings in metallic bodysuits lined up at the front gate. As the maître d' opens the door, music violates all of eighth avenue. Ethan's been waiting for me outside in a snug Todd Snyder blazer, and I, in Darcy's green suit, worry I look like some cheap restaurant hostess who decided to "dress up" for her night shift. The version of this party I created in my mind, the one with NYU students in white gloves serving me champagne and caviar in some industrial-chic bachelor pad filled with New York's tech elite, is fast receding. Ethan and I share a troubled glance and head toward the music.

The townhouse is narrow, and the ceilings are low, and through the feathered headpieces and light-up cowboy hats, I can barely see two feet ahead of me. Ethan leads me through the crowd, soundtracked by deafening EDM and people screaming over the grating synth. The repetitive beat drills into my skull and my thoughts spiral around Jada, the lawsuit, and Darcy's "desperate" push to get acquired—the dirty laundry she bundled up and shoved into a corner I couldn't see. My heart rate starts to climb. *How the hell am I supposed to get it all done in time? Raise this massive round, pay off Jada, and build our "billion-dollar" company? Did Darcy want to sell because of the Jada thing? Is it all connected somehow?*

I need a drink.

A couple walks by holding bright blue cocktails. I trace their origin and nudge Ethan toward the bar.

We push through a crowd of rail-thin twenty-somethings taking selfies with no spatial awareness. Their bodies are taught and topped with rouged, cherubic faces.

"THEO'S TURNING FORTY?!" Ethan screams at me, competing with the drone of La Bouche's "Sweet Dreams." He gives the cherubs a once-over which makes me want to, too, but I refrain. After all, just because they're young and hot doesn't mean they're here as window dressing. Me and Darcy looked like that once—gangly, young, out of place at investor parties—getting ogled by the engineers and hit on by investors who mistakenly thought we were paid to be there and look good.

Dozens of costumed men and women, all in their late thirties or early forties, whir about like college freshman, new and alive with possibility. I feel instinctively forgiving toward the couples here who have kids, wherever they are. For them, this is a rare night off, a chance to drink, reinhabit their tired bodies and remember what it's like to live a little. In my babysitting days, I relished watching couples stumble through the front door after a date night, tipsy on wine and a few hours of freedom.

But a lot of these people aren't parents. I can tell. And they may not even be married. I catch myself feeling sad for them, worried even, and I don't know why.

Ethan eyes a breach at the bar and tugs me forward. He orders us the blue drinks—absinthe dosed with pea flower extract—and we stand in silence, surveying the scene. Out of the corner of my eye, I spot Theo hugging an elderly couple in wizard cloaks and am aghast to realize he's wearing a turban and sequined cranberry vest, some Aladdin outfit gone wrong. Ethan sees me see him and pinches my elbow.

"DO YOU WANNA GO OVER?" he says, awestruck.

"AND SAY WHAT? 'HAPPY FORTIETH? AMAZING FRAT PARTY?!'" I continue to marvel at the Aladdin getup and its blatant appropriation. I don't think Aladdin even wore a turban.

"AND SAY 'HAPPY BIRTHDAY, THIS IS ETHAN, MY BOYFRIEND.' AND THEN I'LL ASK HIM IF HE NEEDS A DRINK OR A SMOKE OR SOMETHING AND WE'LL GO CHAT ONE ON ONE."

He cracks his knuckles. Ever since he got word that he wouldn't make Partner, Ethan's energy has felt more feverish, more urgent. He still hasn't shared any details on that meeting, even though I've asked. I just hope the new non-profit, and finding some solid investors for it, can give him the boost and distraction he needs. On the one hand, he'll always be fine. He could go work for his dad's real estate company, or change law firms, or apply for in-house counsel with any of the Fortune 500 companies he's working with now. He has a JD from Columbia and a BS from Wharton and a powerhouse mom with a network beyond my comprehension. But I know why he's spinning out. Janine makes him feel like he has so much to prove, so much to live up to, and she has to cosign on any career decision he makes. My mom gives me such unbridled, unconditional love—the type of unselfish love only a parent can give. I've always tried my hardest to fill him up with whatever dregs I have after giving to Darcy and my team, but no matter how much I pour, it's like it falls right out his ass crack and onto the floor.

"CAN WE JUST WAIT A BIT TO TALK TO ANYONE," I reply, overwhelmed by the gyrating potbellies in body harnesses and harem pants inching closer. A bald guy in a catsuit slithers by me and hisses in my face. I chug my antioxidant cocktail and ponder how Ethan plans to segue from "nice chain-link jockstrap" to a full-throated ALLMENMATR pitch.

After downing a second cocktail, I tell Ethan I need to pee and excuse myself from the bar. While waiting in line behind a girl in a massive cow suit—udders and all—I hear a single, roaring guitar lick and bone-crushing feedback rip through the air. I shove my index fingers in my ears and search for a view of the stage, where Theo, his turban, and a bunch of guys in newsboy caps have formed an overconfident middle-aged band.

"THE ATHENS STRIPPERS!" yelps The Cow, gesturing an udder toward the stage.

"WHAT?"

"THEY ROCKED CENTER CAMP LAST YEAR. THE STRIPPERS PLAYED RIGHT BEFORE THE BURN."

The burn.

The udders, the harnesses, the barely-there pasties. The complete disregard for how they're perceived. These aren't just New York tech yuppies pursuing their long-lost youth. *These are burners. From Burning Man.* For all I know, The Cow saw Darcy minutes before she died. The catsuit creeper could've watched her fall. The elderly wizards could've camped with her, even heard her last words.

My head is spinning, and I have a thousand questions to ask The Cow, but suddenly, she pulls me into the bathroom with some kimono'd guy and starts bumping coke as the door seals shut.

"Want some?" says the guy, handing me a tightly wound dollar bill and eyeing a line of white powder on the dirty sink. Hazy from the absinthe cocktail and oscillating between feeling empty and panicked, I figure why the fuck not, and bend over the sink.

"Did you guys go this year?" I ask The Cow, who is manhandling her costume so she can use the toilet.

"Go where?" she asks, and I realize between the coke and the pounding music, we lost the thread of our earlier conversation.

"Burning Man," I answer, tapping my foot with lightly clenched teeth.

"Nah, not this year," she says, wrangling her udders into submission while squatting above the toilet. "But I heard it was pretty dark."

"It waaaaaasssss," chimes in Mr. Kimono, and the pitch and modulation of his voice signal to me that he's gay, but I don't want to assume. "Between the dust and shiiit and the rain and the mud and that girl like, dyinggg or whateverrrr," he says, and my heart-rate climbs, "It was baaad energy. Like fucking sinisterrrr honestlyyy."

"What um . . . what did you hear or like, see with that whole thing? Like with the girl who died?" I pry, hoping for I don't know what. All I know is that I'm desperate to fill in the blanks of Darcy's death, to fill my emptiness with more information, as if knowing what she ate beforehand or the last person she spoke to will somehow bring her back or make me feel whole again.

"Oh honey, I stayed faaaaarrrr away from that mess," Mr. Kimono replies, leaving me forever empty. Forever guessing. "I was two tabs deep when it all went down. No wayyy I was asking questions or trying to catch that vibe."

"Oh my god, no way," confirms The Cow. "Talk about a bad trip."

As they share in a giggle, my skin crawls. I quickly ditch the bathroom and charge up the stairs, nearly tripping over my bell-bottomed suit pants. I decide to venture out onto the second-floor balcony to steal a smoke and gather my thoughts.

As I push through the terrace door, the fresh air chills my skin, damp with my own sweat and the heat of other people's flesh. I walk deeper into the night and find a table at the edge of the balcony, where costumed men have gathered to roll and smoke joints. I pick one up and grab a lighter. As the smoke burns my throat, I feel my purse vibrate against my armpit. I grab my phone and scan my texts. Upon seeing who they're from, I get a sudden urge for privacy. I make my way to the lonely chaise lounge on the other side of the balcony, and with my weed and new texting buddy, I feel at ease for the first time since getting here.

> **Dr. Wes:**
> Have you started pitching yet? Happy to review anything. Would be better than bingeing Planet Earth for the millionth time.
> Can't sleep.
> One of those nights.

I've never seen Planet Earth, but from what I've heard from my weed delivery guy, it's a lot of nature porn, like lions giving birth and cuttlefish fucking each other's faces. I'm about to ask if he's seen either before, but then realize I'm too tipsy to type "cuttlefish."

> **Alexis:**
> Not yt. Isabella trying to get me a speaking
> spot at TC disruppt
> Id start pitches after tht
> Puts it dwn to the wire for sure

Maybe I'm too tipsy to be talking to Dr. Wes at all? But some familiar pull in my belly tells me to stay and pivot from work talk. Why would he be texting so late, and on a weekend, if he didn't want the same buzz I'm seeking?

> **Alexis:**
> Im sry you can't sleep but tbh i Ive Planet Earth
> We're just
> Specs of dusttt in the universe
> Dying creatures on a dying planet
> All that jazz

I stare at my reply and feel immediate regret. This blue jungle juice has me overstepping. Or maybe it's the weed. Or the coke. Or all of it.

He's read my response but hasn't answered.

And he won't. Of course he won't. I've gone too far. To feel better, I re-read all of our texts to date, my eyes blurring as I drunkenly squint into my screen.

Suddenly, the tiny dots appear, my new lifeline, and the pull in my belly grows deeper and more urgent.

> **Dr. Wes:**
> Specs indeed
> Curious re Isabella's plan
> You still at the office? phone catchup quick?

I choke on my joint. I cough until my esophagus burns. He wants to talk on the phone? Right now? I feel powerful—clairvoyant even. This man wants to hear my voice. On a Friday night. I knew I felt something when he texted me that first time. I knew there was a "there" there.

But I'm too drunk. I'm too high. He's the only man in-or-adjacent-to Silicon Valley, besides Gordon, who seems to give a shit about me or my company right now. I can't do this. Not now. It would be reckless.

> **Alexis:**
> Would love to but I'm at a party!!
> Thatsa strong word for it actually...
> It's a
> Mid-life crisis rave??lolol
>
> **Dr. Wes:**
> Touché
> Next time then

"Alexis," Ethan screams from a distance, pushing through the sliding door. He slows his pace as he gets closer, realizing I've made a choice to be alone, away from him, even though he needs me right now.

In the throes of my very drunk, quasi-sexting, I forgot he was here.

"Yes?" I answer, quickly placing my phone face-down on the side table next to the lounge chair.

He sets down his drink and scoots next to me, crossing his arms.

"I don't know anyone here. I've been looking for you for half an hour."

"It's been ten minutes."

"You wouldn't know. You've been here *lighting up*." He glares at my joint.

"*Lighting up?*" I roll my eyes. "Okay PBS Special."

"I can't do my thing without you. These people are kind of," he says, trailing off, gesturing to the steam punk dads smoking out the furries a few feet away. "Eccentric."

"Just go back in and do your little dance," I snap. "Invite him to *Mooontaauuuk*. Fly him *priiivaaaateeeeee*."

I'm feeling loose from the drugs and alcohol, and I immediately regret turning sour. He's stressed. He's here. He's trying to make it happen. I shouldn't feel this irritated that he needs me. Relationships are a two-way street, after all, and he's been such a rock for me the last few weeks. But for some reason, I feel resentful. Like *I* need all the oxygen. Like *I* need to do the relying, and not be relied on.

"Alexis," he says softly, but firm. "Look. We need to talk about something." I see his brown eyes turn stern and serious, and he puts his hand on my knee. I pray I have enough sobriety somewhere inside me to feign interest and engagement.

"I said something at a happy hour that I shouldn't have said. With the team." He's burning a hole through my pupils now, making sure I'm paying attention.

"I'd been working on the trade secrets things, the Comcast lawsuit, and just grinding, you know? I got a little too drunk I guess—Manish bought rounds or whatever—and the client was there. She's kinda junior too, right? But—" he trails off, and looks into his lap, like he's about to cry.

"But we've been good. We've been *really* good. And so, like, I said something to Manish about how Jenna's allowed to go on her babymoon? But when my mom invited us to Napa for those four days, like during a quieter period even, they wouldn't let me do it. And I said something about it not being fair, and Jenna getting preferential treatment just because she's pregnant. And I guess my client heard and told my boss about it, and so . . ."

I feel myself zoning into the conversation, processing the gravity of what Ethan's saying, but my eyes suddenly lock in on a petite redhead roaming through the crowd on the second-floor landing.

"I was overworked and hammered, and my mom had been on me about that trip. She didn't want to go alone. I just felt bad, you know? My dad's always in Florida and I'm, like, all she has a lot of the time. And I wanted Jenna to take the babymoon—I did—but it just . . . for a second it felt like my work didn't matter and I didn't deserve a break, but she did."

Looking at the mysterious redhead through the floor-to-ceiling window, I can't see her face, but her hair looks exactly like Darcy's. She's the same height. The same build. That pint-sized hourglass with a waist so tiny it looks cinched by an invisible corset. She's dancing now, her wrists high in the air, decorated with the same gold cuffs Darcy wore to parties just like this.

And before I instinctively rush through the door to scoop her up, hold her and show the world that she's here, she's *alive*, I feel clubbed by the realization that actually, she's still dead.

I can suppress the sense of loss and longing, but it will never truly leave me. I can drink. I can smoke. I can sext. I can work around the clock until I crumble. But her death will find me on every balcony in this goddamn city. It will haunt every moment of my life. And when it does, I won't run. Because I will pursue her memory. I will rewatch every video of her a thousand times. I will Zoom in on all the photos, memorize every detail of her perfect face. I will re-read every conversation, every email, every text, every Slack chain, every word, and I will bring her back to life. How do you let go of the only person who really knew you? How do you say goodbye to the one who taught you how to be?

And what if you never knew her at all? And what if she had secrets? And what if—

"Alexis!" snaps Ethan. "Are you even here? Are you listening? Jesus fucking Christ . . ."

Why is she gone? Why did she leave me? Why did she want to sell? What else is she hiding?

I try to meet his gaze, but I feel cross-eyed and dizzy, like half of my body is pulsing with nausea, and the other half is watching me from afar, limp in his arms.

I bury my head in Ethan's chest and lean with my full weight.

"What?" Ethan asks, worried now. "What's wrong?"

"It doesn't make sense, Ethan."

"No. It does. I take accountability, like, they did the right thing." He purses his lips and closes his eyes. "But I have no idea how to tell my mom what happened. I'm kinda freaking out."

Through drivel and tears, I hug him, and he hugs me back. I tell him everything. About Jada and the lawsuit. About Marz and Darcy's "desperate" plea to sell Savvy to Crafted. My mind may be clouded by its 75 percent ABV but I can still feel the spiderweb, and it's getting bigger. Heavier, too.

I wait for Ethan to stretch out his arms to hold me and kiss my forehead. To tell me it's just the circle of life. And that it can be cruel and random and relentless. But there's no grand mystery. No master plot connecting all my revelations. Just a horrible, tragic accident, and me: my coming-of-age as a new CEO, learning about the darker parts of the C-suite, the messier parts, for the very first time.

"Maybe it was just too much for her," Ethan says, looking down at the floor, his arms crossed.

"But what does that mean?"

"I don't know, Lex. You knew her better than I did. Better than anyone. But yeah, I mean, that's a lot to carry, right?" He replies, a tinge of irritation in his voice.

I sit in silence, confused.

"I mean all the mental health experts I've started researching for the non-profit or whatever," Ethan continues, "They talk about how dangerous shame can be. It's fucked. Like, it's a leading cause of suicide, at least in men. So I don't know. Maybe the lawsuit was too chaotic. Maybe something even worse was going on. And yeah, she was too embarrassed to tell you? That's kind of how I feel right now."

"She wouldn't do that, Ethan," I declare, suddenly feeling like her lawyer, or her publicist. "She was the Roy Horn of wrangling chaos."

"Roy Horn?"

"Yes, Ethan!"

"The one with the soul patch? I thought he died?"

"But he *didn't*! And that's my *point*!"

In my cross-faded rage, I accidentally knock over the side table, and our blue drinks splatter all over the lounge cushion. Ethan's shaking his head now, realizing the night is over and that the last thing I needed to hear, the last thing he needed to say, was that Darcy killed herself in shame.

"Why would you say it, Ethan? Why would you even say it? Even if you thought it, and you *shouldn't* think it, by the way, why would you say something like that to me?" My wild eyes land on the furries, petting each other in syncopation with the muddy rhythm of Theo's middle-aged band. "And why would you say it *here*?"

The dad in the chain-link jockstrap bends over to flip the side table back upright, eyeing us with concern. As he starts drying the soaked lounge cushion with paper towel, Ethan and I simultaneously spy a wad of his tangled pubes, and I know it's time. I know we're done here.

"Let's go," Ethan murmurs, defeated. "And you know what? I'm sorry. I shouldn't have said it. But it's crazy you didn't tell me any of this. And it's crazy you haven't . . . It's crazy you haven't entertained the possibility that yeah, maybe something . . . Maybe something was wrong. I mean," he says, taking me in. The me in mourning. The me in pursuit of her memory. "It's eating you alive, too."

Ethan calls a car, and we briskly make our way back to eighth avenue. The winter breeze sobers me up from the inside, my neck a sheet of slack, exploded skin.

As we weave through the city, I let myself wonder if Ethan could be right. If behind her poreless skin and tailored jackets and aura of mastery and calm, Darcy was a boiling frog, cooked to death by spreadsheets and lawsuits and pressure and defeat. Savvy was her detox and her drug. She started the company in her Saturn Return, believing the experience would reveal her purest form to herself and to the world. In raising money and hiring employees and directing their every move, she found a way to channel her relentless ambition, a way to scratch the permanent itch she felt to be someone, to do something. Savvy was a Hail Mary to make meaning of her late twenties, the hazy, distressing period when everyone you know is either accelerating ahead or falling behind. Some get engaged, then married, then have kids and flee the city, succumbing to a different urgency, the one forged by biological clocks. Others find themselves stuck in some life that they hate but are too complacent or scared to chart a new path. Or they've bottomed out, and they know it, using long nights on cocaine in trendy downtown dive bars to tell themselves they're not settling—they've just chosen *living* over *striving*. But Savvy was Darcy's ticket to something more than all that. A way for her to prove that she wasn't like everyone else. She wasn't going to partner up and head for the suburbs or bide her time at Jetto until a promotion came knocking. She was never going to look at some ordinary life, say "this is it," and numb the death of her potential with key bumps and IPAs.

And then came the lawsuit. The dwindling finances. The threat of layoffs. The insecurity of the raise. After nearly a decade of building and scaling and winning, and *being* a "Winner," maybe Darcy couldn't handle the fall. Maybe the mounting misfortune was so at-odds with the identity she so urgently inhabited—the Founder, the Visionary, the Exception to the Rule—that she could no longer detect what was real, and what was true. Maybe that's why she was looking for help—why she had the therapist's number in that spreadsheet. Was she a resilient startup mastermind facing normal blows on her path to e-commerce domination? Or was she a silly little girl who formed her company on the bathroom floor, now in over her head, and about to prove to the world, and herself, that she was never special? That in fact, she was delusional. Incompetent, even.

Maybe she did jump. If it felt so urgent to start, maybe it felt urgent to leave.

To my right, Ethan is frantically texting, the glow of the screen illuminating his tense, focused face. He's mad about our fight. He's mad that I'm unraveling. I stick my head farther out the window, praying the harsh wind will sober me up even more and shove all my thoughts back down, buried deep where they belong.

I can't keep my team employed and this fundraise on track if I fall into some rabbit hole of grief.

I shouldn't be chasing people down at parties, hunting for answers I'll never get.

I shouldn't be flailing around at investor birthdays, throwing tantrums so childish that grown men in dick thongs gape at me like *I'm* the misfit.

My phone buzzes and I reach into my handbag. It's just a delivery notification, but I fantasize that it's Darcy, from the grave, telling me to ignore Ethan. To remember her, and how she really was. "Ethan's well-intentioned," she'd say, "but he doesn't know me like you do."

After what feels like forever crawling through Friday night traffic, we pull up to our building and Ethan helps me out of the car. I wave past the doorman and head toward the elevator. All I want to do is chug a glass of water and lay face-down in bed. But suddenly, I spot my mom, *my mom?!*, seated on the sofa in our lobby. At first, I'm sure she's a phantom, that I must be too drunk. But when I hear her thick Bronx accent lumber through the air and ricochet off the hallway's artificial marble, I know it's her. In the flesh.

"Alexis!" She yells, like we're not four feet apart. "I'm here baby. Let's go."

She struts toward the elevator in her patent leather platforms. She's a mere five-feet tall but bears a double-D bust and long platinum weave, like a gussied-up chicken on stilts.

"What are you doing here? Where are you going?" The alcohol aggravates my confusion and exhaustion. In the elevator's reflection, I see Ethan push open the front door and hop back in the Uber.

Holy shit. *I've been pawned off.*

"He texted me at the party," my mother says, my mouth still agape with shock. "He said you weren't feeling good. I figured we could use your sauna and jacuzzi so you can sweat it out, whatever you're sick with."

"I feel fine."

"You don't look fine, honey. In fact, you look like shit."

I look down at my own phone, ready to rage-text Ethan for depositing me back at home so he can schmooze with my network in peace, for his own gain, but he got to me first.

> **Ethan:**
> Im sorry to do this and I love you
> I'm in a bind myself
> I really wanna get this thing off the ground and do something right
> Idk
> Im hoping we can talk it out later
> Send my love to Monika

The Raise

I put my phone on airplane mode and wait for the elevator to arrive. To our right, my mom and I both watch as a DoorDash deliveryman waltzes into the building, past the doorman, and lands right behind us with three heavy bags of piping hot food.

"They can just . . . come in like that?" My mom mutters from the side of her mouth, her lips shifting to the right. She thinks she's whispering, but she's not. "Are you safe here?"

I glare at her, embarrassed.

"Yes, mom," I hiss. "It's a guy with some tandoori, not an AR15."

She eyes the deliveryman up and down, then flashes him a big fake smile.

"Did Daddy reach out to you or something?" My mom asks, genuinely worried. The jacuzzi bubbles keep exploding into my eye, leaving a light sting.

"No," I reply, "He hasn't reached out."

"You're lying."

"I'm not lying?"

"If he got a new 'finstagram' then how would you even know? For all we know he's watching everything. He's geotagging you again."

"That's not a thing, mom. And it's fine. I haven't heard from him, and I blocked any of the accounts his phone number makes. You can do that on Instagram. He'd have to get a new phone number and I'm not sure it's worth the visit to AT+T just to stalk me."

I say it, but I can't be so sure. Every nine months, he reappears—like clockwork. A five-foot Scrooge with a martyr complex.

He'll send walls of text, unprompted, telling me that he had to leave for his "sanity," and how my mom was a criminal, a liar, a villanelle. I could never square how a stay-at-home mother became a "certified felon," one with not a single warrant out for her arrest, but he had no trouble making it make sense in his ever-evolving fiction. He is a professional straw-grasper, pawing for as many as his bloated, hairy fingers can hold. He can't deny he was a shit father, and never does, but points to his pile of straws to convince me that this failure was our fault. "Your mother," he writes, "She grew bitter and ridiculous. She was an embarrassment. Rude. Everyone knew it. I held out for as long as I could. And you," he adds, "You were young, I know, but you became her Mini Me, and I expected better. You were so reckless, the two of you. I had to pull away."

He was "driven" to reject us. By us. It wasn't a choice.

One time, while my parents were divorcing, used as a verb because they were in court for nearly ten years, my dad told me he never wanted to get close because he "saw too much of his darkness in me." Another time, he claimed he'd drive drunk and get into car accidents because my mother was "ruining their marriage."

And yet, when he reappears, I still pretzel myself to appease him, deluding myself into thinking that if I just make him feel validated, it will stop. If I give him grace, I'll stave off the next cycle.

And then, no matter what I do or say, he responds with words that sink me. I feel the rawest, the quietest, after I've given him space to wiggle around my brain and fuck with it for a while.

And I pity him, which makes it so much worse.

"So something else then? Ethan?" My mom continues, determined to ferret out whatever's bothering me.

"Oh my god, mom. No. Just stop."

She kisses my hair, smelling my wet scalp. "Fine. But remember that men want a happy girl, not a downer. So don't be a downer, baby."

It always blows my mind that during a genuine attempt to make me feel safe and vulnerable, she starts her "keep sweet" speech and shames me into cheering up. It red tapes any talk about Ethan.

"It's not Ethan stuff," I reassure her again. "It's just Darcy. And Savvy. Everything is so chaotic. It's like, too many big, shitty things falling on top of each other. I don't really know what's going on."

"What do you mean you don't know what's going on?" She nearly screams, aghast. "You're the CEO now! You're gonna figure it out!"

In moments like this, I feel thankful for her and her hard-wired encouragement. If Simon designed the synapses that form my negative self-talk, the voice that tells me I'm incompetent, incapable and undeserving, she created the antidote, the voice that airlifts me out of every spiral and wraps me in confidence. For every Simon, or Janine for that matter, you really need a Monika. Or else the kid has no hope.

"Yeah, it's just . . . I actually don't know what's going on. Really. I'm not doing the 'poor me' thing I'm just learning a lot of stuff really quickly and I have this feeling like . . . I don't know." I purse my lips and taste the chlorine. I can't tell her about Jada or Marz or share any of my suspicions. I'm not in the market for a Stabler to my Benson. I don't know enough yet.

"I guess I just feel like something's off," I hedge. "Or like something bad is going to happen. Or maybe it already happened."

"You need to trust yourself. You need to change the narrative and tell yourself that you can do it." She looks down at the water, and then to me, her olive eyes gleaming. "I know how you feel, though, you know. Like someone's gonna pull the rug out from under you any second. I mean I had everything. We had everything. And it all just disappeared just like that!" She throws her hands up in the air, water spatters on the wall, and her massive breasts jiggle below the bubbles like they're incredulous, too.

"But it's not a disease," she tells me. "It's not following you. Just cuz Daddy hid stuff from us doesn't mean the world's out to get you or there's something, you know, whatever you called it. 'Off.'"

Simon did hide a lot from us. I found out about Nadya when I was thirteen, right before my Bat Mitzvah. She picked me up from school one day, which I always loved, because she reminded me of the senior girls, the cool ones, but even older. In her charcoal eyeliner and big statement earrings, she struck me as too edgy to work for Simon. He ran a hedge fund, after all. But she was like a big sister to me, always kind and inquisitive, and she humanized Simon, who became a little less irritable when she was around.

Driving us to the office, me in the backseat of her Wrangler, she handed me her Razr flip phone and said Simon was on the line. I picked up and he told me he'd be back soon to drive us home, and when I clicked to exit the call, I was met by a string of naked pictures of Nadya in a text chain with "S." My heart sunk in suspicion, but then I saw his nickname for her in the chain—"Nady"—and I knew for sure.

My Bat Mitzvah was that weekend, and she was there. I wore a pair of statement earrings, just like hers, that my mom and I bought at the mall. We threw a massive party at our house in Orange County. They covered up the pool and turned it into a light-up dance floor. Men in little black vests and silver ties served pistachio ice cream from behind our outdoor bar. I curled and highlighted my hair for the first time and wore a floor-length gown in my favorite color, fuchsia, and all the boys told me how hot I looked, "just like Hilary Duff." I spent the entire night oscillating between revery and distress, like somehow, my body knew this would be the last time I'd ever dance in that house.

The Raise

Over the blaring Destiny's Child and Ying Yang Twins, I looked on as Nadya schmoozed and danced, and heard a small voice inside remind me that my dad was fucking her, and that I needed to tell my mom.

Once the men in silver ties were gone and the music stopped, I slipped out of my dress, threw on my pajamas, and dragged myself to my parents' bedroom. I asked my mom to meet me in their bathroom to talk and take off my makeup, but when she got there, I couldn't do it. I couldn't tell her. I wanted to share exactly what I saw, and what I thought I knew, but something told me those three words, "Dad's fucking Nadya," formed the first small thread that would unravel our entire lives. I knew cheating was bad, I knew divorce was a "Shande," but more importantly, I knew that Simon had all the power. I understood, just by living in the four walls of our beautiful home, that he, as the man and the earner, had the upper hand. Triggering the end of their marriage would hurt my mom and me more than it would ever hurt him.

So, as she patted an oily cotton pad to my eyes and wiped off my mascara, tears welled, then streamed down my cheeks. She paused and asked what was wrong, and I told her they were happy tears, that the entire night was just as I had hoped, and I hugged her and choked back the sobs I would later release from the safety of my bedroom.

"Now that you're the Big Macher," my mom says, reaching for her purse and sliding it closer to the edge of the jacuzzi, "Does that mean you pick all the brands at Savvy, all the products and stuff like that?" She starts rummaging through the purse, a Mary Poppins bag filled with empty banana vape pens and four pairs of full-face sunglasses.

"Not necessarily, no. We have a whole team that does that." I remember to use basic, non-technical language to explain how the company works. One time, I tried explaining what our engineers do, using terms like "coding" and "machine learning," and ever since, she asks how our "coding" is going, making air quotes with her fingers, as though coding isn't real because she can't understand it.

"We source all the brands and things we recommend in the digital closet based on all these data points, like what people are actually buying or what product suggestions get the most engagement. I mean I'm sure I have some say, but no, I don't hand-select the brands or anything." She's already checked out, re-applying her Barbie-pink lipstick, even though it's bound to steam off in the jacuzzi in the next five minutes.

"Well, I'm hoping you'll help your mommy," she pouts, returning the lipstick to her purse and retrieving a red phone case with shoddily glued-on eyelashes on the back.

"What . . . what is this?"

"I'm calling it the Coy Case," she beams. "It's a flirty phone cover. It's for the girly-girls, you know. It has its own personality. I was maybe gonna give the colors different names, even. This one is Jessica. I always felt like Jessica was such a sexy name."

After recovering from the shock and depression of her divorce, my mom began her own entrepreneurial journey, and for years has been sourcing cheap shit from China she can flip or change slightly, then retail on Amazon. Once, it was silicon finger gloves for cheesy food, inspired by our nights chugging flaming hot Cheetos and binge-watching *Sex And The City*. Another time, it was bedazzled mace canisters that clipped onto your keys, which she designed when I left for college, and then gifted to all my friends. She once made Darcy a rhinestone Juul case in baby pink, which she winced at, but then graciously accepted and started using religiously.

"And you want me to . . . ?"

"I want you to put them on Savvy. I don't know if you do accessories, but—"

"We don't do accessories."

"But you're in charge now, so maybe you can do accessories, and then Mommy can launch the Coy Case and stop working at the bank?" She nuzzles her nose in my hair again, her way of telling me she's half-joking. "You know they're all such little bitches to me." Her coworkers Jane and Marla, are not, in fact, "bitches." They've got their own First Wives Club thing going on, the three of them, and they love roasting each other. I think it's how they get through the day knowing they're all single at sixty, and nowhere near retirement.

I pull my mom in closer and tilt my head to meet hers. In what felt like the blink of an eye, she went from private school pickups and ladies who lunch to hawking bedazzled rape whistles and "Jessica" on the internet.

"I'm presenting at a big conference soon," I reassure her. "I'll send you the link once they post the recording. You can send it to Jane and Marla and remind them what's what." I throw her a wink because I know she brags about me every time she needs to rekindle her pride.

September 2, 2018

Darcy Lyons 7:46PM
r u ok

Alexis Ecker 7:46PM
what
yah why

Darcy Lyons 7:46PM
you just seem off today

Alexis Ecker 7:47PM
work stuff is fine

Darcy Lyons 7:47PM
??

Darcy Lyons 7:47PM
is it Ethan shit

Alexis Ecker 7:47PM
no no
my dad reached out or whatever
but its fine

Darcy Lyons 7:47PM
fuck im sorry
what did he say

Alexis Ecker 7:48PM
he replied to something I posted to IG saying like, "i was raised by a single mom" or something and he didn't like it

Darcy Lyons 7:48PM
he follows u on instagram?

Alexis Ecker 7:48PM
i didn't realize it but ya
he has a finsta lol

Darcy Lyons 7:48PM
STOP
isn't he like 80
lolol
sorry im just dying at the thought of this
haggard little fuck
making a fake instagram to stalk his DAUGHTER
like sir r u well

Alexis Ecker 7:49PM
lolol no he is not well
and yah he's like 75 I think

Darcy Lyons 7:49PM
what did he say

Alexis Ecker 7:50PM
ummmm u know
that im ungrateful and a liar bc my mom wasn't
single for most
of my childhood
and im "manipulative" just like she is blah blah blah
and im kind of like
ok but functionally ya, she was kind of a single mom
bc you didn't do shit or take care of me or anything so

Darcy Lyons 7:51PM
ya thats fair
i mean he has no right to be saying
any of this
like u can't leave ur family for ur lil hedge fund concubine

Alexis Ecker 7:51PM
lololol

Darcy Lyons 7:51PM
and then nit-pick how ur family processes that
like
just go away and shut up forever

> **Alexis Ecker 7:52PM**
> true true

> **Darcy Lyons 7:55 PM**
> how can I help

> **Alexis Ecker 7:57PM**
> nothing its all good
> rly
> he just puts me in a bad headspace u kno

> **Alexis Ecker 7:59PM**
> i just wish he didn't have that control over me

> **Darcy Lyons 8:00 PM**
> i know
> and im sorry

> **Darcy Lyons 8:00 PM**
> but just know ur amazing
> and ur not a liar
> or a manipulator
> ur a good person

> **Darcy Lyons 8:03 PM**
> in fact
> i think ur the best

After indulging in some cucumber and hummus and killing a bottle of red wine with my mom, I toss an extra blanket in the guest room in case she gets cold and slink off to my bedroom. I hear keys rattling, and the front-door handle hits the wall, like it always does when Ethan comes home a little tipsy.

He greets my mom loudly—too loudly—like he's trying to signal his surprise that she's still here. It's his punishment for leaving me stranded, for outsourcing his emotional labor to the one person he knows would never reject the invitation. I change into my pajamas as their muffled banter ripples through the hall.

"*She's working so hard, I know.*" "*Have you gone to look at rings yet?*" "*Yeah for sure, it's going well. I'm looking into a few new firms. For sure....*" "*I know she says that but I could be dead in three years, Ethan. It's just not fair. I'm ready for my damn grandkids.*"

I bring a clean hand towel into the guest bathroom. My mom's lipliners, nail glue and pill bottles are splayed on the sink. I pick up each bottle: Alprazolam and Zolpidem. I quickly type each into Google to decode the spells they cast, the transformations they promise: Generic Xanax and some Ambien. I remember her going on both right after the divorce.

I shake a few pills of each into my palm and tuck them in my pocket. I look in the mirror and recite the mantra my mom suggested: *I trust myself. I can do it.*

I try it on for size. Again, then again. But it doesn't seem to fit. The girl I see looks unconvinced, and unconvincing.

I don't think I believe her.

September 23, 2019.

> **Yardley 7:04AM**
> need to respond to J and her lawyer. they followed up.

Alexis 7:04AM
call them. say Nov 6

> **Yardley 7:05AM**
> ?

Alexis 7:17AM
we can send the $ to her
by Nov 6
Ssy I'm on a call

> **Yardley 7:22AM**
> ok. They're asking for paperwork tho?

Alexis 7:18AM
ugh

Alexis 7:22AM
ok
ya

Alexis 7:22AM
say our lawyers can prep the settlement agreement
and the liability and NDA docs for her to sign and all that

> **Yardley 7:22AM**
> kk

Alexis 7:23AM
but don't commit to like
a date or a deadline for the papers

> **Yardley 7:23AM**
> what if they push?

Alexis 7:29AM
we need to close the round first and if there's any formal paperwork
or whatever
i think we will need to disclose it in diligence
i'm not sure but
just to be safe

Yardley 7:29AM
ok but
we can
/will
pay her on Nov 6??

Alexis 7:34AM
i mean
i fucking hope so.

10

September 25, 2019.

"He just makes it all look so seamless, especially with all the stress and pressure at the firm. I don't know how you do it," Janine announces to the dinner table after Ethan tepidly explains his plans for ALLMENMATR. We're all at Minetta Tavern—me, Ethan, Janine and Nolan, his dad—because tonight's the night we tell his mom about the whole "Partner" thing. Ethan wants me here as buffer, because Janine *adores* me—or so he says—but I feel off-kilter and foggy. I can't stop thinking about Darcy, and Jada, and how tight we are on cash. I sneakily chugged some vodka from the office freezer minutes before leaving for the West Village. It was a rushed attempt to take the edge off so I could be "on" for Ethan—happy me, conversational me. But now, I'm shoving the free bread rolls into my mouth in a clandestine attempt to sober up, because in a shocking twist of events, the alcohol just made me woozy.

When I usually see Janine, she looks slightly disheveled in a Hillary Clinton-inspired power suit, like she's been running from client to client and popped a button sprinting across the street. But tonight, she's sitting cross-legged in a high-necked architectural cloak, cosplaying as a gallery curator, or Tilda Swinton, and plucking her bread but eating none. Her white hair is in a stiff bob, and she can barely lift her arms to clutch her martini but struggles with a benevolent smile.

"At least I know you're taking good care of our boy," she says, turning to me—like he's a dog, not my adult partner. "Thank God he has you through this non-profit launch. Are you eating enough, sweetie? Is he eating enough?" she asks, first Ethan, then me.

"I'm eating, mom. I'm fine. We're fine." His response sounds loaded and defensive, but no one pries further. I can tell he's nervous. He pulls his index fingers to his lips and starts gnawing on his cuticle.

As I dutifully chew down my baguette and butter, I can't help but feel the contradiction in how Janine sees Ethan, versus how she treats him. She applauds his hard work, his knack for operating under pressure. She considers him her wunderkind but infantilizes him at the same time. Is his work so all-consuming that despite his genius, he forgets to feed himself? And therefore I—his struggling entrepreneur girlfriend with a fifty-million-dollar business—need to remember *for* him? You'd think as a celebrity feminist who runs a preeminent New York law firm, she'd promote a more equitable dynamic—one where I'm not expected to mother him or monitor his diet. But this is *so* Janine. She expects the world from Ethan but quietly doubts he can handle the responsibility, so he's left teetering on her pedestal while she gleefully waits for him to slip right off.

"How's the business, then, after . . . everything?" Nolan asks, clearly wracking his brain for how to talk about Savvy without mentioning

Darcy or the accident. He always looks like he's wearing ten thousand dollars' worth of custom-cut couture, his dark walnut skin aglow in his petrol blue sport coat. He never talks much, and I wonder if the flashy outfits are his way of taking up space around Janine, whose presence is painfully dominant.

"Gearing up for the next raise. Figuring all that stuff out." I force a smile and pray I seem sober. The anxiety I feel for Ethan and his big reveal on losing Partner has only deepened my intoxication.

"I'm sure you'll figure it out, honey," she says, and touches the top of my hand. "Do you think you'll stay at work once Ethan makes Partner? Maybe in the short term, but—" she pauses to sip her martini. "Have you both thought about all that long term, or?"

"Mom, please. Not now," Ethan snaps, and I can tell he and Janine have talked about this already, in private.

"I'm just saying! Two full-time, working parents," she rubs Nolan's back. "It's a lot, as you know. Oh—I almost forgot."

Janine retrieves a framed picture from her purse and wedges it between the bread bowl and our cocktails. It's a snapshot of me and Ethan from the last Butler vacation, smiling like Stepford mannequins in the lush, artificial landscape of Palmetto Bluff, South Carolina. Ethan's standing behind me in a cream linen suit jacket and aviator frames, and I'm wrapped in his arms, mid-laugh, in a spaghetti-strap dress with a cashmere Lily Pulitzer wrap pulled over my shoulders. I remember borrowing it from Janine because I only packed my leather jacket. She seemed a bit too excited to get me on camera, on record, in that outfit.

"You both look so good in this light," Janine says, marveling at the photo, "And I spoke with the property manager again. The takeover fee is *shockingly* reasonable. He said they're starting to book dates for two years' out." She places the property manager's business card in between us, then sips her wine, eyebrows raised.

"Thanks, mom," Ethan replies, slowly sliding the business card off the table and into his pocket, like it's a loaded gun. "It'll be good to have."

"Thanks so much, Janine," I say with a soft smile, holding myself back from reminding her that we're not even engaged yet. I fear that if I don't put physical distance between myself and the dinner table, I might flip it over in a drunken rage: the way she babies Ethan, the hints that I should be wedding planning by now, the way she talks about Savvy like it's a middle school project and I'm just short a glue stick. But instead, I take my anger out on my crusty baguette, ripping it into pieces with satisfying force.

The Butlers keep talking as our starters arrive. Janine goes on and on about some case at work while knocking back oysters, and Nolan quietly nods while nursing his red wine. Ethan bites his cuticles in between swigs of whiskey, and I zone in and out, making sure to perk up any time the conversation inches toward Ethan and work. But Janine is red-faced and drunk within a mere fifteen minutes and is complaining endlessly about some unruly client. It's *her* fault they lost the case—not Janine's. I look over at Ethan who has a sunken, defeated look in his eyes, like a little boy who's been trying to tie his own shoes all morning, but just gave up.

I feel my blazer vibrate but ignore it, not wanting to invite a chiding from Janine, who hates seeing phones out at the dinner table. But when it vibrates a second time, I panic that it's Yardley, or Gordon, so I take a quick peak.

It's worse.

Because it's my dad.

> **Simon:**
> Your mother shared a video to her facebook page of some quack talking about narcissism and narcissists and she said she was "so grateful to be out of her abusive cycle" and I just need you to tell her that if she does ONE MORE THING like this saying I am this or that, I will come after you BOTH with a libel suit. She let herself go our entire marriage and used our money to help criminals and hire them to work in our own HOME and I am done with her not taking responsibility. I bet youre doing the same with your little SAVVY operation over there. Right? She taught you the ropes huh? Me leaving her does not make me a narcissist and if anything SHE is the one. SHE is to blame. I have screenshot the post and sent it to my lawyer as she has blocked me on everything so I can't tell her myself. YOU let her know since you seem to have no regard for my feelings and live in your little LALA LAND together. GROW UP.

"Do you need to step out dear?" Janine says, and I can't tell if she's irritated that I'm on my phone, or genuinely concerned for my wellbeing, but feel safe to assume it's the former.

"Uh, no. Sorry. It's just my dad."

Ethan squeezes my leg under the table and then starts rubbing my lower back. My eyes begin to well up with tears against my will. It's the alcohol—I know. If I were fully sober, I'd have a much better poker face.

"Is everything alright? Can we . . . can we get you anything, or . . ." Nolan drifts off nervously and starts scanning the room for a waiter. I'm not sure what he intends to do, or order, but I'm positive the Minetta Tavern staff is not equipped to fix this. Though I may feel release if I could brutally rip up some more baguette.

"No, no. It's nothing. But thank you," I reply, praying I've aborted Nolan's confusing mission. "He just does this sometimes—contacts me if he wants something passed to my mom. She blocked him a few years ago because he can be . . . well, yeah, he can be a lot."

Janine gently grips Nolan's forearm and pouts, looking at him longingly. And I hate it. Because I feel defined by my dad-less-ness in those moments—in *this* moment. And I can feel the air thicken with their pity.

I am allergic to knowing that they see me as some sort of victim. I may have Daddy Issues, but I refuse to be "that girl." The one you can look at and know that something, or someone, has been missing her whole life. I constantly worry that I wreak of my longing, or even worse, my pain. It was an invisible string that tied us together, Darcy and I, the fact that we both lacked a Real Dad—a TV dad. We never discussed it explicitly, and I never dared to ask, but I felt her longing. I felt her pain. In the early days of Savvy, we used to end our ten-hour working sessions with delivery pizza and Friday Night Lights. We'd watch as Eric Taylor, the fictional football coach and father-to-all, would parent his team and take them in like they were his own flesh and blood. He was, as the show put it, a "molder of men." He taught his players how to be strong yet vulnerable, and how to make meaning of their lives even when things went to shit. He loved his daughter Julie, even through her rebellious phases, taking her to the father-daughter dance, helping her navigate teenage heartbreak, and making sure she felt seen and loved after he and Tami, his wife, welcomed their second daughter. I remember watching these scenes with Darcy, and immediately, the frequency in her living room would shift. An unspoken sorrow coursed between us, saying "I never had that. I don't know what that's like."

But in our unspoken sorrow, we also made a silent agreement: that the pain of knowing we would never be Julie, the sense that we were robbed—the anger, resentment and disappointment—it would never define us. We could never give our fathers that power. Instead, it was something we would use as fuel. Something to move us forward. Because if you don't, you live the rest of your life as the little girl he didn't love, maybe couldn't love, and you never become the woman you deserve to be.

"I'm gonna head to the restroom," I announce, desperate to taste the relief of my Juul in the privacy of a locked stall. Desperate to delete Simon's text or throw my entire phone in the toilet.

"I'll come too," Janine says hastily, leaving her seat. "I should freshen up before my scallops."

"It's always nice to see you, lovey," Janine says through the bathroom stall as I relieve myself, uncomfortable we're peeing through conversation. "Though I don't think I'll ever wear this out again. It's way too high maintenance."

Her muffled grunts tell me she's wrestling off her "high maintenance" outfit.

"Always great to see you guys, too," I reply, before flushing the toilet so I can I suck on my Juul, releasing the smoke into the swirling water bowl and praying she can't smell the mango vapor.

"I'm sorry about your dad," she slurs. "I know your mom went through a lot."

"She definitely did," I reply mindlessly, watching the air go cloudy with smoke.

I'll never forget my mom's face when I told her about my dad cheating with Nadya. Her eyes drooping, as though some hidden battery ran out, after a lifetime performing the role of a chipper and dutiful wife not only for him, but for me. The explosive confrontation went down at the synagogue I grew up in, the Pledge-y smell of its wooden halls and musty pew scent so familiar, so easily conjured, like a bespoke perfume I snorted for eighteen years.

A few months after my Bat Mitzvah, the night I almost told my mom about the affair the first time, Nadya started coming to our synagogue. She was a Russian Jew with no known affiliations, no Rabbi or temple to speak of, and told my family, walking in for Shabbat services that Friday night, that she was "trying out" different congregations. She was "so inspired" by the Rabbi at my Bat Mitzvah that she felt compelled to visit Shalom Emet. My dad feigned surprise. My mom said "that's so lovely." I caught Simon and Nadya exchanging a brief glance, like this interaction was rehearsed in a room we weren't in, at a time we weren't present, and I did my best to keep my discomfort a secret for the entire forty-five minutes of prayer.

I recall this night at temple as my first big brush with anxiety. It was summer, but the room was sufficiently air-conditioned. Most of the women were draped in cashmere shawls and the ones stuck bare-armed folded them tightly for body heat. My ass, though, felt hot and damp on the bench. My internal temperature was spiking, making my thighs sticky and itchy against the temple's upholstery. I could feel my heart racing and wondered if anyone else could hear it. I sat next to Nadya on my left, and my mom and dad on my right. I remember Simon and Nadya's tension—the same tension I feel with Dr. Wes—pulsing through the pews. Sitting in between them, I felt like an intruder. My mom, none the wiser, sang the prayers in her soft, sweet voice, like she always did, soundtracking my mounting panic with her whispered rendition of "Adon Olam" as the service came to an end.

Before sending us back out into the secular world, the temple staff would cart in a massive, genetically-modified Challah to slice up and dole out to its congregants. As my mom embraced our family friends and schmoozed with the cantor, I stood near the bulging Challah and took a piece, carefully peeling and eating the inner dough like string cheese to calm down and distract myself. In my disassociated haze, I watched Simon take a slice of Challah, stealthily hand it to Nadya, and keep her hand in his hand for a beat too long, the bread palmed between them. I immediately shifted from numb to irate. I couldn't handle the audacity of Nadya here, at our temple, feeling up my dad in front of the community I grew up with, infecting the walls and air of a place that felt so familiar, and so mine.

I rushed toward my mom and asked her to join me in the bathroom. I jerked her away from whatever conversation she was in and dragged her out toward the hallway. Once we got to the bathroom, I opened every stall to make sure we were alone and caught our shared reflection in the mirror. Her, with coiffed platinum hair and a black wrap dress to hide her belly pooch, which started to sag in her forties. And me, in a small black skirt and rhinestoned T-shirt, my "clear" braces tinged yellow from the coffee I started sneaking sips of during my mom's morning shower.

There was this passing, brief glitch in the matrix where I never saw the naked picture of Nadya. I never saw that passing glance. I misjudged the Challah exchange, and they were just breaking bread. *Weren't they?*

It felt easier to erase it all from memory, to rewrite the story so it never happened. In the span of five seconds, I told myself I witnessed nothing, and that nothing was wrong, but then caught myself in the lie. Just because I didn't want it to be true, doesn't mean it didn't happen. Just because I shouldn't have to be the one to tell my mom, doesn't mean it'll come from someone else.

The Raise

That spring, I had read from the Torah in front of everyone I knew and loved. I was an adult now, at least according to my religion, so I looked at my life, and my family, and said, "this is happening," even though it felt so wrong, and so unfair.

Age twelve, recently Bat Mitzvah'd, and petrified in the temple bathroom, I took my mom's tiny hands in mine and said it.

"Dad is cheating on you with Nadya. I found photos on her phone."

She stared at me, unblinking. She removed her hands from my grasp and started pacing, her heels clanking the cheap tile and echoing throughout the bathroom. For whatever reason, I expected her to slump down slowly, or collapse into herself. But instead, she was moving fast, darting from one end of the bathroom to the other. She needed to expel energy. She needed to think. She needed to feel her body. She needed to—

At that moment, Nadya waltzed into the bathroom, unaware, tossing her head back and laughing with a person we couldn't see.

And suddenly, the woman with the soft, sweet voice who sang Adon Olam and hugged the cantor and raised me my whole life, lunged toward the young Russian Jew who worked for my dad, and began smacking her in the head with a beaded Fendi bag.

Nadya started screaming and begging for help. My mom, bawling and in a blind rage, still hitting her over and over again with her flaccid, tiny purse. Simon and the temple security guard showed up simultaneously, the guard working to pull my mom from Nadya as Simon used his hands to block my mom's blows. A crowd of lookie-loos formed in the hallway, mumbling to one another while trying to catch a better glimpse of the brawl. My mom went from bawling to screaming, calling Simon a "piece of shit" and "fucking cheater" and "sad, sad man" who only cared about himself.

When Simon finally ripped Nadya from my mom's reach and escorted her out, past the crowd and toward the courtyard, the security guard did the same with me and my mom but brought us into his office. He wanted to keep us quarantined in the event Nadya called the police to press charges.

She declined to, I assume getting a whiff of guilt and showing no sign of injury. But it didn't stop the temple-goers from crowding around Nadya and Simon in the parking lot, offering words of support and sympathy as my mom and I sat alone in the buggy courtyard, calling a taxi to take us home while getting eaten alive by mosquitos.

I try to breathe as I shake these memories and compose myself for Janine, who is at the mirror applying a neutral lipstick and dabbing her lips with a handkerchief.

"A good life with a good husband, a house, a beautiful family. It's okay to want what your mom had, even if it she didn't have it forever." She beams and tilts her head at me. "You know what I mean?"

"I mean . . . yeah," I reply cautiously, unsure where this is going. "Yeah. I know that."

Janine catches my eye in the mirror.

"He's not like your dad, sweetie. He's *my* boy. And if he makes Partner, you can take a break from all the crazy business stuff. Even for a little. He says it's been very hard on you lately."

I feel the words rush from my gut to my lips—"Ethan isn't going to make Partner; he just hasn't told you yet"—but I hold back and stay quiet. Another woman enters the bathroom and slips into a stall. Her pee rushes out like a high-pressure shower, as though she's been holding it in for hours.

The Raise

I quickly do the math on Ethan's potential annual income as Partner at another firm, and what my equity is worth if we sell Savvy at our soon-to-be billion-dollar valuation. I have more earning potential, at least on paper, but it's true Ethan's financial future is more guaranteed, thanks to Janine and Nolan. Weaseled deep down in my gut is the knowing that Ethan offers me a cushion, and that he always has. That's part of the attraction, if I'm honest. Because if Savvy fails, but I'm Ethan's wife, it won't matter as much that I bet on myself and lost.

"Your mom can be the exception—not the rule," she slurs, the martini working its magic, erasing the labor and exhaustion of her long day on-the-clock, and replacing it with a tipsy recklessness she clearly feels entitled to. "I raised my boy *right*. And we *love* you." She pulls me in for a non-consensual hug and my arms stiffen at my side. The flash of intimacy dissolves with the sound of a flushing toilet, and we silently exit the bathroom.

When we return to the table, Nolan and Ethan look uncomfortable. The residue from some tense, unknown conversation of their own still lingers in the air.

Everyone pokes at their food as Janine launches into another diatribe—some client did this, Huma Abedin said that. Ethan squeezes my knee under the table and gives me a wilted smile, as if to say, "I'm sorry."

Because he doesn't tell Janine he lost Partner. Not over our mains, or dessert, or while waiting for his parents' Uber to whisk them back to the Upper East Side.

Ethan and I walk all the way home in silence, but he asks me to hand him my phone once we hit Park Ave, and then he blocks Simon's number. I let it happen but wonder if two broken people can fill each other's cracks, or if together, we'll never be whole.

March 3, 2019

Alexis Ecker 3:46PM
lolol so u know how I worked in service forever like when we first moved here and college etc

Darcy Lyons 3:47PM
ya

Alexis Ecker 3:47PM
so Ethan just texts me
"i rly wish I had worked in the service industry"
"i feel like it would have been character building"

Darcy Lyons 3:49PM
HAHAHAHA
omg
janine would NEVER have allowed that of her perfect son

Alexis Ecker 3:49PM
lolol I kno
i was like
"nice, babe. What prompted the revelation"

Alexis Ecker 3:50PM
and he goes
"i was doing research for a client, and the dole foods guy, like
the guy who makes all the canned fruit, he worked at a gas station"
like he pumped people's gas I guess
"and he's worth over 2 billion now"

Darcy Lyons 3:57PM
yah it was 100% the service job he should go pump some gas on the weekends!!!

Alexis Ecker 3:57PM
i find it funny obvi
but im also like
for people who HAD to do that, like what
we did at diff points
working retail or hostessing or whatever its like
nooooooo. That was not fun. That was
not character building
like
that was absolute torture, sir

Darcy Lyons 4:00PM
no
I would never go back
a customer at the sushi restaurant I
worked at in HS called me a
cunt bc I couldn't seat him right away
and got kind of belligerent
and I gave him some attitude
and my boss fired ME
like
no thank u

Darcy Lyons 4:01PM
my character is fine and dandy
without that experience

Alexis Ecker 4:01PM
ya exactly

Darcy Lyonsm4:01PM
but its Ethan u know
the price of a stable guy w some money

Alexis Ecker 4:02PM
i know I know

Alexis Ecker 4:07PM
what's going on w Henry
is he getting to a 3rd date

Alexis Ecker 4:28PM
???

Darcy Lyons 4:29PM
lolol no
I hate him

Alexis Ecker 4:29PM
????????

Darcy Lyons 4:29PM
we had the dumbest convo last night
just like
him sensing im always rly stressed and
distracted w savvy stuff
aand him just giving martyr vibes
like dating me is such a chore

Alexis Ecker 4:30PM
i don't get it
isn't he like
45??
didn't he work his ass off and have the same stress and sell his
company and shit

Darcy Lyons 4:31PM
ya
but its like
they can do it and maybe he imposed
that stress/distracted
energy on whoever he was dating at the time
or rather on his ex wife lolol
but they don't wanna be on the receiving end
u kno

Alexis Ecker 4:31PM
but then why do they start dating u
or someone like u
it just seems dumb

Darcy Lyons 4:31PM
idk I feel like
Maybe its hot for them and then it's annoying
?

Alexis Ecker 4:32PM
right

Darcy Lyons 4:33PM
or they assume im one of those fake ceo girl types
im "working for myself" but it's secretly for
one of those scary
MLMs I see high school ppl post about

Alexis Ecker 4:33PM
SO SCARY
like no bethany from 3rd grade I do not want to
buy ur fuckin
essential oils

Alexis Ecker 4:35PM
idk
it seems like a simple google search would tell them
exactly who u r
and how legit ur shit is

Darcy Lyons 4:37PM
ya but there's a difference between liking what I sound like or
how I seem vs how I actually am
bc how I actually am is usually the problem

Alexis Ecker 4:37PM
omg shutup

Darcy Lyons 4:38PM
it's true
but honestly I don't care
im already over it slash him

Alexis Ecker 4:38PM
but it's THEIR problem
ur perfect

Darcy Lyons 4:38PM
whatever
I get a free meal and a sleepover
sometimes
that's all I can handle rn anyway

Alexis Ecker 4:39PM
lol ya
believe me
ethan is a lot of work

Darcy Lyons 4:39PM
at least he's a good egg

Alexis Ecker 4:40PM
lol
is he?

Darcy Lyons 4:40PM
he would've benefited from some service
industry work
u kno
to build character

Alexis Ecker 4:40PM
HAHA

Darcy Lyons 4:40PM
but he loves you

Subject: URGENT: need your layoff list
From: Hunter Baker <*finance@besavvy.com*>
To: Alexis Ecker <*Alexis.ecker@besavvy.com*>
September 26, 7:05AM

Hi Alexis,

Per my last email, **if we don't close more cash by November 5, we need to lay off 80% of the team or more by that week—so in a month, basically.** I still need you to review the current team list + salaries and make the call on who we cut. I'll do new projections and see if we can stretch any longer, but I don't think we can. I'll be at the board meeting Thursday, lmk how I can be helpful in getting this $$ closed up…things are looking really, really tight.

Hunter

Hunter Baker
Head of Finance
www.BeSavvy.com
Meet Your Dream Closet

11

September 26, 2019.

The West Village always feels like a movie set with its storied brownstones and corner bistros. Maybe thanks to *Sex And The City*, or maybe because it's really that picturesque. I'm not surprised Victoria lives here. It's any yuppy's wet dream, but it's a neighborhood only few can or will ever afford. I, for one, cannot. But Ethan's trust fund could surely fill the gap.

I pop an Adderall and hit my vape repeatedly as I approach Victoria's place, mustering up the energy to do our prep before the board meeting on Thursday. She doesn't know I've started mainlining nicotine, and that's because I don't want her to. She may have a Xanax prescription, but I've never really seen her drink, or smoke, or indulge in vices of any kind. She'd always make passing, borderline-judgy comments about Burning Man whenever Darcy started prepping: *You do different drugs all in the same day? Aren't psychedelics kind of bad for your brain? Isn't there fentanyl in, like, everything now?*

I take my last pull, my last little hit of happiness, and my phone pings.

> **Dr. Wes:**
> Look who made the list

> **Dr. Wes:**
> www.thesituation.com/10-ecommerce-entreprenuers-you-need-to-know-right-now

I find a nearby brownstone stoop, sit, and rush to open the link, stunned that Isabella has already worked her magic. The Adderall kicks in and the familiar "zing" floods my system, the amphetamines making me feel focused and invincible like I can do anything, be anyone. As I read through *The Situation* piece, the obstacles I'm up against feel a little less daunting, a little more beatable.

10 E-commerce Entrepreneurs You Need to Know Right Now

<u>Ecomm's Katniss Everdeen: Alexis Ecker, Co-founder & (New) CEO of Savvy</u>

In just under seven years, Ecker has helped scale Savvy, the highly personalized shopping site powered by AI and data science, to nearly fifty million in sales and nearly one million registered users. Ecker co-founded the company alongside Darcy Lyons, the late entrepreneur who served as Savvy's chief executive until her untimely and unexpected passing last month. Ecker—taking center stage now after years running operations for the startup—has a lot on her plate. It's no easy feat to change roles, run Savvy and tend to a workforce in mourning. But investors and advisors agree that she's well-suited to face these challenges head on—and win. Mum's the word on Savvy's next move, whether it another round of funding, new launches or further expansion—but take notice. Because while Ecker may have thrived backstage, there's plenty of buzz that this next chapter in the spotlight may be her biggest and boldest one yet.

> **Alexis:**
> Eermm this comparison to katniss Everdeen is
> Rly something
> I havent won the hungergames yet lol
> Like
> Still got this money to raise
> And not sure who gave them that
> One million number...
> But I guess press is safe to fluff

> **Dr. Wes:**
> But its a great piece!
> And youre *this* close

> **Alexis:**
> Not if shit hits the fan first

> **Dr. Wes:**
> What do you mean?
> Whats up
> ?

I'm not sure how safe I feel sharing the gory details of said shit hitting said fan—the lawsuit, the money crunch—with someone I one) barely know and two) want to impress. While he's not on our board, and barely in venture anymore, Dr. Wes is well-connected, like Isabella. For all I know, he's in a busy group chat with his guys from FifteenFive where they swap startup tea or hot tips or whatever men do to suss out ways to make a buck. Women gossip for some semblance of social power, or to bond when they have nothing else in common. But men gossip for money. They find kernels of information—this company's struggling, that founder just left, this or that investor just passed on the Series A—and they use it to get rich.

But Dr. Wes doesn't seem like the type. And I could really use some sort of support system. Until now, he's only been helpful, and he's checked in on me more than anyone else has. I told Ethan everything, and he cared less about my massive pickle and more about the fact that I "took too long" to confide in him. I can't tell my mom about the Jada lawsuit or our money issues, because she, like the author of *The Situation* profile, thinks I'm some hero fit for fiction—a skilled, resilient fighter who is destined to "figure it out" and sell for zillions or IPO. She'd either react with her woo-woo manifestation bullshit or shut down entirely, realizing she'd lose all of her *nachas*. The bitches at the bank would find out about our imminent bankruptcy, our scandal, and my mom would get suicidal. And I definitely can't tell Victoria, who, as one of the few Latinas in venture with her title and seniority, would rightfully flip a shit knowing Darcy blocked Jada from the C-suite. And I can't risk losing Victoria. I need her now, more than ever.

I return to my phone with conviction, the amphetamines coursing through me and telling me to do what feels right, to trust my intuition. I deserve someone to talk to. I deserve someone who will take my side. And he won't judge me. I'm sure of it. I stepped into this mess, after all. None of it's even my fault.

Alexis:
Nothing official has happened yet but
We may have a small legal issue
Well its not really small lol
Idk why I said that

Dr. Wes:
All good Im sure

> What's going on?

Alexis:
No I mean
Basically

I hold my breath, silencing one last squeak of doubt, something telling me to keep it private, keep it hidden. Suppress the vulnerability. That's what Darcy would have done.
But she's the one that got us here in the first place.

Alexis:
We have this lawsuit threat
From a job candidate
For discrimination
She has evidence, and like
Shes in the right
100%
But she wants to settle
And I literally can't pay it rn

It feels so good to *share*. To know that the person on the other end is reading, interested, invested, and going to game-plan with you. This is how Darcy must have felt confiding in *me*.

Alexis:
I have a board meeting coming up
Idk if I should say anything
And ya
I'm basically stalling so I dont have to pay yet

> **Dr. Wes:**
> How successfully

Alexis:
Ish

> I mean
> I have to close the round by nov 5
> And then pay. So I verbally agreed to the settlement
> But im not gonna put anything in writing for a few weeks
>
> **Dr. Wes:**
> Well

Light rain starts to fall and his ellipses fill my screen. He's typing. Now he's not. Now he is.

The rain gets heavier. I get up and scurry from the brownstone stoop back to the entrance of Victoria's building. I duck through the door and feel my wet hand vibrate. I pause before checking in at the lobby.

> **Dr. Wes:**
> First of all it seems like you're handling it really well.
> Smart to stall.
> So props to you
> Second of all, I don't think you need to
> tell your board just yet
> If it isn't "material" and just a threat for now
> And the moneys gonna come out of the C then
>
> **Alexis:**
> Right
> Ya
> Thats what I thought
> Thank u!! phew
> This whole thing has been so crazy I swear
>
> **Dr. Wes:**
> As long as you weren't on any of the
> emails with the candidate
> About the suit or whatever
>
> **Alexis:**
> I wasnt

Im not on any of it

Dr. Wes:
Ok good
Cuz when you do pay the settlement after you have the money
It's all gonna have to seem fresh to the investors
Old ones and new ones
You know?
It can't be that you knew about the lawsuit for a while or during the raise and then never Addressed it or disclosed it
That's a bit more fishy
Even if there's no settlement doc yet or any legal docs yet
You'd technically have to disclose it in diligence
If there's anything in writing at all

Alexis:
lol I mean theres this convo
Right here
Which literally says I knew about it
Like hi
:)
Hello future lawyers
:-P
I know about it hehe

Dr. Wes:
Well I'm not here to sue you
I promise :)

Alexis:
Ya
No
All the emails went to Darcy
And I told my recruiter to handle everything on phone

I hit send, overcome with relief, and Victoria's doorman escorts me to the elevator. Her building is smaller and nicer than Ethan's, with more gold trim and antique furniture, and I can't help but wonder how much Victoria's dad paid for the penthouse unit. Doctor Solis is a retired-surgeon-turned-TV-personality who just wrapped a decades-old talk show on CBS. That means his net worth is in the hundred millions. I breathe through my pangs of jealousy, silence my phone, and find my zen right as I reach the top.

"Welcome welcome!" Victoria chirps, greeting me as the elevator door opens up to her gorgeous, light-filled palace. It smells like basil and geranium, and I'm immediately struck by the decadent, glossy artwork lining the walls. Shelves of color-coded business books adorn her living room, and the closet is filled with furs and coats that look fit for a *Harper's Bazaar* editorial.

"Shoes off, please. You can leave your stuff here," she motions to a velvet bench that probably cost ten thousand dollars. "I just ordered food, if you're hungry."

A petite, pale woman paces around the austere marble kitchen spraying and shuffling and stacking Tupperware, paying me no mind.

"That's the house manager," Victoria clarifies, like she sensed I was trying to decode the woman's identity. "Let's go."

She pulls a bottle of white wine from the fridge, calls to the woman to bring us our food when it arrives and walks toward a sprawling outdoor patio not fit for this cramped, suffocated city. On the way, I spot a framed *New York Times* clipping by the fireplace.

"To build the career you want, you have to take. You can't wait or hope or 'manifest.' You have to believe the career you want, the one you deserve, is within reach. But 'reaching' is active, and women need to remember that."

It's from the big piece on the C-suite gender gap from a few years back, the one that Victoria was quoted in. She offered the most Machiavellian perspective of those interviewed, saying we can't just sit around and complain about the pay gap, waiting patiently for it to change, because it doesn't shift the locus of power away from the men on top. If anything, it reinforces it, by letting them move on their terms, on their timelines. She told women to be loud, fearless and unapologetic in calling out pay discrepancies, to gather evidence and rally the troops, to get litigious if they had to, or quit their jobs en masse. While certain readers took to Twitter to call out her privilege—"easy for u 2 say! ur dad cud pay the crazy $$ fr all the lawyers!" "lolz ofc, bc u cn afford to get FIRED once they can ur woke ass"—she was mostly praised for it. And while I remember feeling some sense of kinship with her Twitter trolls—I, after all, could *not* afford a messy legal battle, or losing my income—today, I feel a little less resentful, and a bit touched she viewed the article as a trophy.

"Darcy loved this spot," Victoria says, opening the sliding door with a light laugh as we pass the framed quote. "I always accused her of coming over for the view. The numbers speak for themselves, you know? We could've run through them on the phone, but she always insisted on coming here." My heart rate gallops at the thought of crunching numbers with Victoria tonight, my incompetence laid bare in the glow of her regal apartment. I shake it off and think instead of Darcy, her growing interest in the finer things, which happens naturally with age, and how she probably loved Victoria's place because it foretold what life could be like, what Darcy herself could have someday if she kept pushing.

We turn the corner of the balcony and the city unfurls before us, a tapestry of lights and trees and tall buildings. I feel like I'm inside a snow globe, the sky a navy dome dotted with tiny diamonds.

Victoria opens her laptop. She's made a list of growth initiatives, each labeled with how much revenue it's expected to generate and how well we're tracking to goal. Over a few glasses of wine, she walks me through busy excel tabs and color-coded spreadsheets, then pulls up pre-written slides I can copy and paste into my board deck. Each slide comes with a script indicating what to say and when, and she forwards me an appendix of other questions the board may ask, and how to answer. This spoon-feeding puts me at ease, but what's even more reassuring is that Let's Fucking Grow is actually *working*—which means we're on track to hit a million customers and close the Series C.

Gordon's gonna flip.

A little drunk and giddy with relief, I find myself softening to Victoria's hardball spirit and manicured life. Over the last few weeks, I've been building up a quiet resentment for her discipline, her ambition, and most of all, her wealth. She has so much less to lose if we shit the bed with Savvy. She has a rich dad, rich brothers. She has a bathroom with a *custom bidet*, for Christ's sake. If I had a custom bidet and a multi-million-dollar inheritance, I wouldn't need to vape away my existential panic. Who knows if I'd even be working.

Suddenly the tiny woman, now screaming into her cell phone, pushes through the terrace door and charges toward our table. She drops a to-go bag from 4 Charles into Victoria's lap and quickly turns away, nearly knocking over her wine before disappearing back into the penthouse. Victoria looks both irritated and jaded, like the woman is a familiar nuisance she has no choice but to tolerate.

As the food's aroma wafts through the air and I start to realize how hungry I am, I let myself think about how we got here, and it hits me that Victoria could have stayed "lost" in that retail job at Anthropologie for much longer. She never needed me and Darcy—not really. But she took a chance on us and threw herself into building out Darcy's vision for the company, just like I did, and bet her entire early career and reputation on two girls who vaped on the bathroom floor and called it a "mid-day break."

"Thank you," I say, feeling tipsy and vulnerable, and hoping I can lighten the mood. "For getting us on track, for helping me out with all this. I know it's been weird to figure all this stuff out." I gesture to my computer screen littered with dozens of open tabs and financial documents. "I'm sorry if . . . if I've made it harder in any way. You were right about LFG and . . . I don't know. I should have been more open-minded. It's just been, like, survival mode since Darcy died. I don't always feel like I'm doing it right."

"I get it," Victoria replies, opening the 4 Charles bag triumphantly and handing me the charred broccoli and a plastic fork. "I feel the same way. Not so much about work stuff, really. But I'm still, I don't know . . . processing the whole thing." She picks at the button mushrooms and looks out at the gorgeous view, and I can tell she's thinking, weighing something.

"What was it, um . . . what was it like for you?" I ask cautiously. We've never been open like this with one another, not even after the accident, and I want to get it right.

"The Darcy stuff?"

"Yeah."

"Well, work was already, like, a tense thing for me? If that makes sense?"

"Because of the workload, you mean?"

"Yeah. But more like, it's kind of an issue? In my family? That I didn't pursue medicine like my dad did, or my two brothers. I mean Manuel doesn't do it anymore, really, since he's back in Chile. He's doing healthcare tech consulting, or whatever. He's a data nerd. But still, she sighs, still not looking at me. "It was a whole thing when I was working the floor at Anthro. Definitely worse. My dad couldn't believe I'd be, like, a sales associate at a store when he could've gotten me into the best med school in the country. And I had the grades."

Of course she did.

"But I don't know. I didn't know what I wanted to do, but I knew for sure it wasn't medicine. And I knew I was really into fashion, like my mom."

"What happened to her?" I ask, aware that Victoria mentions her dad from time to time, but never talks about her mom, at least not to me.

"She died when I was really young," she says, turning to meet my gaze, her eyes a bit glassy. "Cancer."

"I'm so sorry."

I study her lush lashes, her sad almond eyes.

"Thanks, yeah. I mean it sucked. I just know if she were still alive, *she'd* at least be proud of me."

She gives me a soft smile. Sometimes I'm shocked by all the broken young women, because their dads couldn't see them, or love them. Or never even tried.

"Are you, like, talking to anyone about it? A therapist or anything? I feel like that's—"

"No," she replies sharply, like the question is patently ridiculous. She catches herself, then softens. "I mean, there's just so much work to do. There *already* was, you know, from the dropship debacle, and then when everything happened with Darcy, it's like it doubled. And I know the team was freaked out. So I've kind of just put my head down and focused on them, and whatever work is in front of me." She eats a fork-full of mushrooms and shrugs. "It just feels like there's no time."

I nod furiously, because of course I understand. "Sometimes remembering to eat is a win, which sounds so bleak." I pop a wad of broccoli into my mouth.

"Yeah. I never understood how you or Darcy made time for it all. Even like, dating, you know? At this rate I'm like fuck, okay, *single forever*." She takes a sip of wine and sighs. "Ethan must be a really patient guy."

I laugh, a bit thrown. "Darcy made time for dating? *Did she*, though?"

I raise an eyebrow and drink in silence.

In my book, going for hour-long drinks in between work sprints and never getting to a second date does not qualify as "making time for dating," but maybe Victoria, saddled with a demanding schedule of her own, is trying to do some version of that. I don't want to outright knock it. I don't want to be rude.

"I mean she was leaving tons to see that guy," Victoria replies, cocking her head. "Or at least, I assumed she was leaving to see a guy."

This is news to me. Much like the buddy-buddy acai bowls and war-room goji berries, but the sense of betrayal feels sharper. It feels worse.

"What guy? Are you sure she wasn't leaving for Long Island? Like, to see her family?"

I can tell she's surprised by this interrogation.

"It was over the last few months, really," she says, confused. "I thought maybe it was to see her family, but when she'd leave my place after a Friday brainstorm or data review or whatever, she'd like, do full on makeup and fix up her hair. And she had a suitcase and everything."

"Her mom can be really intense about that stuff," I answer, reclaiming the conviction that I know her best. That I'm right. That there's no way Darcy had some secret guy in her life and rendezvoused with him behind my back. "Cecilia is a total perfectionist."

"Yeah, that could be it," she says with a sigh, and we silently agree to drop it.

The Raise

Victoria refills our glasses with the crispest white wine I've ever had—it's even nicer than the first bottle. We start sharing what our lives have looked like for the past few weeks without Darcy, revealing where we were when we found out she died, and the moments we spent alone, in mourning and in shock.

Victoria was still in Miami for her revenue retreat, and I was home with Ethan, heading out for a couple's massage. While we waited for our elevator down to the lobby, I got a call via Instagram from Darcy's brother. I didn't know Instagram calls were possible, so I ignored it at first, thinking it was some sort of mistake. But then he called me again. And again. I finally picked up, and he told me with chilling calm that Darcy had died "at her event"—those were his exact words—and I could hear Cecilia wailing unintelligibly in the background. I screamed *"what?"* into my phone maybe a thousand times, because it all felt like a glitch in the matrix, some colossal misunderstanding, like a lie that would surely get retracted if I challenged it with all my breath. I was waiting, pleading for a "never mind" that never came, and then the call was over, and I collapsed to the floor and threw up on the hallway carpet.

Ethan called the doorman to clean up, then paced aimlessly while I spoke to Gordon, then Isabella, then my mom, who came over right away. I kept calling Victoria over and over and over again, but she was flying back from Miami, so it took forever to get in touch. By the time we connected, Burning Man had just tweeted an alert about Darcy's death, so we both started getting incessant, frantic phone calls from employees, friends, and our other investors. My mom put my phone on silent and told me to go at my own pace. Ethan helped me make a list of everyone I needed to contact, and the most urgent things I had to do. I drafted a quick, somber email announcing Darcy's passing to the team and our shareholders, knowing that as soon as I sent it, the calls might stop. I didn't have all the information yet, nothing about the art car, the forty-foot fall, and it would be days until everyone learned the whole story, but I knew saying something was better than waiting and saying nothing. I knew I needed some time to process and plan without having to perform or "take shape," so I gave everyone a few days off, then a few days to work from home, and we all reunited in person the following week with a leader to mourn, but also, a business to run.

By then, I'd signed all the necessary paperwork to take over for Darcy and everyone knew what happened, and how she died. The fact that she toppled off a massive, mutant school bus reworked with metal scraps and LEDs seemed so freakish and Lynchian that for everybody, not just me, that first week back in the office felt fictional and surreal. We were millennial zombies, physically going through the motions, checking our emails, taking meetings and calls, but inside all of us, something had died. A sense of security, a sense of stability, a degree of certainty around how life unfolds and who bad things happen to. For the most part, we were all school kids during 9/11, and the energy in our office felt the same as that of my elementary school class the day of the attacks: like there was no such thing as security or certainty, and even Darcy Lyons, even America, could fall.

"But we fucking made it," Victoria says, raising her glass to cheers mine, "and you're gonna crush it Thursday. I'll be around in the morning if you need to debrief on anything, but I really think you got this."

We clink glasses and I sip my wine, which is lukewarm now, and I notice that her faith in me has taken the edge off, has smoothed something over. I don't need to stress about what Victoria thinks of me, and whether she finds me worthy of my newfound power. I don't need to compare and contrast us. And I shouldn't hold her wealth against her, even if it means she has less to lose if we fuck up this raise and Savvy implodes. Because, ultimately, we're in the same boat. We're both trying to honor Darcy's legacy and keep Savvy alive, trying to heal from losing her, and trying to prove ourselves to an industry, to a world, that never stops looking for evidence that we're not good enough, or that we don't belong. I had no idea Victoria and her dad had such a strained relationship, and I understand her so much better now: her drive, her relentlessness, her need to be the best.

"After this raise, you're gonna be the Chief Revenue Officer of a *billion*-dollar company," I tell her, staring out at the stars, thinking about Darcy and how in the multi-verse, she's still here, sharing in our wine and the breathtaking view.

"It's so crazy," Victoria sighs with a slight smile, her cheeks flush from the wine. "It was like fate when she found me that day, you know? I had no idea who I was supposed to be, or what I was supposed to do. But here? It's like all the puzzle pieces fit? I don't know. I don't think I'd ever be in a position like this or doing this level of work had it not been for her."

"Trust me—I get it."

"But sometimes you find a person," she continues, "or they find you, and it's like—"

"Besheret."

"What?"

"Besheret," I repeat, taking a final swig of my wine. "It's Yiddish. It means 'predestined,' kind of. Or like, 'intended.' Like the universe planned it.'"

She nods silently, and I look for Saturn and its hazy yellow light, wondering if it's finished orbit, back where it was when I was born, putting me to the test; wondering whether it's returned to push me forward; wondering what "forward" even looks like if I fail—if I don't nail tomorrow's meeting, close the round, and pay Jada what she's due. I can't see Saturn, but I know it's there. Because this chapter feels urgent, it feels ruthless, like getting pulled up and down a Gravitron.

Victoria takes our empty wine glasses back inside while I peer over her balcony and look down for the first time. It's steeper than I expected. I feel my toes prickle and my soles start to throb.

I automatically think of Darcy tumbling through the open sky, and how scared she must have been. My chest gets hot and my throat tightens, but then I start to focus on the cars below, the people walking to and fro. *You're one of them now*, I can hear Darcy whisper, like she was there in my bedroom when I moved in with my mom after the divorce, like she laid witness to my sense of stagnation, my envy toward everyone going from Point A to Point B. *You're plotting now. You're striving. You're in motion.*

May 27, 2019

Darcy Lyons 11:03PM
im gonna murder gordon
i swear tg

Alexis Ecker 11:03PM
oh no
what now

Darcy Lyons 11:04PM
legit texts me some girl's LinkedIn
and pitch deck
like
"do u think she has what it takes"
"i don't understand the market"

Alexis Ecker 11:06PM
what's the company

The Raise

Darcy Lyons 11:07PM
a party planning startup
they handle the invites and do sms reminders + shit
like eventbrite but cute idk

Darcy Lyons 11:07PM
but apparently he's never planned a party before so
he needs me (???)
to vouch for her (??)
Im like
dude I don't know this chick and
I don't plan parties either lolol
I HAVE NO LIFE BRO
IM UR LITTLE STARTUP SLAVE

Alexis Ecker 11:08PM
wtf does he think ur doing
having other founders over for like
lil tea sandwiches lolol

Darcy Lyons 11:08PM
fuck if I know

Alexis Ecker 11:09PM
what did u say back

Darcy Lyons 11:10PM
I didn't answer right away bc Im working
on the Q4 strategy stuff
so obviously
he called me

Alexis Ecker 11:10PM
STOP

Darcy Lyons 11:10PM
ya

Alexis Ecker 11:11PM
it's 11pm here

Darcy Lyons 11:11PM
id venture to say he pays 0% attention to
what time it is here
like
hes on his own planet
always

Alexis Ecker 11:11PM
omg

Darcy Lyons 11:12PM
so I told him to FUCK OFF
jk
i told him I'd check it out tmrw
but bw this and his lasik surgery lolol
im on edge
like
he can't rly see right now
he's a little blind
for real
so I have to send voice notes for evvvverything
like the man can't read an email or review a deck
and idk when it will end

Alexis Ecker 11:13PM
omg
wait
so he needed u to review the party planning deck
bc he legit
can't *read* it

Darcy Lyons 11:13PM
this is what I'm saying
im losing my mind

12

September 27, 2019.

"EYE CAHNT HEEYA YOU YET!" Jürgen screams from his Zoom square into the depths of Tai Fraiser, where the other board members, who are here in person, are taking their seats and settling in for our quarterly meeting. I can't see him, but I can hear the sound of harsh winds and crushed ice bursting through the room's speaker system. His assistant cautioned he'd be dialing in from the slopes of Sölden, Austria, even though this call has been on the books for nearly three months.

Gordon pours himself a cup of coffee, telling Jürgen there's no rush, and to take his time finding service. Isabella rolls her eyes at me, clearly peeved by their behavior.

"He can at least mute himself," Isabella huffs under her breath, her hostility toward Jürgen growing with each wasted minute. She looks sharp and expensive in silk-blend suiting that must be The Row or Jil Sander.

As Gordon takes his seat at the head of the table, he's in stark contrast with Isabella. I notice he's wearing cargo pants and FiveFingers running shoes, which are like rubber gloves but for your feet. This choice means we can all see the curves and contours of Gordon's ten toes, which feels too intimate. Too exposed. I hear Darcy giggle in my ear and whisper, faintly, that it's some ill-conceived attempt to play "alpha," a way for Gordon to assert dominance by making everyone else in the room feel uncomfortable.

Laney, a childless, fifty-something former Etsy exec that Darcy wooed years ago with an offer for equity in exchange for a board seat, is dialed in too. Even though we only ever see the top half of her body because she lives in Marin, the fanciest part of San Francisco, she's always dressed in ivory or soft, subtle beige, like she's Diane Keaton's body double in a Nancy Meyers movie.

Gordon sits upright at the head of the table and clears his throat before leaning into his MacBook speaker. We can still hear crunching and crackling coming from Jürgen's line.

"Okay team. Let's queue up," Gordon says to the room, before turning to face his screen. "And Jürgen—hey man—can you mute yourself, buddy?" He looks at me and Isabella and tips an invisible cowboy hat, as if saying, *"Here to help, ladies."*

Although I practiced this exact moment in advance, twice, I futz around with my bluetooth for a bit too long, struggling to sync with the monitor. This is the first board meeting I'm leading solo, or leading, period, so I spent lots of time this week rehearsing every single step: the tech setup, my operations overview, the growth slides Victoria gave me, and my closing remarks.

I was able to stay up late and keep prepping thanks to caffeine and cigarettes. No benzos. No alcohol. No uppers. I decided to forego my evening Ambien, which I stole from my mom, and I didn't take or pack any of her Xanax either. It's been weeks since I raw-dogged my life like this, but I got home from Victoria's the other night feeling stronger and more capable than I had in ages.

While my system may be squeaky clean and substance-free now, it's pulsing with nerves. It's working on overdrive to keep my anxious thoughts tight and buried, and I'm all too aware of the looming lawsuit, our dwindling cash reserve, and how important this board meeting is. It's the first domino in a chain reaction that'll secure our Series C financing, so if I fail now, the entire thing collapses. My mind is racing, but I have to remind myself of what's true, and what's real: it's been days since my last conversation with Yardley, which means we're successfully stalling Jada, and like Dr. Wes said, the lawsuit's not "material" yet anyway. That, and according to our revenue, our customer count, and every data point I have, Victoria's plan is going gangbusters.

Once my presentation finally syncs to the screen, I surprise myself and take shape, chasséing through the slides. I hit every beat. My words feel light and airy leaving my mouth. My voice sounds confident and firm, like I'm Darcy.

"As you can see, we've gained ninety-five thousand customers since turbo-boosting our growth efforts," I say, my mouth drying out like cotton from the subtle but persistent anxiety I've been choking down. "The trend line shows us hitting one million customers by the end of December, which we can confidently project to all the potential Series C investors." I click to reveal a line that shoots up and to the right as the slide rains animated confetti.

"So just in time," says Hunter, right on cue. As our Head of Finance, his role at this meeting is to be male and reiterate how urgently we need our Series C money from the board. If I say it, it seems worrisome and existential. But if he says it in his ill-fitting khakis and Patagonia vest, it just feels like finance. Like businessmen doing business. "Our model shows 'money in' on November fifth. So if Alliance and the rest of you plan to reinvest more money, we may want to chat through that now and do it sooner rather than later."

"That's right," I nod forcefully. "The timeline is pretty tight. We'd like to get your checks in by October."

My brain rips through our growing list of expenses and the toll Operation LFG has taken on our runway. There's the conscious, logistical part of me that knows we must bag the cash as soon as possible so we can prevent the lawsuit, make payroll, pay our office rent, and stay in business. That knowledge never leaves me, and I run through the same list seventy times a day.

But below, there's the deeper, egotistical part of me that wants the money so I can beat the odds and join the almost-zero percent of women that raise a Series C, boast a billion-dollar valuation and proudly lay claim to some self-made-boss-bitch narrative about grit, confidence, and of course, *resilience*. I rarely indulge these thoughts, though, because this outcome is so rare, the probability is so stacked against me, that it feels foolish to let myself want it. But I *do* want it. I want the story. I want the glory. After all I've sacrificed for this company, after everything it has put me through, I want my Katniss Everdeen moment.

No. I don't want it. I *deserve* it.

The deepest, hermetically sealed voice inside me, though, the one that only leaks in little whispers, nervously wonders who I am without Savvy, and what my "story" is if there's no glory in the end. If there is no outcome, and it all just falls apart. It taunts me, tells me I'm no one without the splashy fundraise announcement and startup founder halo. It warns me that if the money doesn't appear, and the raise fails, which means *I've* failed, my status slithers down the drain, taking all my career currency and self-worth along with it. I regress back to the girl trapped at my mom's, the one with no purpose, no direction. The version of me Before Darcy, before all this.

"We might as well start diligence, then," Gordon says, and that magic word—*diligence*—is exactly what Hunter and I were hoping for.

It means Gordon, and Alliance, are planning to reinvest more cash once we find a new lead investor like "Golden Daddy" Fisher Jing, who was on the Board of StockX and Skims. They just need to go through some financial and customer data before cutting the check. Hunter shoots me a quick wink and a smile, and we both know we've made it past our first major milestone.

"I mean the growth is there," Gordon continues, my nerves subsiding, relief taking their place. "And the numbers—at least what you've shown me—it all looks good. The rest of the fundraise will go much faster if you and Hunter start prepping the docs and send everything over to us."

"It's safe to assume we'll find a lead investor, Alexis," he continues, clearly trying to hide his surprise. "I'm gonna start making intros tonight, let everyone know we're ready to rip."

"No no—not yet," insists Isabella, finally looking up from her phone. "We should let them come to us."

"LET ZEM COME WHEYA?!" Jürgen crackles through the speaker, giving all of us a jolt. Isabella stands and adjusts her blazer, and I'm 99 percent sure she's about to come up from behind and mute Jürgen from my laptop.

"Savvy is strong. *Look*," she says, instead gesturing to the marigold and pale pink slide that says **GROWING 40% MONTH OVER MONTH.** She walks the room like a general, her chest up and chin high. "That's gold right there. *We* have the prize. So we let them come to us. *They* hunt. *They* pursue. That's why I got Alexis a headline slot at TechCrunch Disrupt," she pauses to survey her audience, her Cartier cuffs clanking in delicate applause.

Holy shit. She got me the gig. I honestly can't believe it. I was nearly blackout when I wrote that presentation draft the other night.

"Alexis can tell the full story," she continues. "Show off our prize. The round will peak and close before she even leaves the stage. A lot of my contacts have already read *The Situation* piece I secured, so we've whetted their appetites. They're impressed. But we need to keep the power."

"I like it," Laney chuckles through the speaker, and I imagine what it's like to be her, a cashed-in corporate servant who spends her days pruning hydrangeas and muddling herbs, who doesn't have to worry about pitching her vulnerable tech startup to nearly ten thousand people, who never knew and will never know the existential pressure of starting your own thing and keeping it alive. "It feels bold. Confident. And I think Alexis will do a wonderful job."

"Well, I *don't*," Gordon cuts in, before going sheet white. "I mean . . . I don't . . . I don't deny Alexis will do a great job. That's, um, that's not what I meant. I'm not comfortable—I mean—I don't necessarily like the idea of us delaying this raise when it's already—"

"That's *your* problem," Isabella replies, blinking at his FiveFinger toe shoes. "This decision isn't about what makes you comfortable. It's about what has the best chance of working. Whatever can get us the most capital at the best valuation."

"Exactly," Laney chimes in. "I mean just look at the numbers, Gordon. You said it yourself. We can afford a little risk here! I think she should do the presentation and start pitching after."

Everyone, in unison, turns to look at the growth slide. Gordon massages his chin with one hand and his rubbery left foot with the other.

"Hunter, what do you think?" Gordon asks, his eyes still on the slide.

"What?"

"*What do you think?*" Gordon reiterates, agitated. Hunter looks confused and uncomfortable.

"Um . . . well . . . I don't technically count, you know, as a board vote. . . . But . . ." He turns to look at me, his boss, who is the subject of this debate, or rather, the one on trial. Because what Gordon is really asking is, *Is she good enough? Likable enough? Smart enough? 'Savvy' enough to pull this off? To bet an entire raise on one presentation?* Hunter begins to mumble before—

"I'm just not sure how it'll play with Marz speaking too," Gordon interjects. "Sharing the stage with a competitor nearly twice your size. It messes with the framing. It makes you look small."

I recall our showdown at The Battery House, Marz badmouthing Darcy, then threatening me. I remember his arrogance, his comments about her inability to execute, and immediately tense up.

"It doesn't *make* us look *anything*," Isabella scoffs, pulling up the TechCrunch Disrupt schedule on her phone. "I checked the lineup. First of all, he's on a five-person panel at 8 a.m. that day. No one's there that early. And second of all, he'll probably say six sentences tops."

The thought of seeing Marz again feels like returning to a bad dream, awake but paralyzed.

"Did you not know?" Gordon asks, and I realize he's looking at me. "I thought he would have told you."

"What . . . what do you mean? Why would he have told *me*?" *It's fine. It's nothing. He doesn't know about my meeting with Marz. He's just—*

"Because you met up," he replies. Isabella and Hunter look up from their phones.

Fuck.

"Oh right," I scramble, composing myself. "When he . . . when he asked to get coffee."

"He asked to get coffee with you? When?" Isabella demands. I glance at Jürgen and Laney's Zoom squares, and they look equally concerned.

"Yes. But . . . but it was nothing," I stammer. *I'm the Talented Mr. Ripley. I'm Catch Me If You Can. Stay calm and composed. Don't fidget. Find a reason.*

"He wanted to pay his respects," I state calmly. "He and Darcy go way back. They did G Calibrator together. Gordon met them both back then, I think."

Gordon stops massaging his foot and leans back, releasing a long, loud "mmm," which I cling to as vindication.

"Yes," he says, but now I can't tell if he's buying it. "Same batch."

"Right, well, he wanted to come to the funeral. But he couldn't. Because . . . well, it was sweet, actually, he um . . ." I search for a lie, some viable excuse, because of course I can't share the real reason why Marz and I met, of course I can't tell them about Darcy's acquisition plea, and—

"Darling, I know you're newer to all this," Isabella interrupts, a bit alarmed. "But you should never meet with a competitor while raising capital for the business. It could cause rumblings that the company's in trouble and, you know, hoping to *sell*."

A lump forms in my throat and I swallow it down. Because that's exactly what Darcy was trying to do. *And I still don't know why.*

"So regardless of why you took the meeting, it doesn't *look good*. At The Battery House, no less. It's swarming with founders, investors. The types who take notice. I'm shocked none of this was obvious to you?"

"She's right," Gordon adds eagerly, thrilled he and Isabella can agree on something. "One of our analysts was there and told me in passing. Thought it was kinda weird. Maybe we're overthinking it, but if we want to hedge our bets here, you know, if word starts to spread, it may be better to start raising now, to show we're in good shape and going strong."

"No," Isabella says, shaking her head as she slides her notebook and phone into her Celine bag, before getting up from her seat. "You've been outvoted. Laney, me, and Alexis are the majority. We're waiting to pitch. But trust me—" She locks eyes with mine. "Don't do it again. You're lucky the growth looks this good. And on the heels of such tragedy, no less," she says, nearly licking her lips, like Darcy's death is the perfect amuse-bouche for investors, all of whom want to see a business plan, traction, and numbers, of course. But nothing writes big checks quite like a juicy story.

Gordon and Hunter shuffle their papers, preparing to leave. Laney shoots me a "good luck" message before dropping off the Zoom, and I notice Jürgen is already gone. Isabella slips on her camel trench coat and snaps a picture of the revenue graph on the screen.

"Just hype up the user growth and really own it," she says, giving one last glance at the screen. "And if anyone's worried we wanna give up and sell, this slide should shut them right up."

Alexis:
Crushed it. TY

Victoria:
Knew you would

Alexis:
Marz is doing TC disrupt
Wait
Lol
I'm doing TC Disrupt
Isabella told me today. she got us a spot
Its so fucking soon tho

Victoria:
AHHH!!!!!
Yessss
I'm around tn for prep
Do you need any help?

The Raise

Alexis:
I think I'm ok

Victoria:
....?

Alexis:
I swear! Lol I'm good

Victoria:
Ok ok
I trust you! lol
No help then
I just know its sometimes hard to ask for it
I have ptsd from when stop the bleed imploded
I know that wasn't all your fault, but...

Alexis:
I did ask for help!!!! I asked for a project manager
I knew it was on the road to disaster
Darcy said we couldn't do it
Bc of budget etc

Victoria:
Well
In my book you should've had help
We ended up losing so much money anyway
W the checkout breaking and losing all those orders

Alexis:
I know
But look at u
U made it back for us in no time

Victoria:
Aw shucks :-P

Victoria:
R you celebrating tn

> **Alexis:**
> Not doing shit
> Gonna eat leftover Thai and flop
> Ethan's getting drunk w his Michigan crew
> So im AWOLLLLLL

I put my phone down and submerge in the hot bath water and its lavender bubbles. I reflect on the board meeting and getting caught on my coffee date with Marz. Thank *God* the growth looked good. Otherwise, I'm sure Gordon and Isabella would've come down much harder on me. But then again, if the growth's been looking this good, why did Darcy want to sell to Crafted? And who was that guy Victoria said she was seeing? Was that a thing? The familiar anxiety I've been stuffing down consumes me again, and I hear three consecutive pings on my phone.

I click my screen open with wet, pruning fingers.

> **Ethan:**
> Hi
> R we ok
> ?

> **Alexis:**
> Wat do u mean

> **Ethan:**
> Idk
> U just seem off since dinner the other night

> **Alexis:**
> R u drunk?

> **Ethan:**
> No
> I had three beers

The Raise

Alexis:
Ok
Sorry
I mean I feel fine
I had a great board meeting today

Alexis:
What's on ur mind

Ethan:
I just feel like
U don't appreciate or acknowledge that
my shits also a lot rn, too
I'm worried about the work stuff
And telling my mom

Ethan:
Its hard to talk abt this
Sorry
I just don't know where we r at

Alexis:
Is that why we r texting
And not talking

Ethan:
Ok so ill call u in 5

Alexis:
I'm in the bath
Idk that I have it in me rn after the board stuff tbh

Ethan:
Let's make time to talk about it then

Alexis:
Ok
We should

Alexis:
Maybe doing the non-profit thing rn is too much
And better to focus on moving firms first??

Ethan:
Ya
Mayb

Alexis:
Im like
On the fucking fritz here
I'm rly sorry if u feel like things have been off
A lot on both our plates

Ethan:
Ok
I mean
Ya I get it
It just sucks

Alexis:
I know
I can't rly predict when this is all gonna level out tho

Ethan:
Right

Alexis:
And I feel like I have to do this
U said I could do it and that I deserve it

Ethan:
Yes
I did

Alexis:
Right
So wat do u want
Like

The Raise

> **Ethan:**
> I just want my old gf back

> **Alexis:**
> Ok

> **Ethan:**
> Or at the very least know what ur rly thinking
> Don't make me hack into ur notes app lol

> **Alexis:**
> Omg

> **Ethan:**
> What?

> **Ethan:**
> ?

> **Ethan:**
> ????????
> Wtf

I leap out of the bath and towel-dry as quickly as I can, clumsily calling an Uber with wet, dripping hands. I grab an oversized tee and Ethan's sweats, the closest pair of pants I can find, and dress my still-damp body. My heart is racing as I wrestle my wet leg into Ethan's pant-hole and watch as the car emoticon inches closer and closer to Park Avenue.

I rush down to the lobby and hurl myself into the backseat. I nibble on my hand skin again, my teeth gnawing at the wrinkles around each knuckle. I pull and tug and grind the skin until the Uber suddenly stops at our office. I fall out of the car and rush toward our back entrance, fumbling around the keys to the door.

I burst into the pitch-dark office and nearly trip over the umbrella stand as I paw around to find the lights. I'm welcomed by the familiar smell of fig, sandalwood, and a hint of rotting trash. I gag and wonder if I should bring our bins down to the street.

With the kitchen light now on, I hurry toward Darcy's office. I'm possessed by my need to know. My need to understand. I want to reincarnate her and tie her to her Aeron chair and plead with her until I have all my answers: why she wanted to sell the company, why she didn't tell me about Jada, why she was so on edge when I bungled the drop-ship launch, and why she never said sorry.

As soon as I pull her laptop out and crack it open on her desk, I find laser focus. I stamp her password into the keyboard and scan her applications for what I know I need.

Reminders . . . no.
Keynote . . . no.
Contacts . . . no.
And then, *there it is*.

The little square icon with its rounded edges. A mini piece of paper with a yellow bar on top. The Notes App. The Holy Grail. The app promises a portal to Darcy's most ad hoc thoughts; her most vulnerable realizations; her musings; her to-do lists; her 401k password; a bazillion links to tops she never purchased and apartments she never leased. I'm shocked I didn't think of it before, but she was never the most open book. If her family struggled with vulnerability, she did too, inheriting their inability to "go there." She rarely shared how she felt, or what she needed, or how the highs and lows of our journey affected her mental and emotional state. It's why I learned to read her eyes, the slight twitches of her shoulder, and decode the hidden meaning in the things she *didn't* say.

I take a deep breath before double clicking the Notes app icon, and brace for impact as I enter this new world, the one she built alone. Without me.

And with one quick scan, I know I've done it.

I know I've hit the jackpot.

The Raise

August 3, 2009

Im never going back to b bar ever again

I dont fucking care if James Franco is there auditioning GFs okay!!! im NEVER going back!!!

I was waiting in line to pee and Jackson came up wasted and was like

"I haven't seen u since senior yr but I still read Dean's piece abt u all the time so it feels like we've stayed close"

I almost socked him I swear tg like how repulsive can u get

And I was like "that's a nice way to put it its not rly a piece abt me its more like Dean used me for his art or whatever and didn't tell me he recorded anything" and now everyone at school knows I sucked him off and how he felt watching me

And he was like "oh he always told me u knew that he was recording and he was gonna write about it that's the only reason I feel ok reading it"

????

Like ok ur legit telling me at the bathroom line of bbar in all our sticky shoes and 2 sober braincells that u "read this piece all the time" like ok r u hard rn bro>?? Wtf

He used my full name!!!

And the teacher wouldn't even do anything he legit let him read it in front of the entire class apparently, Lucy told me

Im only pissed I never saved the pdf cuz ya maybe I am a bit curious what it feels like to watch me do that, who wouldn't be

I feel like that's the least I deserve after what he did

I didn't wanna read it at the time bc I felt like if I did I couldn't be mad about it or something

But tonight I couldn't ask Jackson for it so I just had to scream at him and pee and leave and now im waiting in line for a corndog

June 17, 2019

Baby names

Girl:

Ava
Rae
Quinn
Harper
Charlotte
Paige
Delaney

Boy:

Miles
Alex
Hudson
David

May 28, 2009

last night Elisa had a panic attack and I feel like it fixed everything just for a few hours

The Raise

Graham was over and his finger was inside me and my phone buzzed and It was Elisa, and I called her back. she said she smoked too much and she was too high. And she thought she was dosed with something like not just weed. She has a broken foot also and its in a boot now. she went hopping through her apartment halls screaming for help because her "brain was burning" but no one was home.

Even tho her boyfriend Jackson was w her Elisa said she rly needed me to go to the hospital asap

So I showered the sex off of me and got dressed to go and im thinking, she'll def calm down before midnight, and I strutted to the L in my hot pink skort and studded black heels and a see through top bc I figured id go out after w graham.

I stopped to get us all bagel sandwiches for dinner and we were there literally until 2am.

Elisa had taken azo pills for her UTI and she accidentally peed her white sweatpants in the hospital bed so it was just this big neon orange puddle of piss on her butt all night

The nurses said Elisa had a panic attack and her heart rate wouldn't go down but that nobody dosed her. Elisa didn't believe it.

I think everyone in NY feels lonely all the time

Especially when they're alone

so I was rly glad to have spent a night w Elisa and Jackson and Elisa's other two friends came too later

We were all chatting and laughing while Elisa was in her own pee on the gurney bed and I felt like, I was happy to be doing that instead of going w graham

Elisa just kept us laughing and laughing even tho she didn't mean to and was panicking the entire time but I think we all stayed til 2am bc we were all afraid to feel lonely again

At least that's why I stayed

I feel so fucking lonely all the time, like, even when I'm with ppl

But at the same time I had this sense of like, I never wanna be Elisa. I never wanna be that girl. I couldn't believe she was like that in front of Jackson it was CRAAZYYYY

If my mom ever knew I had azo pee all over me in front of a boy , on a gurney, in front of my BOYFRIEND????!!! Lolol she'd kill herself I can't

She was so not in control and so out of it and such a mess

I feel like if it were me id go to the hospital dead solo and pray no one I knew ever fucking saw me

January 5, 2010

Why I broke up w graham and we r not compatible

- he acts like dating me is a burden bc I "work too much"
- He doesn't know who he is or what he wants
- He thinks the clueless thing I wanna do sounds "childish"
- Hes not exciting
- Hes basic aka he only eats quesadilla or pizza and WE LIVE IN NEW YORK
- He needs a lot of validation like at his core he rly need someone to always be telling him he's so smart and great etc and its exhausting
- I was bored
- I don't think he rly believed in me
- he made me feel insecure
- He's actually 5'8 not 5'9 and a half like he says

The Raise

November 30, 2012

The app

- curation and scale
- Lots of shit that works for ur body type and color palette. There has to be a LOT to look at
- True spring, true summer, cool spring, cool winter whatever
- Can use kibbe body type test or something else and they upload a pic and the platform tells them their type and color palette???

Pulling in ecomm listings from other sites or we r hosting? Owning????

If we host from other sites, —> we take commission if the customer orders

If we own it all its more $$ but we have more control and margin

WHAT DATA DO WE COLLECT UPFRONT TO MAKE IT GOOD BESIDES THE PALETTE AND BODY SHIT

How do we make it not too much work.. is it a quiz??

Intro box?

To do:

- find Etsy pitch deck online
- Find stitch fix deck online

April 8, 2019

he feels exhilarating

The beginning of something

Like getting pushed down a zip-line

May 24, 2019

- makeup wipes
- sav blanc the one w the starfish on the front
- Amy's Mac and cheese
- Amy's veggie lasagna
- Cucumber juul pods
- Condoms
- Jergens tanning shit
- get waxed (bikini, lip)
- Highlights w Jen
- Eyebrows

May 1, 2019

I told him he needed a haircut and he sent me a picture of his egg salad

I reply

It continues

I wonder if he's gonna wish me happy birthday

I googled him but beyond what I already knew I found his grandma's obituary and his mom's twitter which is private

I always thought I wasn't beautiful or smart enough for him

But we'll see

Who feels exhilarating?

Whose egg salad?

Who needed a haircut?

And why does she have a recent log of baby names? Why is she buying condoms?

These intimate "notes to self" have me feeling both touched and betrayed. To meet Darcy at age twenty-three, before she caught my eye on LinkedIn that fated night, before I even knew she existed, feels like the most beautiful gift. To access her young and unfettered brain, a version of her that feels so innocent and free of investor pressure and board meeting chaos and deadlines, is like traveling time and space to meet the love of your life in her purest form. But it also feels like trespassing, invasive and crude and vile, because I know, deep down, all of this was meant for her eyes only.

And I hate her for that. I hate her for hiding from me. But more than that, I hate the wound that made her feel like she had to keep her full self a secret. I want to know who put it there. And I want to hurt them. I want to handcuff them to a locked cage and pry their eyes open with metal clamps, show them every beautiful word she wrote, every tender thought she had, and slice their skin open until they bleed out screaming "I'm sorry" for teaching this young girl to shut up, to grin and bear it, and mute the most delicate and complex parts of herself for the outside world. I never knew about this incident with Dean, the fact that he hooked up with her, recorded it, and published some trashy story about it for the entire school to read. I never knew she felt so lonely, even with her friends. I never knew she could be this open and vulnerable.

Did I ever really know her at all?

I pace around Darcy's office trying to shake off my sudden sense of betrayal, racking my brain for clues as to who she was dating. I remember what Victoria said on her balcony during our board prep—

that Darcy was dating someone who wasn't from New York. She mentioned Darcy would get dolled up at her place before leaving for the weekend, and that Darcy had a suitcase with her.

Did she ever tell me she would be gone for the weekend? Did she tell me where? I think and think hard but hit dead end after dead end. I finally succumb to the deflating fact: Darcy was dating someone she really, really liked. Someone she liked enough to brainstorm baby names for. Someone "exhilarating," as she put it. And I had no idea.

But why?

I migrate from the Notes app to her calendar and her inbox.

Was she flying somewhere? Where was she going?

I hover my mouse over her inbox search bar and type in the word "FLIGHT."

I cross-reference her calendar and comb through Amex notification after Amex notification, all confirming flights for work trips I knew she was taking or for the occasional wedding or bachelorette. I spend another twenty minutes bleary-eyed and beholden to the screen, matching emails to her color-coded Google calendar events from the last two years, hoping somehow, I'll catch a discrepancy.

But nothing.

Until Friday, April 7, 2019.

I catch a thin orange line, representing a mere fifteen-minute event on Darcy's jam-packed calendar, titled "Acela 2248."

But that doesn't confirm she went anywhere. She could have had a friend in town and wanted to keep tabs on their train and arrival time. The Acela spans Philly and Washington, where some of her friends moved to settle down and start their families, so it could be anything. It could be anyone.

We have our weekly exec team stand-up every Monday morning, which guarantees she was in New York to start the work week. She hasn't missed a Monday standup since her appendix exploded in 2017. And even then, she was back in action by Tuesday afternoon.

I skip to April 9 and 10, that Sunday and Monday, to see if she logged a return trip. If she *did* leave to visit some suitor, she would have had to be back in the office by 9 a.m., which is when we all gather to share department updates and how we're tracking to our revenue goal.

And there it is. Sunday.

Another thin, orange line. "Acela 2255."

I rush to Google the train numbers, but it's impossible to pin anything down. Both trains make stops in Washington, D.C., New Haven, Stamford, Boston, Wilmington, Baltimore. For all I know she was cozying up to some Bain exec with a mansion in Stamford, or serving as the mistress to a horny politician in D.C.

I quickly pull up her Notes App again and feverishly skim for clues. I search the names of each city, each state, and read as quickly as my tired eyes and rabid brain will allow. I try not to get distracted, but it's so hard when she feels reincarnated by each entry, each word:

June 22, 2014

- Sav blanc

- Popcorn

- Amy's Mac and cheese x 8

- Amy's Mexican casserole x 8

- Granola

- Chobani

- Cucumber juul pods

June 18, 2014

Sometimes we don't want to know what anyone thinks of us

But other times all we want is to know what someone thinks of us

September 29, 2018

I can feel myself depreciating

As each neck wrinkle gets steeper

And my legs become not only hairy but a dry I can't lather away no matter how hard I try

And all the little starter-pack girls come to work w their tight ponytails and tight glowing skin and they all have yet to pay $3,000 every 3 months just to stay like that

I wish I had known how good I had it and been more out there instead of spending an entire decade in this office

And they wanna be me but they have no clue, like

Its literally me versus them for everything now and even tho im smarter and have more experience and have learned way more they still have the thing any investor wants or any guy wants which is the youth they feel slipping

Just like I feel it slipping

I swear tg i feel like my 30s is me just fighting for my life, for relevance, for higher eyebrows lolol

And so its like why

why would u wanna be me??

The Raise

If im just a wrinkly neck on a pair of dry ass legs stuffing needles into my face so I can be YOU and my wisdom counts for literally nothing and im too old to be single but too young to have any real respect

I know I could've settled down and all that but it just felt too easy

and wtf would I be known for, then ??

Literally id be known as "that girl" from college, the one Dean wrote about. He wrote about every single thing we did in bed that night and read it to the class and everyone in school knew and that's it. That would be my whole

identity

she got married to John Hammersmith "the third" at a lovely country club in rhode island, cuz he had no idea about the Dean thing!!! About her body count!!! About what a whore she was!!

But I wanted no excuses

No excuses for not going for what I want

Bc if John Hammersmith gave me the world

Would I even need to make my own?????

After another fruitless dive, I pivot back to her email inbox and search the names of each city along the Acela line.

Baltimore. Nothing.

Washington. Nothing.

New Haven. Stamford. Wilmington.

Nothing. Nothing. Nothing.

Boston.

Bingo.

On May 19, an email receipt shows that Darcy took a Peter Pan bus from Port Authority Bus Terminal to South Station Bus Terminal in Boston, Massachusetts. On May 21, she returned by train.

The hairs on my arms stand up, and my internal temperature starts to climb. A small voice within, as low as a whisper, tells me that I know. I know who it is. And maybe on some level, I've known all along.

I revisit her Notes App and type in "south station."

May 16, 2019

9am

Gym

Wax

Eyebrows

Trim

12pm

PA bus to south station

take redline 4 stops Kendall/MIT

The Raise

I stare at the screen, biting my cuticles.
Boston. South Station. MIT.
Of course.
Darcy Lyons was fucking Dr. Wes.

13

September 28, 2019.

As I struggle into my umpteenth jumpsuit of the afternoon, I try to quiet my spiraling thoughts about Darcy's obsession with her appearance, her resentment toward aging, and of course, her relationship with Dr. Wes. Isabella demanded I trek to an overpriced, minimalist boutique in Cobble Hill called "Piper Muse" to find a suitable outfit for my TechCrunch Disrupt presentation. She's close with the owner and told her to find me something "chill, eye-catching, yet composed." As such, the slim, early-twenties retail associate has dutifully filled my dressing room with oversized jumpsuits ranging from beige to eggshell to a very bold Victorian pewter. She keeps serving me Prosecco in a clear and stemless plastic wine glass even though it's 3 p.m.

"Show me the Nili Lotan once you're in it," the girl calls out from the stock room. The store is empty, and there's no one strolling the streets. "Pumped Up Kicks" by Foster the People floods my dressing room, and I wince.

The Raise

I shimmy into the jumpsuit legs and stare at my breasts. I feel an unexpected surge of confidence, a newfound attraction to myself. It's true I've lost fifteen pounds since my CEO saga began, leaving my body leaner and tighter than it's looked in years. But I can also make out a fresh yet invisible stamp of approval on my chest because Dr. Wes noticed and liked Darcy, and now, he likes me. I don't want it to matter, and I tell myself it doesn't, but I know deep down it does.

I feel conflicted about their secret affair. It kept me up all night. On the one hand, I'm happy she felt this type of crush and companionship before she died. For the near-decade I knew her, she never let a man excite her. She never inconvenienced herself like that, traveling to Boston and back on her precious weekends. The men she entertained had to fit squarely into her life, and existing routine, or else they got the boot. And she never discussed a desire for children. But here she was, ranking baby names.

On the other hand, there's something about her obsessing over and physically transforming for Dr. Wes that feels too anxious, too needy. I think about Darcy pining for him from afar, stalking his mom on Twitter, reading his grandma's obituary, pulling and tweezing and tanning and scrubbing herself to perfection before catching the train to Boston. I knew she Google stalked potential investors in advance and contorted herself slightly for Savvy, dressing more conservatively than usual for board meetings or slicking back her wild red hair before Town Halls. I know she cared about appearances and maintenance and all that for her own self-image, for her own pride. But there's something about her stalking and fixing and grooming for a man, and then hiding him from me, from everyone, that feels unnerving.

"Did you throw on the gray one yet?" the associate asks.

By the volume of her voice, I can tell she's hovering right outside my dressing room now. "We close in twenty, so just checking in."

"Not yet," I reply, realizing I've been zoning out and still have twelve jumpsuits to wiggle into. "Sorry."

"What's this for again?" the girl asks, her voice floating farther away.

"It's for a big presentation," I belt, hiking a too-tight eggshell option over my thighs. "It's basically a pitch to a bunch of investors. For my company. To get money from them."

"Oooo sounds fancy!" she replies giddily. "Like how much money? Is that weird to ask?"

"No," I huff, shoving the eggshell jumpsuit off my body. It doesn't fit over my breasts, which are still plump, despite the weight loss. "It's seventy-five million dollars. That's what we're trying to raise, at least."

"Oh my god! Wow, okay. I'll stay open a bit longer then. We've gotta find the *perfect* fit!"

I take an olive jumpsuit off the rack and brace myself for another disappointment. I've never paid this much attention to my appearance before. Beyond buying those "serious-looking" reading glasses and loading up on black this and black that over the years, items I can lazily throw together while still looking "chic," I never prayed for higher eyebrows or softer skin or the glow of youth like Darcy did. I always sensed it, but her Notes confirmed that she had a base need to seem perfect, to seem sewn together with invisible string. I don't know if it's because her beauty excused her aloofness, creating a gorgeous walled garden people wanted to trespass, but never could, like Gramercy Park.

Or maybe this is just what it takes to be in the spotlight, like she said. Maybe it went no deeper than that. Her beauty kept her current and gave her currency. As a woman so squarely in the public eye, she couldn't bear to depreciate right before our eyes. And she simply thought what all women think, on some level: the older I look, the less power I have.

Either way, there is something so lonely about staying so beautiful. Even though I feel a thrill when eyeing my smaller frame and fantasize about what Dr. Wes will think when he finally sees me in the flesh, I've also never felt more isolated than here, in this dressing room, contorting and fixing and perfecting my look for a presentation that will last all of five minutes. Finding the perfect color, the perfect fit, the perfect length in the arms and legs and torso to perfectly hug and perfectly communicate my body underneath. It won't matter what I say. It won't matter how much we've grown. If there's a pucker near my tits or I have outgrown roots or camel toe, no one will listen. I'm shocked Isabella didn't book me a Botox and threading appointment, too.

 I tie the olive jumpsuit, and it's too big. Too boxy.

 I hurriedly unzip another option. It makes my legs look stumpy.

 I unbutton and rush into a charcoal option, with a metallic belt around the waist. And this one, finally, feels "perfect."

Subject: Tomorrow
From: Marz Davis *<MarzDavis@gmail.com>*
To: Alexis Ecker *<Alexis.ecker@besavvy.com>*
September 30, 9:03PM

Good luck.

You need it.

M

14

October 1, 2019.

"I'll be at the cafe in ten," I explain on a call with Isabella, who tells me that actually, she can't meet for coffee before my big Disrupt pitch today, because she ran into potential investors for her fund.

"I'll try to talk my way into the green room later," she reassures me, whispering into her phone. "But I'm ten million short and these Coinbase guys cashed in big-time. I'm sure you understand. Go on and I'll find you."

As I pay for my burnt Americano and start weaving through the investors, founders, wannabe entrepreneurs and press, all sardined and desperate for caffeine before embracing the day's relentless talks and panels and schmooze breaks, I'm stopped dead in my tracks.

I spot Marz and Golden Daddy, Fisher Jing, breaking bread at the table to my left. They're talking so close that their foreheads nearly touch. I pull behind a burly man before either of them knows I'm there. My phone buzzes.

> **Laney:**
> My golden poppies are wide awake
> We're finally in full bloom!
> And so are you <3
> I'll be live-streaming and cheering
> You got this!

I've gotten texts like this from everyone. The classic "break a leg, kiddo" from Gordon, who says he'll be here soon, "I'm proud of you," from Ethan, that trolling-ass email from Marz last night, and of course, incessant "???"s from my mother begging for a full-length picture of my outfit. I snap a quick selfie in the grey jumpsuit I got from Piper Muse.

My mom doesn't reply, which means she doesn't approve. I immediately follow up with a closer face selfie, my cheeks stained with Darcy's signature coral blush, my lips lined to beige perfection. At this, she sends a heart, before telling me to put more concealer under my eyes. "U look blue?? kinda corpse-y," she writes, completely impervious to the fact that any talk of dead bodies, even in jest, is wildly insensitive given Darcy's accident.

That said, she's not wrong. My pores are secreting the Adderall and all-natural ginseng pills Victoria keeps bringing to my office. She doesn't know I dabble with prescription amphetamines, or that I've continued to take stolen Xanax long after she drugged me at Darcy's funeral, so it's been days of her showing up with ashwagandha powder or nootropic capsules from whatever DTC wellness company is in her Instagram feed that week. It's felt excessive at times, but I'll take all the help I can get. I've been pulling back-to-back all-nighters prepping for this day, this very moment. If it takes a vat of controlled substances and woo-woo placebos to reach the finish line, so be it.

I type out a quick "thank you" to Laney and resume spying on Marz and Fisher Jing, who are still yakking it up at the table. Another investor I don't know leans over and joins their huddle, and I faintly overhear Marz tell him he's "itching to get out of here" now that his panel's over. My heart sinks as I realize he likely did Disrupt as a favor to some investor or even Mike from TechCrunch himself, while Isabella and I pleaded with him just to get my foot in the door for a random pitch slot. It makes me feel like a second-class citizen.

Marz, Fisher Jing, and the unknown investor suddenly disperse, and I rush toward a seat at one of the cafe's garish yellow tables. I need to find the instructions and the map I got from the Disrupt planning people, because I'm supposed to meet an admin at the show office and have no idea where it is in relation to this florescent circle-jerk.

I screenshot the details and make my way through the hustle and bustle of the Moscone Center in all its glass and gloomy glory. On the outside, it looks like every other new building in SoMa: stark and clinical, a muted, silver office building piercing through the ominous fog of the the San Francisco sky. Whenever I'm here, I have this prophecy that SoMa is where the aliens would land first, a "fuck you" to the tech elite who thought they could predict and build the future. I get an immediate itch to flee as soon as I've landed on Silicon Valley soil. The energy always feels foreboding and cryptic.

On the inside, the Moscone Center looks like a refurbished airport terminal, a place they'd turn into a makeshift hospital when the aliens finally do come and lay waste to the Twin Peaks. Everyone buzzing about looks exactly the same. I wouldn't be surprised if they broke out in a silent flash mob, organizing themselves by vest shade or Allbirds SKU.

I squeeze past hundreds of retractable vinyl banners plastered with either unoriginal or *too*-original startup names like Squeeker and Bleepr and Sneakr and Farmio.AI. Their keepers, the founders who printed them, start groggily wiring up monitors or plugging in laptops.

The Raise

It's a catalogue of crazy: crazy ideas, like the company promising to "solve aging" through cell reprogramming, and crazy people, like the founder of Farmio, who appears to be setting up a small pen of live sheep. The chaotic conference floor is made somewhat cohesive by the identical black table covers next to each vinyl banner, the shiny grey floor supporting the weight of the growing crowd and its collective delusion of startup glory.

I'm almost at the show office, I think, when a mousey blue-haired girl appears to my right and starts matching my hurried pace. She's at least ten years my junior and her pink skin is flushed, like she's been bustling about for hours.

"Alexis Ecker?" she asks sheepishly, before looking down at a clipboard of faces with my name and headshot on it.

"Yeah," I reply, still gliding through the busy conference floor. "That's me."

"Okay great. I'm Kylie with TechCrunch," she says more confidently now, marking a big "X" next to my name and reaching for my forearm. "I'm actually gonna steer you this way," she continues, gently guiding me in a new direction. "It's a faster shot to the green room and I know you're on kind of soon."

Kylie releases her light grip and goes on to explain how much she loves Savvy, and how sorry she is about Darcy's passing. She started using the platform after a bad breakup last summer, overcome with an acute awareness that she needed to reinvent herself on all fronts: career, style, "everything." I immediately think back to that afternoon at Jetto, smoking Darcy's Juul together on the bathroom floor, hatching a "me" that I sensed would get me further in life. I was right around Kylie's age.

"It's hard to explain," she continues. "But yeah. It's like I slowly molded to him, or toward him, and didn't really notice? And then once it was all over, I was like, *oh my god bestie. What have you done?*" We're stalled in a small crowd of people, and she lowers her voice. "I wanted to feel new, or different. So I had to *be* new and different? I don't know. All I know is I popped onto Savvy after seeing it on Instagram. I was like, fifteen-dollar starter box of clothes to kickstart my single era!? *Slay.*"

Still stuck behind a mass of men, I ask about her experience with the subscription and if there's anything she'd change. She is lackadaisical but pointed with her feedback about our slow customer service and inaccurate size matches, and it's clear she's either thought through these improvements before or vented about us to her friends. After rattling off her wish list, she shyly mentions that she knew I was Alexis Ecker when she asked for my name a minute ago but felt "starstruck."

"It's just crazy what you guys did," she says, tapping her Apple Watch to check the time, then standing on her tip toes to see past the hoard of people that won't seem to budge. "Like I read all of Darcy's press stuff and you know, all the fundraising? My friends and I were amazed. Like Crafted was always so mid, and you came along and—"

The crowd starts to clear, and we try to regain some momentum, both of us taking a more urgent pace so we can make it to the green room. Kylie reaches for my forearm again but before we hit our stride, I hear a voice cut through the crowd, loudly calling my name.

I spin around looking for its origin, staring through the row of faces and bodies behind me, but everyone's preoccupied with idle chit chat or full-on networking. I hear my name again, even louder now, and realize it's coming from—

"Nice to meet you, Alexis," says the voice, now attached to a pinstripe-suited body and stunning, golden-brown face. She reaches for a handshake, but her eyes are still locked on mine, unblinking.

"I'm Jada," she says firmly. I stare dumfounded as our hands touch. "I assume you know why I'm—"

"Yes, I know," I interrupt, all too aware that Kylie is here listening, observing, and privy to whatever happens next. I can tell Kylie senses our tension, her back straightening and eyes widening while Jada and I stare at each other in silence.

"I've been patient," she says kindly—more kindly than I deserve, given the circumstances. "I didn't want to make this a problem for you, I really don't. I know your friend died. But we both know she screwed me, here. I've been trying to do the right thing, but—"

"I appreciate your patience, I really do," I interrupt, eyeing Kylie as the three of us drift to the edge of the crowd, mutually aware that walking while talking feels inappropriate for this conversation. I'm desperately trying to hide my irritation and mounting anxiety. I don't want to ruin Kylie's perception of me, and I don't want to insult Jada by fending her off and telling her to leave it with legal. I feel empathy for what Jada is going through. For the email, for the blatant discrimination. That must feel like shit. And if it were me in her shoes, I'd be livid. But a larger part of me feels defensive and angry. *This isn't my fault. This wasn't my doing.* I didn't even want to be here, in this role. Darcy died—she's *gone*—and here I am trying to clean up her mess, pay Jada off, raise the money, make investors happy, get the valuation, chase the growth, then IPO. There is no light at the end of the tunnel. There is only darkness. Every. Single. Day.

And you know what? I'm not even sure how crazy and messed up it was for Darcy to say that stuff in the email in the first place. In this industry, men *do* have it easier. They start all the companies, then they bag the best investors, then they raise all the money, then they *make* all the money. Was it really so awful that Darcy wanted a leg up? That she wanted to juice her chances by forming an executive team that investors could get behind? We killed ourselves for years to build a real company that deserves to grow and shine and prosper. All Darcy wanted was the right window dressing so we could finally stop investors in their tracks and turn a "hey, let's give them a look" to a "hey, let's give them a *shot.*" It's fucked up that the way to do it is by putting more men in power, but Darcy's not to blame for the inequities in Silicon Valley. Is it so nuts that Darcy wanted to make life, to make raising, just a *little* bit easier for once? Wasn't it smart of her to know how to beat the odds so she could keep the company going, keep paying people, and create even more opportunities for even *more* women, like us, and like Jada, down the line?

"We're twenty out from your pitch," Kylie says, a bit jittery. To my relief, the crowd thins even more, leaving a clear path for she and I to book it straight to the green room. "If you guys want, I can find a um . . . I can find a private place for you to talk after, maybe?"

"That totally works," I cut in with a forced smile. I turn to Jada, praying she'll acquiesce. "I do want to talk, really. But I hope, I hope you understand. I have to go onstage in a beat, but I know how important this is . . . I swear I'll find you later."

Kylie and I start walking, and my head continues to spin. As my thoughts dart from Jada to Darcy to Gordon to Marz and Fisher Jing to what the fuck I'll even do if this pitch doesn't land, I realize Jada's right there, matching our stride, still talking at me. I force myself to look down.

"It's been weeks, Alexis," she says, lightly panting as Kylie and I continue to charge forward. "And my papers are drafted, just so you know. But look—I mean it when I say I'm trying not to make this a problem. I really don't want to front the money for a lawyer, and I know you just took on an entire company and I'm sure it's a lot for you," she continues, and for some reason her empathy makes me want to ugly cry.

"But if this isn't handled by next week I *will* go to the press. *With* the Darcy email."

I don't know how to respond to the threat, and I don't know what to say. I can't promise it will be handled by next week because I have no idea when I'll get the money, or even *if* I'll get the money. The green room comes into view and my body feels preliminary relief, like it knows this firehose of shame and guilt and truth is about to dry up. Gathered near the green room, I spy Isabella laughing performatively for two men I assume are the Coinbase guys, and a few feet from her I see Dr. Wes, who throws me a beaming smile and a wave. This gesture soothes my insides like a hot cup of warm milk, but only for a fleeting moment, because Jada is now standing in front of the green room door and refusing to move until she hears me speak. She wants something, anything, and I'm still struggling with what I can offer to make her and this whole thing just go away. I summon Darcy and wring out my memory searching for what she would do, what she would say, praying all the while that Dr. Wes and Isabella are preoccupied and looking elsewhere, lest they sense our tension and my chaotic, unglued energy. I've already given up on Kylie, who I'm planning to hand an NDA by day's end.

Just do the next right thing, Darcy would tell me. *Handle whatever's directly in front of you—don't spiral over what comes after.*

"I'll handle it," I say confidently with a firm nod, then offer a handshake. "I'll handle it all by next week." I peek over at Isabella, who is still cozied up to the Coinbase pair, and Dr. Wes, who is chatting up a girl who isn't me, his blue eyes and black hair looking more inviting than ever. I pray this is enough to make Jada disappear but have absolutely no clue how I'll "handle" anything, let alone in the next six days. The most I can do is nail this pitch. And pray.

"I'll hold you to it," Jada snaps, declining my handshake before gliding away. I thank Kylie for her patience, pry open my purse, and bust through the door to the greenroom.

As I weave through a few speakers and moderators to find a pocket of privacy, I riffle through my bag to find the only thing that can take my heart rate down from a sprint to a stroll. I nibble on half a Xanax and survey the rest of the space, desperate for water or something stronger to down the pill and wash away my panic. The green room's massive water jug is empty, and it's too early for alcohol, at least in San Francisco. If I were still in New York, the wine would be out by now. But I know it's somewhere. There's a panelist and speaker happy hour slotted for later this afternoon.

In the back corner, I notice a table draped in white tablecloth and various cardboard boxes peeking out from underneath. I know how props and product are typically hidden from when we promoted Savvy at different trade shows over the years, so I hurry toward the boxes and crouch down behind the table before anyone can see, and peek inside. I find rows and rows of twist-off white wine, warm but otherwise drinkable. I crouch even lower to ensure I'm out of sight, twist open a bottle and toss some Chardonnay down the back of my throat. I put the cap back on and slide the bottle inside my black Mansur Gavriel tote bag, pop up from the floor, and exhale.

Within a few minutes, I'm at my desired homeostasis: the Xanax settles in like a weighted blanket, numbing the pulsing anxiety from the Jada conversation and the pivotal pitch ahead of me. But the wine keeps me sharp and limber, converting the calm into something less zombie and more elastic. Around me, about a dozen people are talking to each other or pacing around and practicing. I debate doing this, retreating to my private corner and pitching audibly to the wall, but I don't want to stumble and jinx it, and then get anxious all over again. Right now, I'm perfectly calibrated, and I can't risk a pre-pitch spiral.

"Fifteen minutes!" Kylie barks in my direction, as I suddenly realize she's been here, babysitting me this whole time. "In five or so we'll head to the stage and stand in the wings."

The Raise

I nod and continue running through the beats of the presentation in my head when my phone rings. I grab it, hoping it's Isabella or Dr. Wes, checking in with one last verbal fist bump, but it's Victoria. For all I know, and given how the day's gone thus far, there's some unsolvable issue with Let's Fucking Grow, or someone quit, or the office is on fire. I worry it's risky to chat, but something tells me to answer anyway.

"Hey Vic, I'm about to go—"

"I know. That's why I'm calling! I know you have like thirty seconds or something, so I want to get this all out before you go. I know this is a really big day for you and for the company. I know you've been busting your ass and came into this role so suddenly and there was so much shit to get done and so many impossible things that needed to happen," she says hurriedly. "But all we wanted to say was that Darcy would be so, so proud of you. Seriously. We're all at the office live streaming and cheering you on and I got some skin contact wine for everyone so we can celebrate you when you're done and just know you're gonna crush it and investors are gonna FLIP when they see our growth! So basically—YOU GOT THIS!"

I hear rowdy yips and claps and hurrahs in the background and my heart melts, realizing the entire company is dialed-in and eager to watch my presentation. I've been so buried in my fundraising prep and refining this pitch that I've barely seen the team in days. Because of the Xanax dose I can't really tear up, and thank God, lest I smudge my mascara, but my insides swell with the tight burn that comes before a good cry. Smiling ear to ear, I thank Victoria and the team, hang up and put my phone on silent. I close my eyes and savor the last sixty seconds of my pre-pitch life: a life that has felt so brutal and relentless, both challenging and precarious, but also so vulnerable and rich.

Kylie appears and escorts me from the green room and toward the backstage holding pen. From my vantage point stage left, I peer into the crowd and see my communications team, Isabella, Dr. Wes, and Fisher Jing all scattered throughout the pews. I keep scanning, but I can't find Gordon. He's either in the bathroom or running late, per usual. Kylie says something to me, but as my adrenaline begins to build, everything starts to sound muffled and fuzzy. The "Me" of mere weeks ago—sweaty, birdbrained, and nervous at Darcy's funeral—would be shocked to meet the "Me" of today, of this moment. I spot an empty seat in the audience, and I wish so desperately for her to appear and beam up at me. I wish she could flash me her approving smile. The smile that says I've done right by her. The one I see in the darkness, and in my dreams.

The sustainability founder currently on stage says his closing line and takes a bow to lukewarm applause. Kylie taps me on the shoulder and her eyes go wide. She holds up her hand and uses her fingers to slowly count up to five. The lights go dark and suddenly, once her thumb flips up, the song "Fighter" by Christina Aguilera starts blaring through the speakers and rumbles the stage. It was Isabella's pick. She said it communicated my "resilient spirit" and the beat had "warlike" energy. Kylie gives me a final nod and my mind sharpens into focus, like the race car driver I never was but am now becoming. I power walk onto the stage as green, yellow, red, and purple lights swirl and pulse through the air, the crowd jeering and clapping as I take my place in front of a massive, glowing screen. My heart explodes with pride and excitement, and I'm ready to rip.

I'm ready to own this.

The crowd dies down, and I'm caught in the glow of a harsh blue light. Through the haze, I spot Jada in the crowd and my stomach curdles. A dormant voice, now screeching from deep below, remembers how dire this pitch really is. *I need the money. I need to get rid of her. I need to beat Crafted. I need to figure out why the fuck Darcy wanted to sell. I need to know if she killed herself. I need to know why.*

The Raise

I need to know what happened.

I choose to swallow the intuition that something's wrong, that something's not right, because I have no choice. I look for Dr. Wes, who is not Darcy, but he's beaming up at me nonetheless, and remember I'm in charge of where I look, where I focus, what I say, and how this pitch unfolds. I decide to do the next right thing, just like Darcy would've, and take control.

In an instant, I transform, just like I did at the board meeting. I am holding the audience captive with my confidence and the strength of my delivery. I'm not the fluffer anymore, that's for sure. *I'm the star. I'm the center. I'm the main event.*

I walk the audience through Savvy's origin story, explaining Darcy's ingenious creation, how the company was really decades in the making, because she thought it up in high school. I quickly play a snippet of the scene from *Clueless* when Cher uses her desktop's "digital closet" to plan her outfit for the day. The crowd laughs with "ahas" and intrigue, completely captivated by the boldly feminine approach to the presentation and format, which everyone in the room knows is so rare in this industry. Isabella and I decided it would be risky—the marigold and pale pink brand colors, the *Clueless* clip—but pay off in spades if it actually landed. And she said if I was wearing a neutral, more masculine color onstage, I'd be fine.

I then commend Darcy for her vision and leadership, and we all take a coordinated moment to honor her legacy. I do a rapid-fire product demo, carefully curated toward the most magical moments in the customer experience. There's no sign of Kylie's platform feedback, no mismatched sizing or slow customer support chat, because of course, the demo has been pre-recorded to perfection. I eye Fisher Jing throughout this section, praying he's impressed with the product and its capabilities, because from what I've read, that's his number one obsession. *Creating magic.* I see him smiling and whispering to the guy next to him, who I assume is another partner at Precursor Capital, and my vagina flutters. There is something undeniably arousing about putting on a good show, wooing your prey. I impulsively glance at Dr. Wes now, hoping he can smell my pheromones from the stage, that he's fascinated by me in the flesh, the way he was with Darcy.

I move on to the presentation's climax: the growth slides. We're inching toward a million customers, and our traction over the last month or so has been explosive. You can quite literally see the hockey-stick moment, the inflection point where Let's Fucking Grow, our painful, deliberate, and expensive push to the top, starts to skyrocket our customer count and revenue. It's the graph every investor looks for, the one that signals the business is real, the users are happy, and the money's flowing in. The room roars with every milestone I share, picking up on every queue and every crumb I drop. Isabella is plastered to her seat, eyes gouged open, nodding unblinkingly like a giddy robot.

Maybe this was my destiny all along. Maybe I really am this impressive, this shiny, this powerful. Maybe Darcy's passing was all part of some twisted plan God had for my self-actualization. As soon as I think it, I feel a pang of guilt flicker in my chest. I would never have wished for her death. I would never trade her life for where I am now, for who I'm becoming. But somehow, in this moment, it feels like everything is finally coming together, like I'm taking shape for real.

I stand tall and proud and deliver the last few lines of my presentation, thanking everyone for their time and attention. I ever-so-casually hint that those with "checks to write and unicorns to build" can find me later on the conference floor. I don't explicitly say we're fundraising or looking for cash, but everyone important can decode the cipher.

As I bow, then stride off stage to a reprisal of "Fighter," the audience erupts in thundering applause, with some even standing as I fade out of view. To Isabella's credit, I do feel like I just returned from war, holding a head on a spike in one hand and a sack of gold in the other. Emerging through the flaps of the backstage curtain into the green room, I'm received by the founders-in-waiting as a startup celebrity. They hoot and holler and pat me on the back, seemingly enamored by what I've just done. Kylie, my temporary assistant, pulls me from the crowd to hand me a bottled water and a printed conference directory.

"Thanks," I say panting, my mouth dry and sore from the ten-minute stretch of smiling and talking. I gulp down some water and close my eyes for a few seconds, savoring my moment of glory. "Wait, what's the directory—"

"Because I want your autograph!" she giggles, a bit embarrassed. "That was SO, *so* good. You *ate*, Alexis."

I consider asking what this means, but I'm smart enough to infer that it's good. I sign the directory, down more water, and walk to find my purse. The founders in the green room continue to forego their own pitch practice to congratulate me and ask for my Twitter handle or attempt to pitch me on whatever they're building.

"Let's get you out of here," Kylie mumbles, realizing I'm nearing sensory overload. She creates a physical buffer between me and the growing pack of people as I finally find my tote and head toward the door.

On my way out, I eagerly check my phone to see if I have any messages. I've got a cascade of unread, exuberant texts from everyone from Victoria to Laney to Isabella and my communications team, but the one that matters most is the text I just got from Gordon.

> **Gordon:**
> **HEY KIDDO**
> **DINNER TONIGHT?**

Instead of feeling nervous or apprehensive about seeing him tonight, or disturbed by his incessant need to feed, I feel grateful and excited. I can't wait to eat on his dime and recap the reactions to my undeniable, triumphant pitch. I'm sure he's getting bombarded with emails about how well I did and requests for intros from investors looking to get in on the next fundraising round. *I can't believe I pulled this off.*

My pitch was scheduled just before the day's lunch break, so when I emerge from the green room and onto the conference floor, everyone is filing out of the auditorium and bustling about to find the food tents and some free grub. To my shock and awe, Fisher Jing is waiting just beyond the exit, leaning up against a wall, clearly inspecting me.

We lock eyes, and he walks over. *Be cool be cool be cool be cool.* I straighten my back and take a swig of water, praying I don't cough through the conversation given my dry throat and exhausted vocal cords.

This is your chance, Alexis. Seal the fucking deal.

"Alexis," he says, his voice bright and perky. He's in a crisp white button-down and black Arc'teryx vest, which is basically the three-hundred-dollar version of the one-hundred-dollar Patagonia vest everyone else is wearing. It's an obvious and heavy-handed flex, but he's Fisher Jing, and he's invincible. "That was quite the presentation. Kudos to you and the team." He holds his hand out and I shake it with mine, concerned I hadn't thought to sneakily wipe it on my jumpsuit on the way over. Kylie retreats backwards at a fast clip and fades out of view.

"Thank you," I say, toeing the line between assertive and bashful, trying to embody Darcy, how she seemed so commanding but so harmless. "The team has been firing on all cylinders. It's been a hell of a quarter."

"Yes, yes, I can see that," he replies, and I can tell he's aroused by the idea of winning. And he wants to win *me*. He wants to lead this deal. I can see it in his eyes. All I have to do now is lean in and let him perceive me, then elegantly shape-shift into the "founder" he's conjured up in his head. If Darcy were here, she'd say as few words as possible. She'd let him take up more space. She would be noncommittal, but still kind.

"Are you free for coffee or lunch? Tomorrow?" he asks, and now I know, officially, that I've reeled him in. *Gordon's gonna lose his goddamn mind.*

"I'll get back to you on that," I answer, recalling Isabella's instructions to seem *busy busy*. "Let me reconnect with my board and see what we've got lined up for the week. There's a lot of demand," I say, deliberately trailing off and looking around the room, like I'm the prize, and *he* must hold *my* attention. But with a smile. I want to preserve his dignity.

"Makes sense," he says, smirking, and it's clear he understands but respects my game. "You can let your board know, then, that I'm curious as to where you're at on your next round, and how you're thinking about what growth funds you'd want to partner with."

Before I can even respond, I notice there's a small crowd that's formed behind us, waiting for their turn to meet me. Kylie reappears by my side. She asks if I want them to form a line, and what she should do, and I pull out a stack of business cards for her to give out. Fisher Jing takes one from my pile and nods before walking away. I've gained cache by standing here with the Founder of Precursor

Capital. I don't have to talk to anyone today. It's *better* if I go and leave them wanting more. Which means I can finally escape this bland, grey prison, lock myself in my hotel room, and find a delicious stretch of sleep.

As I make my way out of the shadowy, stuffy conference hall and walk toward the light, the prickly intuition that something is still off, something is still wrong, reawakens. Jada expects a "solution," also known as her wire transfer, by next week. Darcy trying to meet Marz. Marz, today, meeting Fisher. I can't tell what's real and what's delusion, what's insomnia or premonition, what's the Xanax and what's ashwagandha powder. But I realize I may not need to worry. Because very soon, it'll all get smoothed over, like pouring concrete over corpses. Because maybe, given how well the business is doing and the inevitability of this round closing, I can finally talk to the board about Jada. I can get an early check from Isabella or Gordon for whatever she needs, three-hundred-thousand, four-hundred-thousand bucks. Just a small bridge until I get my term sheet. It's in their best interest to help me and for us to give her the money. Nobody wants bad press. Nobody wants a lawsuit. So I'll just tell them the truth. I can be vulnerable with them now. I'm a winner.

I walk down a branded escalator, each step plastered with the event hashtag "#movefastandbreakthings." I arrive at the landing and spot Dr. Wes eating with a colleague at a high-top table.

Aglow from my performance and feeling alive, I decide to zip on over.

"Hey hey," he says as he spots me, wiping his hand on a napkin, but leaving no stain, even though he's eating a sloppy sprouted tofu wrap. "Great job. Really. Was a very cool presentation," he continues, holding up his kombucha to cheers the air. "Jim, this is—"

"Alexis Ecker," I chime in, realizing they're barely halfway through their meal. "I didn't mean to interrupt. I mean, I did just interrupt. But I'll catch you later. Just wanted to say hi and thank you for coming."

"Oh," he says, raising an eyebrow at his tofu wrap, then at Jim. "It's my pleasure. Darcy would've loved that pitch, by the way. I'm sure of it."

It is this sentence that makes my entire groin tingle and my throat go tight. I now know that he sees me, that he understands exactly what I needed to hear in this moment. The electricity between us is so obvious, so stirring, that when his aqua eyes squint as we say goodbye, I feel like I'm falling.

If he was good enough for Darcy, he's good enough for me. But more critically, *I'm* good enough for *him*. The way I felt when his eyes embraced me, knowing he used to give that look to her, to Darcy, it was like looking in the mirror for the very first time, seeing myself in all my glory.

I float my way toward the building's entrance and pry open its heavy glass doors. As soon as I'm out in the fresh air, my face cold under the cloudy sky, I feel tears fall down my face and into my mouth. My body is overcome with a sense of joy. A sense of relief.

I did it. I just saved us. It's all going to work out.

I immediately pull out my phone to text Victoria, intermittently wiping my tears on my jumpsuit while I dig through my purse.

Alexis:
We did it.
We r gonna get the money
Thank u sm for everything!!!!
AH

I call an Uber back to my hotel and relax into the next few minutes of blissful, quiet waiting. I so rarely get moments like this. Moments where I can just linger and listen and breathe. I feel full and warm like I do after a tender moment with my mom or when I get a text from Dr. Wes, but the warmth isn't coming from someone else now. It's coming from me, *for* me. I have never felt prouder of myself. I have never felt more in my power.

With two minutes to spare before my driver arrives, I click open my phone and pull up Darcy's number. I dial it, even though I know she'll never pick up.

"Dee, it's me," I say once I hit her robot voicemail, my wave of tears returning, "I miss you. So much. And . . . and Savvy is doing great. I'm doing great. I'm doing it, you know? I'm doing it for us. I wish you were here. I met a girl today. Her name was Kylie. She loved us. I just knew, that like, she realized she could do whatever she wanted because *we* did it first. And we showed her how."

My Uber pulls up, and I get in.

"I love you," I say, the tears trickling into my mouth. "I love you and everything is going to be okay."

Gleeful and light after a five-hour nap at my hotel, I Uber past a homeless man shitting into a Styrofoam food container, his pants at his ankles, and I don't even blink. It's a rare, fog-free night in San Francisco, and the atmosphere finally feels less ominous. It may even feel promising.

From the backseat, I whip out my phone to text Dr. Wes.

> **Alexis:**
> So good seeing u in-person :-)
> Ty again for coming
> Was helpful to focus on u during the pitch
> Instead of all the vultures lolol

I'm shocked when his reply immediately starts to percolate, those delicious eclipses promising me the butterflies and validation I need so badly.

> **Dr. Wes:**
> I'm really glad I came
> You were magnetic up there
> How you feeling?

I start brainstorming my reply, but then the driver stops and drops me off a couple blocks away by accident. I swap apps and blindly follow my Google Maps to Baan Yaai, Gordon's restaurant of choice, overcome with the pride of a gold medal champion. I just gave dozens of business cards to Silicon Valley's biggest investors, the decision makers at every firm, from funds that had never given us the time of day before. Based on the glowing tweets and endless Instagram tags I poured over on the way here, there's no doubt I emerged as Disrupt's One to Watch: the phoenix rising from the ashes of my co-founder's passing, the reluctant but prodigal leader, the bold, brave archetype these people love to create and deify. Isabella texted to let me know she was getting swarmed, too, and I even exchanged numbers with Golden Daddy, who's already texted me to meet for coffee first thing tomorrow morning. I have so much good news to share with Gordon, it feels like it's all piling up in my throat, ready to fall from my mouth and into his elated ears.

I spot the Baan Yaai awning and enter the restaurant, immediately eyeing the kitschy, cheap decor and dirty laminated menus. The place smells like garlic, curry, and comfort, and I suddenly realize I'm starving. I haven't eaten since leaving the house this morning, and that coconut RX Bar barely got me through the day's frantic, thrilling chaos. I notice Gordon seated at the farthest table from the other patrons, nursing an ice water as he mulls over various printed documents. I prepare for an unsolicited bear hug or proud dad fist bump when he sees me, but instead, he remains seated and gives me a soft, half-hearted smile.

"Hey kiddo," he says, still marking up the documents, eyes avoiding mine. He must be in the throes of diligence for some urgent deal. I should never expect to be his sole focus or his priority for the day, or even the moment. I know by now there's always something.

"Hey hey," I say cautiously, trying to match his energy. "We missed you out there today."

"I'm sorry I couldn't make it," he replies, finally looking up. "We've been prepping diligence for a few different companies, like Savvy, and things just . . ." He trails off and furrows his brow, like he's weighing what to say, or how to say it, which never happens.

"Things just got a bit crazy today," he adds, before picking up the menu. "Let's order?"

We both sit in silence and scan the menu, and I wish I could eat everything in sight. I want fat noodles and greasy protein and crispy gyoza galore.

I am excessive and indulgent with my order. Gordon loves to feed me, after all. Gordon alerts the waitress to his peanut allergy, and she kindly reassures us that they're well accustomed to special requests around gluten, specific ingredients and the like, and he seems satisfied. She refills our water before leaving, and I take the opportunity to catch Gordon up on all the Disrupt success, spilling every detail from the strongest beats of the pitch to the funds I met to getting Fisher Jing's personal number. I obviously say nothing of Jada, who is still gnawing away at my psyche with her press threats and firm handshake, in the hopes that news of my presentation success will soften the blow once I ask for an urgent bridge of cash to pay her off and hold us over, but only for a few weeks, because Fisher and his fund are *dying* to lead our Series C and give us money. I'm planning on asking tomorrow after my coffee date with Fisher so I can give even stronger signal that their support is a done deal.

Gordon listens wide-eyed and calm, as though he's getting hosed down with too many flashy updates and needs a beat to process. I'm nearly out of breath once I'm done with my monologue and move toward my water and some gyoza to refuel.

I slowly dunk my pork dumpling into some tangy sauce while Gordon sits still and silent. I look up at him as I chew down a delicious, juicy bite of meat and try to read his stoic expression, wondering what Darcy would do and think in this situation. Does he feel competitive with Precursor now that the raise is real and definitely happening? Is he preparing to tell me that Alliance wants to lead instead? I wouldn't be surprised. Now that I'm shiny and Savvy's a hot commodity, Gordon and Alliance could easily be changing their tune, hoping to throw in more money so they have more equity, and more upside, in the business.

"There's something we need to talk about," Gordon finally says, looking into his lap. He hasn't eaten a single gyoza, and his napkin is still neatly folded on the table.

"Erm . . . okay," I reply with my mouth too full, before swallowing a massive bite of fried dough. "If it's about the round, though, don't worry about the hype. We'll obviously make as much room for Alliance as we can afford to make, and I think the other funds would just—"

"Thanks for that," he says, and puts his head in his hands, like a tortured boy who doesn't have the answers. I suddenly realize we've been talking past each other, and something is terribly wrong.

"Something's . . . wrong," he confirms, and my digested dumpling meat cinches together like it's a rocket preparing to dislodge from my stomach. At this very moment, the waitress returns with my Thai buffet, which now feels like an unhinged and embarrassing amount of food. The once-tempting smells now disgust me, and I feel the grease and oil and steam of the restaurant settle into my hair and mouth.

"Okay," I reply calmly as my mouth goes dry. I feel heavy in my seat and my adrenaline drops, my body now registering the sharp discomfort of the square-back beechwood chair.

Gordon rifles through the papers at our table which are lightly drizzled with gyoza sauce and condensation from our glasses. He plucks one from the pile and puts it in front of me.

"Something's not adding up here," he sighs, as if he's been waiting to tell me this all day. I quickly realize that this, these papers, this problem, is why he wasn't at the Disrupt pitch. He's likely been cooped up in an office with the analyst who's been pouring over the data Hunter sent them, trying to interpret and then unsee whatever he's about to show me. But whatever it is, it was clearly too troubling to ignore.

I look deadpan at the paper and see a bunch of numbers, dozens of shipping addresses, and a few simple line charts. Despite my strengths in operations and logistics, I've never really been a numbers person. I have the same hot and panicked feeling as I did when I was at Victoria's to prep for the board meeting, anticipating a data deep-dive that thankfully never came. But I'm backed into a corner now. No one's here to spoon-feed me the obvious. I have to face the data and digest it, so I can start to understand what's "wrong" and then make it right—at any cost.

"What we're seeing is," he says carefully, "that if you snapshot the company's revenue in a given timeframe—in a cherry-picked timeframe—the numbers look solid. But—" he continues, clearing his throat, "because of how your subscriptions are set up, it's all very misleading."

"*What's* misleading?" I blurt out, anxious and eager for him to get to the point.

"When customers sign up, they commit to a three-month starter subscription, right? That's forty-five dollars."

"Right."

"But the way your billing's set up; the customer's card only gets charged fifteen-dollars for the first box. See here," he says, pointing to the oiled-up print-out. "That fifteen-dollar charge happens as soon as they place the order. Their card gets charged for the next two months though, the remaining thirty dollars, at the start of month *two*."

"Yah, I'm aware. It's my business. We set it up that way because—"

"Were you aware though," he interrupts, "that a good forty percent of your subscriptions over the last few months get canceled around the same time, *right* before month two? Which means your team is 'counting' three months of subscription revenue because that's how the product is packaged, but you're only making money on the first month, or that initial fifteen dollars. And in most cases," he adds, leaving a brief, loaded silence between us, "you're even refunding the first charge. So you're—"

"Counting sales that aren't really there," I whisper, on the verge of throwing up.

He nods slowly and purses his lips. A heavy brain fog sets in, and my eyes start piercing in pain, like I'm brewing the biggest migraine of my life. I feel both weightless and immobile, and whatever questions I have, whatever I want to say—the words just won't come out. Much to my shock, Gordon finally lifts his fork and stabs a dumpling. The dough rips under the metal force as fatty, shiny gunk oozes out and onto the plate.

"I . . . I don't . . ." I stutter, stunned by the revelations and distracted by Gordon's chewing.

"Wait," he cautions, his mouth still full, "there's one more thing." He swallows, and I pray for my assassination, for the homeless guy I saw shitting in the street to rush into the restaurant with a loaded rifle. *How is there more? What the hell is happening?*

"The cancelled orders," he adds, casually wiping the grease from his mouth, "they're all going to PO Boxes. It's pretty weird. We wouldn't usually go this deep, but after everything with Theranos and LightSail all these crazy-girl schemes the last few years, our LPs are on our ass about catching this shit before it's too late. To be honest, I'm not really sure what's going on, but if we were able to find this in just a few days, then—"

His phone rings mid-sentence. He immediately reaches to read the screen.

"Give me a beat," he says, urgently getting up from the table and throwing his paper-white napkin onto his seat.

"We're closing on Farmio for three million, but he's pushing back on pro rata," he laments—like I'm supposed to both process and care about this information, when all I want to do is stab his wrinkled neck with my knife and scream so loud my eyes pop out.

He leaves the restaurant and goes outside, and I can see him flailing his arms as he paces up and down the street. As I watch him, my rage expands inside me, filling every crevice with blazing anger and thickening spite. The man just told me that nearly half of the revenue we've booked since launching Let's Fucking Grow, our silver-bullet for the Series C, is fake. And after dropping that bomb, he prances off to take a call with another founder? He leaves me here alone, tormented, to tend to someone else—*to a company he doesn't even work with yet?*

The Raise

I can feel it settling in now: the throbbing migraine, the toxic spiral. I am whiplashed and frenzied, the high from Disrupt warping into a dangerous, lawless adrenaline fueled by a deep sense of betrayal. The betrayal is compounded by not yet knowing who to blame, as though I've been assaulted by a masked figure with no discernible features, no scent, no identity. I don't know if this is some covert assault coming from the outside, from Marz, in a cruel attempt to bungle our raise from within. Or if we've fallen prey to some widespread e-commerce fraud by rogue international agents who are buying and reselling our boxes on the black market. Whatever it is, it's a problem. It's a *huge* fucking problem. It's a problem that, if exposed, could derail our Series C, or worse. If this got out, if other investors like Fisher Jing knew that the growth I just boasted on and on about was completely *fake*, Savvy would collapse. And I along with it.

Maybe this is why Darcy was so desperate for an acquisition. Maybe she knew it was happening. Maybe she knew who it was. Between this and the lawsuit, she must have been falling apart. *Why didn't she tell me? Why didn't I know?*

My head spins as I keep my eyes on Gordon, who is now laughing and tossing his head back. It looks like he and that Farmio founder are really chumming it up—on my time, in the throes of Gordon dropping this bomb. For all I know, they've come to an agreement, and now they're making plans to go golfing or skiing or yachting or whatever these rich guys do when they're not screwing me over.

My sense of betrayal is peaking, seeping into my veins, my fingers, my heartbeat, and with every passing second, my body grows warmer with the heat of revenge.

I hear the bell of the restaurant's front door and Gordon's bombastic, cheerful voice spills into the room.

"I still got it," he boasts, light and airy as he walks toward our table. "He totally caved."

He still hasn't looked up from his phone.

"I'm gonna hit the loo. But don't let me hold you up—those noodles won't eat themselves," he says, patting me on the back a little too hard before heading to the restroom. "When I'm back, we should ping the board with what I've got here. Keep everyone in the loop."

Fuck.

He can't tell the board yet. I've barely wrapped my head around what's going on. My head is too fuzzy and my eyes are too blurry to effectively process all this paperwork. I haven't talked it through with Victoria yet, who will surely give me more amo—anything—to better explain how this happened, and how we didn't catch it. What if they think I'm incompetent? Oh my god. *I am incompetent.* What if they ask me a million questions I can't answer yet? *They're going to. Of course they will.* What if they decide to kill the raise? What if they tell other investors? What if they vote me out?

What if they take Savvy away from me?

I'll have nothing. Literally nothing.

Darcy's dead. I'm about to get sued. And apparently, my company is a total sham.

How did this happen? *How is this happening?*

Cortisol rushing through my body, I feel like I've entered a fugue state. All I can think is *I just need to hold him off for a little bit. I need time. I need to talk to Victoria, or the retention team, or both, to understand how we got here, and why no one caught it. If he starts wheezing just a little bit—if he just gets a bit itchy and breaks out in some hives, I don't know—he'll have to handle that, and all this board stuff can wait 'til tomorrow. That's fine. It'll all be fine.* And in that moment, my body springs into action to protect me. Without conscious thought, and barely even aware that I'm doing it, I reach

The Raise

over, take a spoonful of crushed peanuts from my Pad Thai and drop them in Gordon's coconut chicken soup.

It happens in a millisecond, and immediately after I do it, I come to my senses and regret it. I don't know the extent of his allergy. It's probably safe to assume it's minor, because Gordon exaggerates absolutely everything, but a kid from my elementary school nearly died at recess from some other fourth grader's Nutter Butters, so who am I to assume?

I immediately reach back over the table to fish the peanuts back out, to take it all back, but before I can slip my spoon back in, they slide below the surface, imperceptible.

Gordon saunters back toward our table and rubs his belly. Seemingly ravenous after a very macho, very successful negotiation, he shoves his spoon into the soup and starts slurping down his soup with the fervor of a hungry child. The mushrooms, chicken, and furtive peanuts mingle together in the cloudy broth before entering his system. I stare at him, my mouth agape, completely clueless as to what happens next. *Maybe he just gets indigestion. Maybe he bloats. Maybe he outgrew the allergy, but he doesn't know.*

"Where were we?" he asks, unfolding his napkin.

"Um . . . well you . . ." I stammer, trying to divert us away from texting the board, and toward something else, "you were explaining the . . . the PO Box issue."

"Mmm, right," he replies, enjoying his bite. "So, did you know about this? Or I guess the better question is, how did you *not* know about it?"

He swallows.

I gulp.

"I um . . . well, you know, prepping for a fundraise is a full-time job," I explain slowly, trying to overcome my mounting anxiety. "I had the big pitch, too. And, you know, I've been . . . processing? Darcy's accident? And we're not necessarily, um, monitoring trends in shipping addresses or anything like that. We're kind of incentivized by you guys, by our investors, that is, to grow, grow, grow. So, if that's happening, then it's kind of like, we're good here. Do you . . . do you see what I mean?"

He nods profusely, his mouth full of mushrooms, and I take that as a signal to keep talking.

"Right. I didn't—I didn't know because with the sales tracker and all that, money's still coming in. Like, whatever subscriptions are getting cancelled are still getting replenished by new customers in month one, so I . . . I didn't know to be on alert for . . . for something like this."

He chugs his water and I notice his face is turning red. His eyes widen as he drinks. As his cheeks grow ruddier, my heart rate starts to climb, but I feel compelled to fill the silence, to act normal.

"I'll look into it immediately," I conclude, attempting to keep my voice as level as possible while knowing full well this man may collapse, or choke, or worse, right before my eyes. I nearly gaslight myself into thinking I didn't do it, that I never touched the soup, but whatever lever I used to pull to unsee, to un-know, to believe my own bullshit, it's broken now. It jams up when I try.

"I'll ping Victoria immediately, as soon as we're out of here. And Hunter. I'll fly back to New York tonight. I'll rally the team and get to the bottom of it, but I'm not sure what it means for the raise if—"

Before I can finish, Gordon's eyes freeze, unblinking, in a moment of existential fear and shock. His face is cherry red now, and he frantically brings his right hand to his throat, unable to speak. His lips are pink and swollen, his eyes look puffy and bruised. He's shaking his head violently and pointing to his backpack. My heart racing, I scream at full volume to call an ambulance while tearing through his bag, which smells like rotten sweat. He makes a signal by flicking his thumb, like he's pumping a needle, which I take to mean I'm looking for an EpiPen. I find climbing shoes and a belayer, a loose bag of magnesium chalk, an unused journal, a crumbled hoodie, a handful of granola bars, and a Farmio-branded flat-brim hat. I'm scrambling like my life depends on it, like Gordon's life depends on it, but in the clutter, the EpiPen is nowhere to be found. All the other restaurant patrons are frantically zipping around, summoning useless glasses of water or calling the police.

Time is passing at hyper-speed but every second feels like forever. Gordon's coughing now and his nose is running, and in mere seconds, he's keeling over and slumping toward the floor. Luckily, we hear the ambulance siren surging louder from a distance. I kneel to the floor, petrified, and check Gordon's pulse. He's still alive, but he's rapidly declining. I sit next to his limp body, embrace the chill of the tiled floor, and not knowing what else to do, or where to go, gently rest my hand on his back until the medics rush in to fix him.

I have no idea how much time passes, but once help finally arrives, I peel away from Gordon and quickly explain what happened. "He ate peanuts," I say, "and he's allergic. I couldn't find his EpiPen. He's been having an allergic reaction for what feels like five minutes, but I'm not sure."

They shoo me away, open a medical kit and get to work. I find myself walking backwards, toe heel, toe heel, until I'm nearly at the door. I hear a medic say "we got him" in a voice that's sprightly and alert, and as soon as I know he'll live, my feet move faster, pushing me out the door and into the street, away from the scene of my crime.

❖

Alexis:
Urgent
Im coming back early
We need to talk asap
Ill come to u
Plz cancel ur stuff for the day

Victoria:
Omg
What happened????
????
?
All fine Im sure??

Alexis:
Ill let u know when I land

15

October 2, 2019.

If my company's about to implode, I can't afford another Uber. I decide to train into the city once I land back in New York, taking the E line from JFK. My hands shake on the platform as I pull an Adderall from the wallet in my backpack. I swallow it down with my spit and drag my suitcase into the subway car.

Within minutes of fleeing the Thai place last night, I booked a red-eye back home. In the event I'm able to salvage this, I can go back to San Francisco whenever, fly into the fog just as quickly as I fled it. I'll still meet with Fisher and everyone else once everything is fixed.

That is—*if* I can fix it.

I feel groggy and cloudy from my six hours in the air. I probably shouldn't have mixed Ambien and red wine after takeoff, even if it was just a few sips. But I couldn't bare the weight of my mental load sober, and all I wanted was to escape Silicon Valley. Escape what I'd done. I had nonstop nightmares on the flight home, trapped somewhere in between the reality of what I did and the terror plaguing my subconscious.

I couldn't sleep.

In one dream, I'm still in the restaurant, but the tile floor—the whole scene—is warped to look like the bathroom at Jetto. I'm sitting with Gordon, my hand still on his back, but he has no breath, no pulse, and he won't wake up. There's no one else around, no restaurant patrons or staff or paramedics. It's just us, cramped together with the greasy table and cheap chairs in the bathroom stall, the one Darcy and I used to vape in, and Gordon's hunched over, cold, with his eyes open and staring straight at me.

In another, I'm strapped to a seat in a pitch-black room watching the restaurant security footage. My eyes are pried open with metal clamps, and Darcy's there, slicing my forearm skin with a knife as she replays my crime over and over and over again: me, the peanuts, Gordon's steaming soup.

In the worst one, I'm naked and tied to an active oven at the restaurant as I watch hooded, unknown figures burn the line cooks and waiters with piping hot utensils. I hear them screaming in agony, calling out for their family members, or begging for mercy, as the heat from the oven slowly roasts my bare back. I know that by not owning up to the crime, I've put the restaurant in a horrible position. I feel guilty, but I didn't know what else to do.

As we inch closer to Manhattan and the robotic subway voice announces each stop, my heart pounds faster and faster, and I wonder what Gordon knows, what he thinks, and what happens next. Last night at the airport while waiting for my flight back, I sent a handful of texts and emails to the team and to current and potential investors, writing as little as possible because I didn't trust my mental state. I couldn't trust my judgment. I told everyone to work from home for the next three days, lying that I hired some company to do a "deep clean" of the office. I texted Fisher Jing to postpone our next-day coffee date. I told him I was double-booked with another fund, but that I'd follow up on Monday. I texted Gordon to see if he was okay, but he never responded, which made me anxious, especially because in the wee hours after his anaphylaxis, he Tweeted up a storm. He outlined the entire incident and even posted a picture from his hospital bed, alerting his followers that he intended to sue the restaurant for "borderline manslaughter." He also used the opportunity to promote an at-home allergy testing kit that Alliance invested in a few years ago, linking out to their website and a promo code for a discount on your first order.

I don't know what I was thinking. I don't know what's happening to me.

All I know is the walls are closing in. If our growth is completely fake, is the raise even feasible? And who would coordinate an attack on our company? Could we eke out some more *real* growth in the next three weeks while I close the round, and raise *something*? Anything? Do I tell Isabella? Has Gordon told Isabella? Has he told anyone else?

I need to get these questions out of my head, or they'll kill me. I need a sounding board. I need a partner. I want Darcy.

But the only person I have is Victoria. She may not have all the answers, but she can help me find some, and if we need to recover the fake revenue with real revenue in record time, she's the one to make it happen. At minimum, she'll give me some context, maybe a few talking points, to help me explain all of this to the board.

I plug her address into Google Maps when I get a brief window of cell service underground, then stare at the dirty documents Gordon brought to the Thai place.

It doesn't make any sense. All the credit card numbers are different, so they're *real* customers. *Real* people. The PO Box thing is super bizarre and leads me to believe this is some sketchy operation, a bunch of random criminals ordering our boxes to ambiguous, untraceable locations, so they can resell the inventory for more money on eBay or Etsy or something. The USPS can't give out PO Box numbers or disclose who they belong to. After the divorce, my mom pivoted to a PO Box after she found our rental in the city. She didn't want Simon to know where we were, or how to find us.

    I near Victoria's with puffy, pink eyes. One stop away now, I use my compact mirror to survey the damage. I gently pat my swollen skin and naturally think of Gordon, his face ballooned and blushed, inflamed eyes bulging from his head in panic. When I comforted him and rubbed his back on the restaurant floor, there must have been a silent, invisible transfer, because his panic is mine now. It's living and growing inside me. Mine's not from literal suffocation. I can technically breathe. But it feels like my spiraling thoughts around the future of Savvy are choking me from within. There's simply too much to lose. If this all goes belly-up, then Jada goes to print and destroys Darcy's legacy, we get sued, I ruin the company my best friend worked her whole life to build, I put hundreds of people out of a job and prove to the entire world that women are reckless, ineffective leaders—that you can try to play alongside the boys, you can try to beat them, but you'll always come up short.

    I stumble out from underground and emerge into the light, nearly sprinting to Victoria's building, my wheeled suitcase crashing against the cracks in the sidewalk pavement. I arrive, warm and musky under my crumpled sweatsuit. The doorman calls Victoria to let her know I'm here, and escorts me to the elevator.

    I feel a chill as I enter, the cold metal box cooling my forehead sweat. I get to Victoria's unit and take a deep breath. I have no idea how she's about to react to this news. I fear that as soon as I tell her,

I will transfer my panic, and I've never seen her under real duress before.

Victoria meets me as the elevator opens, her insanely beautiful apartment laid bare.

"Alexis?" she says cautiously, surveying my dark, tired eyes and disheveled outfit. She's in a casual, cream-colored silk set, her hair gelled back in a tight, chic bun, her ears decked out in dense, gold hoops.

I immediately break down, bawling and wailing against my will. I know rationally that as a CEO, I owe it to Victoria to sit her down calmly, walk through this emergency in delicate, slow detail, and bring her potential solutions that I want her feedback on. And that I should have at least combed my hair. But as a person, I can't "take shape" right now. I can't play the part. I need someone, anyone, to hold space for me and my deepening grief.

"Alexis," Victoria says empathetically as she pulls me in, squeezes me tight and hugs my backpack. She smells like fresh linen and soft citrus. "Look, we're going to get through this. Whatever it is. We will figure this out, just like we've figured out the last few months and the last seven *years* together. I promise. It'll all be okay."

Her affection drop-kicks me into a new layer of despair. I am touched by her softness, by her inclination to hold me. I suddenly realize how lonely I've been these last few weeks. How distant I've felt—even in my own body, in my own life.

Victoria leads me deeper into the apartment and I float behind her, my eyes still wet. She pats her manicured hand on a lush, ivory sectional and I collapse onto its lap.

"You sit here. Put your feet up and relax," Victoria instructs as I notice a four-hundred-dollar Diptyque candle burning in the background. The room smells like tuberose and Windex.

The Raise

"I'll be around the corner making us some tea and making you something to eat. I have leftover cauliflower casserole. It's vegan. You look frail as fuck," she says, and I let myself smirk a little.

"Walk me through it," she hollers from the kitchen, where I can hear glasses clanking and drawers zipping open. "You crushed the pitch, right, and then what?"

I pull one of the couch's cashmere throws over my body and talk Victoria through the events of the last twenty-four hours. I reference the dirty pile of documents, which I've been clutching since I snatched them from the Thai place, and explain the oddly-timed subscription cancellations, the PO Box mystery, and Gordon sounding a five-alarm fire on the raise. Overcome and overwhelmed, I ask Victoria how this happened, and why she didn't flag it, attempting to sound curious but coming off as accusatory.

"Building the customer machine and retaining those customers are totally different things," she calls out in a bright, perky tone, trying not to sound offended. "We need to pull in Oren from customer success. Because once I get them on the three-month plan, his team basically takes over."

"Fuck," I reply, annoyed with myself for inadvertently blaming her, when in reality, I was so thrilled with the growth graph that I never even bothered to meet with Oren in the last month. I didn't think to care where the customers were coming from, or if they cancelled, or if they were new or old or real or fake. It was my blind spot, not hers. "I'm, yeah, I'm sorry. I didn't mean to sound—"

"No no, it's okay," she reassures me, still out of sight. "His team's been flailing lately. I'm not sure what's going on. But you have to give yourself some grace, you know? You just took on the company and shit's been absolutely crazy. You can't keep tabs on everything. And the most important number, *my* number, was moving in the right direction, so . . ." she trails off, distracted by her kitchen duties.

I hear the kettle come to a boil.

"There's just so much to do," I say with my head in my hands, exhausted, worried the tea she's brewing might make me even sleepier. "Should I tell Oren to meet us at the office?" I scream, trying to pierce through the shrieking kettle. "Or would here be more comfortable and less, like, scary? I mean, would you mind? I don't want to freak him out, you know? It just feels like there's too much."

I rub my eyes and yawn. My mind is racing, but I urge my body to keep alert. We have so much to unpack. So much to figure out. I pull my phone out to text Oren.

"Let's just, like, put it all on the table before we involve anyone else," Victoria chimes in from the kitchen. "You know, walk through it just us. I think that's fair."

I look up, and I realize she's no longer in the kitchen. She's frozen in the doorframe with a mug in each hand, staring at me with an empathetic tilt to her head and concerned, soft eyes.

Victoria walks over. She hands me my mug, gently moves the throw and sits next to me on the couch.

"I know you loved her like a sister," she says softly, one hand on my knee. "But we both know Darcy wasn't well. We both had, you know, moments with her before she left where it was pretty clear she was having trouble, um," she says, clearly searching for words that won't set me aflame. Ones I might hear. "Holding it together."

"No," I say definitively. "If you're about to imply she did this, or had something to do with the fraud, then no. She wouldn't do this."

"Alexis," she says, clasping my hand, her eyes pleading. "Come on. This whole thing has her name all over it."

"It doesn't, though. She wouldn't cheat like this."

"Maybe not, but I think we need to suspend our disbelief a little bit. It's not what you want to hear, but between the lawsuit and the raise and just, years of pushing and pushing—"

"Who told you about the lawsuit? She told you about the lawsuit?"

I release my hand from her grip.

"She told me, yeah."

"When did she tell you? Why didn't she tell me?"

"You idolized her. Like, you made her a god or something. She said she didn't want to disappoint you."

"N–no," I stutter, confronting the possibility that Darcy hiding from me was *my* fault. Realizing I did put her on a pedestal, and maybe Victoria's right. Maybe she felt pressured to stay there.

"That's not it," I say, tears welling up in my eyes. "That's not fair."

"It's true, Alexis. We would Slack about it. We would talk about it here, on the balcony. Why do you think she came over so much? Just because she liked the wine? The view?"

I stare at her blankly, unable to speak.

"She loved you, but she felt, you know, suffocated. She felt like she had to perform for you. Babysit your feelings a little bit."

"No," I squeak, weighing Victoria's words. "It really wasn't like that. I swear."

She gets up, affectionately squeezes my shoulder, and heads back toward the kitchen, presumably to check the progress on my vegan cauliflower casserole, though I've completely lost my appetite.

It's true Darcy's entire identity and mood was wrapped up in Savvy. And my identity and mood were wrapped up in Darcy's. If the company was doing well, she was doing well, and I was at ease. If the company was struggling, she was struggling, and I was an anxious mess. And while she was feeling more tense in the lead up to Burning Man, I don't think she would have gone off the grid for five whole days if she was secretly spearheading this fake order operation from behind the scenes. And what about that acquisition text to Marz? I don't think she would have knowingly sold him a company with fake revenue. She would *never* have given him the satisfaction of knowing that she was some sort of crook.

And in looking through all of Darcy's documents, Slacks, and emails over the last few weeks, I didn't see anything that would confirm what Victoria's claiming. Of course, she has a private, non-work email inbox, which I don't have access to. And of course, there are other ways she could have been communicating that I couldn't and won't ever see—like her texts. I nearly tell Victoria this, in a reflexive need to rush to Darcy's defense. But I remind myself that my snooping may come off as pathological. So I hold back.

"I just know some stuff," I say instead, still belting a bit so she'll hear me from the kitchen. I notice the casserole smell wafting toward the couch. "And based on what I know about her, and her situation, I don't think she could have done all this. Or kept it from me. From us. I don't think she would lie."

She peeks her head out, and I stare at her, waiting for her to agree, praying she shakes her head and says, *"Silly me, you're right, Alexis. She wasn't capable of this. And you definitely knew her best."*

"It's possible," Victoria replies, and my heart sinks. "I just, based on what *I* knew, and what she told me and wrote me and just, you know, being around her those last few weeks. Like, being exposed to her mental health or whatever before she jump—"

"Before she what? What the *actual* fuck?"

"Before the, you know, the accident . . . Or whatever it was. She was dealing with a lot."

First Ethan. And now Victoria. Accusing Darcy of giving up. Of ending her life. My rational mind can look at all the clues and circumstances and understand their perspective, but my heart, my gut, my deep knowing of this woman—they all tell me it's a lie. They reject this accusation outright, and every time.

"She was under pressure, sure. She was, you know, dealing with a lot. But lots of CEOs deal with a lot. *I'm* dealing with a lot. It doesn't mean I'm gonna go off myself in the desert," I snap. "And the fact that you think she was that weak is ridiculous. And really sad."

"I'm sorry. It's just . . ." Victoria places both hands in the door frame, leaning out with her head down, pensive. "The fraud starts slow you said, right? Then accelerates as we get into the raise? And this person, whoever is doing it, is outsourcing somehow so it's isolated, or like, untraceable. And you said it's all anonymous—the PO box shit or whatever? So this isn't, like, a dumb person doing this, or some random outsider reselling our boxes. It's timed to our needs. And she had the most to lose."

I watch Victoria rack her brain for a convincing explanation, untangling the web of deceit and fraud I've brought to her doorstep. *Is it possible this woman knows Darcy better than I did? Is it possible she met a version of Darcy that would concoct this con, desperately and unsuccessfully try to offload her company at the last minute, and then kill herself?*

The accusation is maddening.

Even so, the demands of this job drove *me* mad, so mad I nearly killed my investor. I flash back to Gordon in the Thai restaurant, suffocating from within. *Who's to say Darcy was immune to the madness? Who's to say she deserved to be on that shiny pedestal I gave her?*

"And honestly," Victoria adds, interrupting my train of thought. "It's in our best interest, you know. It being Darcy. If we can explain all this to the board, then—"

"Wait," I interrupt, newly provoked. "You just wanna definitively say, with no evidence, that Darcy did this? Like, publicly?"

"From a self-preservation lens, for both you and me, and the entire team, I mean . . . yeah."

I feel like I might throw up. Victoria is still perched in the kitchen doorframe, her eyebrows raised.

"I'm not trying to sound, like, callous," she continues, sensing my disgust. "We could tell the board the truth, and get them to see, you know, her lived experience and really come from a place of empathy. And *invoking* empathy. And then we can get a bridge or something to make up the numbers with real growth. We only need like three months of new money to make up for everything that happened, and you did so, so good at Disrupt. I feel like they'd give it to us. To *you*."

"I can't believe you're saying this. I just can't believe this, that any of this is happening." I pull the throw blanket closer to my body, wishing I could shove my face in it and scream.

"Think about how hard you worked, Alexis. How much you sacrificed. It's not fair for this to fall on you, right? For the company to implode just because she, you know, did this crazy thing behind the scenes. Because she was *unwell*."

"Stop saying that."

"I'm just saying. I don't think it's fair if the road ends here. Not after all we've been through. And what's your alternative? I think we can empathize with where Darcy was at, and why she did it, but not let it fuck us. I mean, does that seem fair to you?"

The oven beeps, and the smoke detector starts ringing. Victoria rushes into the kitchen and out of sight.

A familiar impulse snakes up inside me, eager to let Victoria be right. Eager to absolve myself of really knowing, or of putting up a fight. Part of me wants to listen to her, the part that's still a little girl, weighing the pros and cons of telling other people's secrets. The part of me that, after the fallout of my parents' divorce, felt ashamed and guilty for doing the "right" thing. The part that now, today, feels like I was naive—maybe even stupid—because in telling my mom about Simon, in listening to my gut, we lost everything. The part that abdicated my adulthood, my career, and handed it to Darcy, because I couldn't trust myself. I didn't trust what I would do, or could do, with my own life.

The impulse is so vocal, so strong, telling me to hand over my power. Telling me to look away, and let Victoria drive the cleanup. To give her control of the narrative. To finally understand that no, I don't know best. And I never did.

But instead, I riffle through my bag to find my phone so I can pull up Oren's number and let him know to clear his day tomorrow. Because even in death, I believe Darcy over Victoria. I believe the Darcy that took me in and taught me how to be. I cannot conceive of a Darcy that would accept the role of guardian, and become my big sister, only to deceive me. That's not who she was.

She wouldn't do that to me.

There must be another culprit. Some other explanation.

The smoke detector keeps ringing, and the entire apartment now smells like sulfur-y farts and burnt vegan cheese.

Opening my iMessage, I realize I left Dr. Wes on read. I never replied to his last text.

> **Alexis:**
> So srry
> Got caught up in a shitstorm. Everything is unraveling
> Ill ping you tn to explrjkkk

I hit send, and I hear a loud "ping" from the living room shelf, where the four-hundred-dollar candle is neatly merchandised alongside a copy of Doctor Solis's recent and ironic cookbook, *From Our Kitchen to Yours*. He tries to brand himself as a big happy family man, the kind of guy who cooks and dazzles his ambitious, hungry children after they've all had a long day. But I can tell from what Victoria told me the other night, and from the look and feel of this place, that he's never here. I wonder whether I would've preferred an absentee father to my outright malicious one.

> **Alexis:**
> **Explain

I hit send and hear more pings from the shelf, loud enough to pierce though the still-shrieking smoke detector. My heart starts to race before my mind can piece together why I'm nervous. I instinctively sit up and tiptoe toward the bookshelf.

I send one more text.

> **Alexis:**
> Talk later

And there it is. The last "ping."

I rush to the shelf to hunt down the source of the glaring ping, the ping that rang and in one swooping sound signaled how fucking stupid I am, how naive, how goddamn idiotic I must be to have thought—

And then I see it. I see the phone. My hand shaking, I click to reveal its screen, and I see all of my text messages to Dr. Wes plump, primed, and waiting to be read.

By Victoria.

The alarm stops shrieking. The room falls silent.

"I can explain," Victoria says, now standing mere feet behind me, her eyes dark and unblinking.

"What the fuck is this."

"Just sit back down, I told you I can—"

"What the *fuck* is this, Victoria?"

Like a wind-up doll, this revelation, this knowing that I've been duped and manipulated by someone I thought I could trust, is the key that unlocks my body's stored trauma. It's the answer to why I've felt so unsettled, like something deep and fundamental was broken. Was not right. I felt it at TechCrunch Disrupt, right before my pitch. I felt it for weeks in the office, roaming the halls Darcy and I painted ourselves so many years ago, clad in overalls and dirty sneakers. I felt it in that first growth meeting with Victoria, the indigo acai bowls leaking condensation all over the conference room table, taunting me.

It's been months of this familiar weight, that everything is not as it seems. It's the haunting sensation that the reality you're in is not reality at all. It's a simulation someone has staged for you, to manage your perception. To wield control.

I start to shake violently, my hands quivering as my legs go numb. My head feels light, and I worry I might faint. I am overwhelmed by Victoria's betrayal, but even worse is the deep sense of shame. I am ashamed of my gullibility. My innocence. My conviction that Dr. Wes, a forty-something multi-millionaire bachelor who chose Darcy, the most beautiful and fascinating woman in New York, would want *me*. Would pine for *me*. With my see-through skin and peach fuzz and drooping arm fat, like the most delusional woman on the fucking planet.

I reflect on my interaction with the real Dr. Wes at TechCrunch Disrupt, my knack for projection clearly working overtime. It felt so charged and erotic, when in reality, he probably forgot who I was and was just trying to be polite. I reflect on the convenient timing of our missed FaceTimes and calls, and realize it was Victoria, every time, ringing me when she knew I couldn't answer, using the prospect of a real conversation to augment this artificial reality, this sense that the real Dr. Wes was yearning for me on the other end of the line.

I have a knack for seeing things that aren't there and ignoring things that are.

I am clutching the newfound phone for dear life, praying I can keep my grip. Victoria eyes the phone and walks slowly toward me. With every step she takes, I take one of my own toward the elevator, so I can flee.

"Why don't you sit back down and have your tea, okay?" she says all too calmly. "I know how this looks. And I know why you're hurt. But I swear it was for your own good. For *Savvy*. I could tell you were drowning, but you wouldn't talk to me about it, so I—"

"So you decided to spy on me? You decided to catfish me? Are you serious?"

"I didn't necessarily see it that way."

"There's only one way *to* see it! What does that even *mean*?"

"I was trying to give you a safe space. I wasn't sure if you'd, you know, open up to me like Darcy did," she says softly, batting her deep, almond eyes and carefully inching toward me. "You were shouldering so much, and I wanted you to have someone to talk to. I was worried you were gonna put on this—I don't know—this *charade* that everything was under control and that you had everything figured out. Especially after Stop The Bleed and you fucking up that whole rollout, and everyone knowing."

I weigh her words. It's true that I've been performing, forcing resilience and a bold, brave front for her sake, for the team's sake, for our investors. I wanted Victoria to think I was capable and sharp and that everything *was* under control. I wanted to impress her. I wanted her to feel like I was worthy of taking over, because then maybe I'd feel worthy, too. But all the while I've been privately agonizing over

The Raise

Darcy's mysterious acquisition plea and the lawsuit and our finances and the fact that she's not here to fix it. Clearly, things have *not* been under control. And as it turns out, I'm not capable after all.

I look into Victoria's eyes, and I can see the fear in each iris, worried for her career, worried she's lost my trust, worried I think she's categorically insane.

"I want to talk this out," she says. "And I want you to know how sorry I am. I really am. I know it wasn't the right thing to do. It was a crazy, stupid thing to do. But after seeing you at the funeral and how vulnerable you were, and watching you collapse at her casket and wailing and freaking out—"

"You saw that?" I ask, surprised and embarrassed.

"Yeah," she sighs. "Yeah, I did. I never said anything because, I don't know. Again, like, you were *not* in a good place. And in a way, you had so much more to lose than I did. I wanted you to have someone. I just figured that if Ethan wasn't even at her funeral—your *live-in* boyfriend—would *he* get you to that better place? Would *he* help you through it?"

Some hidden dam breaks inside me, like for the first time in a long time, I can feel myself being manipulated. I feel compelled to trust myself more than her, more than anyone. I feel firm in my reality, and there's nothing Victoria can do or say and no one she can blame, to convince me she's the Good Guy, or that this made any sense.

"I figured if I could be someone you and Darcy liked and admired," she continues, "a man you could actually trust for once in your life, then I'd know what was really going on with you. And I could help."

"It's not an excuse. You're disgusting. You're fucking insane."

I grab my suitcase, strap on my backpack, and begin pressing the elevator button, desperate for its arrival.

Victoria hovers right behind me, still eyeing the phone in my possession.

I scurry into the elevator as soon as the door drifts open, and as I descend to safety, I hear Victoria's muffled screams. "What are you gonna tell the board!? Alexis! We need to fix this!"

It feels like I've lived five full lifetimes between landing back in New York at the crack of dawn this morning and now, turning Savvy into my investigative headquarters. I still haven't heard from Gordon after last night's peanut incident, either, but I shove down that anxiety because there are more pressing matters at hand.

I arrive at the office and sprint to Darcy's desk with the intensity and focus of a NASA mission controller for Apollo 11. It's almost 10 a.m., and the office is empty. It's dirtier than I'd like, which makes me wish those "deep cleaners" were real and actually coming. But luckily, I have the building all to myself, and enough Juul pods, Redbull, and Diet Coke to sustain breaking into Darcy's computer and creeping around for as long as it takes.

Victoria said she and Darcy Slacked about her mental health.

That she was broken. Devolving. And hid it all from me, her longtime business partner and best friend, because I worshipped her. I smothered her. I "put her on a pedestal," then cut off her circulation.

But if it's all true, then it'll all be in here. In their chat history. Right where Victoria said it would be.

I spend a few hours pounding caffeine and gnawing at my cuticles, patiently scanning months of conversations between Darcy and Victoria. I search my name. I scroll and scroll. I download attachments.

The Raise

June 1, 2019

Victoria Solis 1:56PM
D! I got accepted to the revenue retreat!
Here's the one pager if you wanna review or anything
📎

Victoria Solis 1:56PM
If okay with you, I'll take off Aug 30 thru Sep 1
The retreat is weds + thurs and ill stay in
Miami thru the weekend
But I can check in all 3 weekdays ofc

Darcy Lyons 3:01PM
all good
have fun

Darcy Lyons 3:01PM
and no need
I'm gone that week too

Victoria Solis 3:02PM
Ohhhh yes
"The burn"
Okay

Victoria Solis 3:03PM
Are you still gonna lead the C suite sync that week
Or no

Darcy Lyons 3:08PM
No
I prob won't have service

Victoria Solis 3:09PM
Do you want me to do it?
I can dial in from the retreat on weds :)

Darcy Lyons 3:10PM
Alexis is doing it

Victoria Solis 3:10PM
Oh
right
Ok!

May 21, 2019

Darcy Lyons 8:03AM
when do you think you'll have the q3 projections ready? i have to share it with Gordon soonish, ideally by tues next week

Victoria Solis 8:03AM
Yah I was meaning to bring this up in our 1:1 tmrw
Once Oren sends me the retention stuff I'll be good to go that's why we're delayed
:(

Darcy Lyons 8:04AM
hmm okay
i know he was out last thurs fri
his dog got hit by a car...poor thing

Darcy Lyons 8:04AM
Do you want me to ping him to help move things along? was gonna check in on him anyway

Victoria Solis 8:05AM
No no, I got it
Thank you :)

Victoria Solis 8:08AM
But
I do think it's worth bringing up in his July review
That he missed the deadline

The Raise

Darcy Lyons 8:09AM
Did you remind him of the deadline
Or had a direct convo about any of this yet
?

Victoria Solis 8:09AM
Not yet

Darcy Lyons 8:09AM
Let's start there then

Victoria Solis 8:10AM
For sure
I do think hearing it from his manager would be best
But I got you
:)

Darcy Lyons 8:22AM
Ty!

August 24, 2019

Darcy Lyons 9:46PM
Growth looks rly good

Victoria Solis 9:46PM

(Takes a bow)

Darcy Lyons 9:46PM
where is it coming from

Victoria Solis 9:47PM
What do you mean?

Darcy Lyons 9:47PM
Like, what's our most performant channel
What's driving the surge

Victoria Solis 9:47PM
Paid acquisition, for sure
36% of new users are coming from Adwords, the "competitor set"
Which is us bidding against Crafted and their key words
It's expensive but working

Darcy Lyons 9:47PM
cool

Victoria Solis 9:48PM
It IS cool

Darcy Lyons 9:48PM
Are there any demographic trends
Like do we know where they are based or how old they are
The 36% of new users

Victoria Solis 9:49PM
I can work with Product on that before you leave for burning man
We have the age ranges from the initial quiz
Ill need to check on location tho
May need a few more days for that...but on it!

Darcy Lyons 9:50PM
Nice ty

Darcy Lyons 9:58PM
One more thing actually

Victoria Solis 9:58PM
?

Darcy Lyons 9:58PM
Can you also do an analysis on the same info
But only for users who keep using us after month 2?
Seeing a spike in order cancellations after month 1
Not sure what's going on

> **Victoria Solis 9:58PM**
> Sure!

> **Victoria Solis 10:07PM**
> I'll get it to you first thing Monday.

To my delight and relief, their conversations are notably stilted. They don't chit chat or gossip. They never share inside jokes or words of encouragement with one another. Victoria plays the dutiful employee, and Darcy plays the slightly aloof, yet discerning boss. There is no whiff of intimacy. No confessional tone. Not an ounce of vulnerability from either side.

They don't have what we had.

And I knew it. I knew I was right. I knew Darcy loved me.

But the relief quickly morphs into sharp stomach pain and a queasy, paralyzing intuition.

Because not only did Darcy notice the suspicious orders in the lead up to her death, but Victoria lied to me. Outright.

I zip open my leather backpack and pull out Gordon's documents, the ones he showed me at the Thai restaurant. The number of users starts to slowly climb in June and picks up steam in July. But the orders and cancellations really start to build right before Burning Man, in August, and then sustain through Darcy's death all the way to today.

Would the con really continue, and *accelerate*, even with Darcy gone? In the off chance she was behind this, it means she told the anonymous fraudsters to ramp up orders in August no matter what, and at all costs, even without real-time guidance or direction from the CEO.

I don't think that makes sense. She'd never anticipate not being here, her cold body buried beneath the Long Island dirt.

The second, and simpler explanation, is that whoever's spearheading this scheme is still very much alive and has a vested interested in making us grow—or making it *look* like we're growing.

Someone who needs our numbers to look as impressive as possible. Someone with something to prove. Someone bold enough, and vain enough, to put the entire company on the line to boost their own agenda.

Someone who's not afraid to "take."

> **Victoria:**
> I called you
> It went to VM
> I wanted to say sorry
> I know your going thru a lot
> I think we should meet first thing tmr to talk thru everything
> Anything I ever did was to help Savy and you
> I hope you see and understand that
> Bc its true

Ethan hounds me when I finally come home around midnight, asking for every detail of the past twenty-four hours. *Why are you back from SF early? Where have you been all day? What's going on? Are you alright?*

He can see on my face that I'm war-torn and broken. But all I share is that Gordon and Alliance ran into a small issue during diligence, and that I'll know more soon.

I lock myself in the bathroom, sink into the tub, and open a bottle of wine. I dunk my head under the scorching hot water and stay down there for as long as I can. I count the passing seconds with each suppressed breath and think about Victoria, and how much deception she's capable of. It's freakish.

She pretended to be Dr. Wes. She catfished me for weeks on end. And she knew Darcy was suspicious of our sudden spike in sales and order cancellations. She keeps lying to me about how close the two of them were, too—and why? To be my "support system?"

To keep tabs on me?

Or to keep tabs on what I *knew*.

The mere thought overwhelms me. My best friend just died a few weeks ago. And now I'm in bed with a corporate psychopath?

I imagine what it might feel like to let go and live safe under the water. But I know my body would fight it. I'd enter multiple rounds of respiratory arrest and eventually start convulsing, shaking myself upright and above the water line. But depending on how much water I've inhaled by then, maybe I could swing it. Maybe I'd make it to those last few terminal gasps.

I imagine Ethan's face when he breaks through the door and finds me bloated and floating face-down, like a mannequin out at sea. I imagine him shaking me endlessly, trying to force me awake. I imagine him screaming and punching the mirrored cabinet—then calling his mom.

But when my count hits thirty, my body instinctively pops up for air. I'm alive. I'm breathing. And Ethan's not here holding my heavy, limp body. He's working from bed, finishing a bottle of wine of his own, apparently finalizing his first-ever pitch deck for ALLMENMATR.

I submerge my head again and hear a knock at the door. It's Ethan. I hear a muffled question: do I have a few minutes to give his pitch a once-over?

I pretend not to hear him, come back up to breathe, and eventually see his shadow disappear below the door. That itch I felt back at Theo's birthday party—the mounting resentment toward Ethan, the stress of being needed—is flaring up again. I keep reminding myself that Ethan has no idea what's going on with me, because I haven't and won't tell him until I'm closer to the other side of this mess. But the animosity is starting to stick regardless, like the hard water stains in our bathtub I can't seem to scrub away.

My phone buzzes relentlessly. I screen a call and a string of texts from my mom, who shares blurry, pixelated screenshots of me on stage at TechCrunch and notes of congratulations from the "bitches" at the bank and all her Facebook friends. I screen a handful of texts from Victoria, too, who keeps asking how the board meeting went, and when we can meet again in person.

I can't believe I fell for her ruse.

I can't believe she took advantage of me like that—so vulnerable after Darcy's death, so desperate for an ally.

But most of all, I can't believe her audacity: calling me, texting me, asking for board updates—as though she never deceived me. As if she didn't do something so egregious and cruel that she forced me to confront the edges of my sanity. *How could I be so gullible? How could I be so trusting?*

The Raise

I pause to toggle my phone to silent, but before I do, I see a rapid influx of messages from Hazel, our old HR consultant.

> **Hazel:**
> Please call me. Urgent.

> **Hazel:**
> Alexis. Call me.

> **Hazel:**
> Alexis.

> **Hazel:**
> I just watched a replay of your Tech Crunch Thing
> And there's something I need to tell you asap

> **Hazel:**
> About Darcy

I frantically scramble to get a grip on my phone so I can call, but my fingers are too wet. I spring from the bathtub and skid toward my towel, nearly tripping on the tile.

I wipe my hands on the towel and try calling again. She picks up at the second ring.

"Alexis," she says sternly in her southern twang. "I've been trying to reach you. Why haven't you called me back?"

"What do you mean?"

"I texted you like four times since the funeral."

"I know, but I thought it was cuz you just, like, wanted to stay in touch since I took over. Or you wanted me to hire you or something. It's happened with a lot of Darcy's people. And we were so strapped on cash, so I was like, I'm not gonna—"

"That's not why I called."

I crouch down in the corner of the bathroom, the heat from the tub fogging up my phone and making me sweat. I listen nervously as Hazel explains her last few interactions with Darcy in the lead up to Burning Man. I knew from snooping her Slacks with Victoria that Darcy was suspicious, but I had no idea she had enlisted and paid Hazel to separately investigate the spike in orders, and subsequent cancellations.

"I guess she was seeing a ton of customer disputes, people disputing the intro box charges with their banks. Claiming their credit cards were stolen. So she sent me all of that," she continues. "And I had my technical guy here look into the IP addresses for all those orders, which basically lets you see where the orders were actually placed. Like where the computer physically was when it placed the order."

"Well, it's obviously Victoria. She clearly hired some randos to steal credit card numbers and place the orders and send them to the PO Box addresses."

"No, actually. You're right that likely, all the fake orders were placed with stolen credit cards. You can buy fake credit card numbers in bulk on the dark web, test them out, see which are real and which are bogus. But all the IP addresses were obscured by a VPN. The VPN hides the real IP address for the computers, sadly. So my guy couldn't catch the locations for—"

"Well then why are you even calling to—"

"For *most* of the orders. The first fifteen or so, though, the first fifteen intro boxes that were ordered and then cancelled, we tracked to two IP addresses. It looks like whoever did the ordering either forgot to connect to the VPN for these first few, or only thought to install the VPN afterward."

"And they tracked to Victoria's address in New York?"

"I can't confirm the exact addresses, and I can't confirm it was Victoria. I'm sorry. I don't know who it was. Darcy just asked me to help identify where the orders were coming from."

"Just fucking tell me!" I hear my voice jump an octave, like I'm about to cry. Because I am. Between the bottle of wine and the suffocating condensation and the suspense, I feel unmoored and unstable, like I'm in a stuffy, hazy nightmare.

"Alexis. Breathe. That's what I'm trying to do."

I take her advice, and breathe in, then out. Ethan knocks on the door to ask if I'm okay—and I say yes, then beg him to leave me alone. My ear is pressed to my phone for dear life, like I'm hearing Darcy's last words before she fell.

"There were two computers placing those early intro box orders with the stolen cards, then cancelling them," Hazel continues, "one was in Southampton," she says, and my stomach drops. "And the other was Santiago, Chile?"

Still crouching, I lose my center of gravity and go numb, slowly slouching down the wall behind me. I feel a sense of relief. A small sense of triumph. Because I'm not crazy. I'm not wrong.

I have it now. *I have proof.*

"And you told Darcy that? Darcy knew that?" I pry, my words rushing out.

"I texted her exactly that on August twenty-seventh. I could see she read the text, but I never heard back."

That was the first day of Burning Man. Two days before she died. Which means she arrived at Burning Man fully aware of the fraud. She was likely overcome with a deep sense of anxiety and betrayal when Hazel shared those two locations over text. Victoria's from this luxe commune called Vitacura in Santiago, and her family's East

Coast vacation home is in Southampton. *Didn't Victoria say Manuel, her brother, was back in Chile when I went over there last week?*

It all makes sense now. That's why Darcy texted Marz. As soon as she got that text from Hazel, she could smell it was game over, and clueless as to how deep or intricate the fraud was, or how many people Victoria had involved. I bet as soon as she got to camp on the Playa, she scrambled for service immediately. To plan a way out of Burning Man and get back to work, back to me, and back to Hazel, but also, to reach a soft landing for her company. For *our* company. And to keep the fraud from spiraling further in her absence. Burning Man is a week-long commitment, after all.

She must have been panicked. Frantic. Stuck on the Playa knowing full well she was right to be suspicious, and that Victoria was to blame.

But her beautiful, cockroach mind found the last trapped door—Marz, merging with Crafted—even if it killed her to come to him. Even if it bludgeoned her ego to be vulnerable and ask for his help.

"That's all I have," Hazel says with a sigh. "I was gonna come to the office this week if I didn't hear back from you soon. I know you needed space but, it really messed me up, not knowing if you knew about this or not, and then seeing you up on that stage. Darcy said you didn't, so I figured—"

"Yah," I reply. "There's a lot I didn't know."

"She loved you. I think she wanted to protect you. And maybe she was a little ashamed. A little embarrassed."

"I would've loved her anyway," I say, my voice shaking, my body naked on the tiled floor. "I would've helped her. She didn't need to hide it from me. I would have loved her still."

"Sometimes people don't know that, or they don't realize. They think love is conditional. That they need to be a certain way to keep the love, or seem a certain way to be worthy," she replies, her therapist voice creeping in. "We never talked about this stuff, by the way. I'm just guessing. But I know she really cared about you. *That's no guess.*"

"I know."

"She wasn't trying to hurt you or deceive you, though. That's not how I see it. From where I sit, she was doing what she thought she had to."

I clutch the phone close and thank Hazel for her persistence, for getting a hold of me. Then I splay face-down on the floor, like a starfish, and let the sense of relief—of vindication—baptize me in the fog.

It's 4 a.m. and I can't fall asleep.

Before crawling into bed to cuddle with Ethan—a gesture to make up for avoiding his pitch deck, though every cell in my hunger-panged frame yearned to gorge on pad see ew and pass out solo on the couch—I texted Hazel to send me all her documentation. Then, I set an emergency meeting with the board for tomorrow morning to share details of the fraud and all the proof that's about to hit my inbox. I'm anxious about Gordon, and whether he's somehow realized I turned his meal into poison soup. I can't stop thinking about what Hazel told me: that Darcy learned about the fake orders right as she arrived on the Playa, that it was Victoria's scheme all along, and that Darcy kept it all from me on purpose. To avoid shame. Or embarrassment. Or maybe, just maybe, to keep herself neatly situated on the pedestal I constructed for her so many years ago.

Phone and pinot noir in hand, I scroll endlessly through Darcy's Instagram grid, which she hasn't posted to in about three or four years: a picture of us curled up on the couch during Jetto movie night nearly ten years ago, looking fresh-faced and green; a selfie of us at the kitchen counter in Darcy's old apartment, sharing earbuds, about to do our first brand pitch for Savvy; a grainy shot of us chugging champagne on the sidewalk after closing our very first investor check. I miss her so much it hurts. All I want to do is call her right now and vent about everything and hear her say "it's okay" on the other line.

Ethan's snoring now and I'm jealous. I'm jealous he can sleep so easily. I'm jealous he has his parents, who will always catch him when he falls. And I'm jealous that his toughest battle to date is finding a new law firm to work for. I'm not sure what to do with this jealousy, or where to put it. I was once so attracted to his stability, but now, I fear it's starting to repulse me. At the very least, I'm not ready to tell him what's going on, and what I know. It feels like more work to explain the whole thing. I don't have the energy. And I don't trust he'd be helpful.

Still wired, I keep swiping and clicking and scrolling away. And suddenly, I freeze on a photo of me, Darcy, and Victoria applying stick-wallpaper to our old shoebox of an office—back when it was just the three of us. Back when things were so simple and wholesome and optimistic and right.

I click the tagged profiles and pull up Victoria's Instagram for the first time in nearly a month and click through to her main feed. Like me, she hasn't posted anything since Darcy died.

I tap to stalk her tagged pictures, and nearly drop my red wine on our white duvet.

Hands shaking, I carefully put my glass on the bedside table and zoom in to the first tagged picture on her account.

The Raise

It's a snapshot of her and some girl standing in front of the furry double decker bus, the one Darcy fell from. The photo was posted and tagged thirteen minutes ago by the artist who conceptualized and decorated the bus.

> @burnerbabedezign
>
> wat an honor to decorate this beauty <3 this design took me nearly a year and 42 different scraps and fur and materials!!!
>
> missing my fave @iamVickySolis jetting in from Miami (!) girl I love you sm u know ur my girl. so proud of u <3 plz visit lisbon soon??
>
> tbh hesitated posting these for a bit due to the accident. but this pic to me captured the essence of the burn this year b4 things went haywire :(
>
> laughter, smiles, sun + lots and lots and lots of DUST!!! was impossibly hard to see this year without goggles (even with tbh!) and I wishhhh I took more pics before we got on site, but I'm so proud of the work of me and my team and idk if this badboi will ever ride again!! so RIP to our beautiful creation and
>
> darcy baby, rest in peace my lovebug <3

My mind abuzz with confusion, I can barely keep my thoughts straight. I frantically zoom into the photo and see her dusty, fuzzy frame: Darcy, bedazzled Juul in hand, boarding the bus. Her head is tilted back, her long, red hair glistening against her golden skin. Stuck on the Playa. Knowing her company is imploding slowly, from the inside. And that it's all Victoria's fault.

I barrel out of bed and into the living room, pacing around like my soles are on fire.

Something's not right. Something's not adding up. Victoria was there?! She was fucking there. But she said she was in Miami that whole weekend? That's what she told Darcy in their Slacks about the retreat . . .

I crouch into a ball on our living room rug and start biting my knuckles, piercing my skin. My breathing gets heavy and fast, and I try to suppress the guttural, primal scream that's brewing inside me.

It's not adding up. It's not possible. It's not—

Wait. Hold on. She must have flown into Nevada some time that weekend and didn't stay in Miami after all. She didn't call me back after Darcy died that Sunday because she was stuck on the Playa—she wasn't flying back from the revenue retreat, like she said at the time. She was there all along. She did it. She killed her. She did it. She—

My head is spinning, and my thoughts are sprinting so fast I can barely hear them, one by one. I stumble toward the kitchen sink to get some water, careful not to trip or hit my head on the way. I try to put the pieces together: the tagged photo, her Slacks, the fraud, and all her lies.

She pretended to be Dr. Wes so she could keep tabs on me—on what I knew. She wanted me to think she and Darcy were buddy-buddy so I would trust her and need her for growth stuff. She had that frantic, focused look in her eyes when she told me they were close—that they shared meals, they shared secrets. She needed me to believe her so she could avoid suspicion about all of it—the fraud, the catfishing, the murder. Like a desperate person.

Like a guilty person.

Before the water hits my mouth, I start gagging in the kitchen sink, suddenly repulsed by our dirty dishes.

I force myself to take a few breaths so I can rush back to the phone and screenshot the picture—so I can have proof.

Victoria was there. She was at Burning Man. She was with Darcy on the bus. And Darcy knew about the fraud. Did she know Victoria was coming? Was there a confrontation?

Did Victoria push her?

I refresh my Instagram a dozen times, like an addict pulling the slot machine. But I'm too late. It's all over.

The picture—my only proof—is gone.

16

October 3, 2019.

Two hours later, I'm hungover and running on no sleep, staring at Isabella in her tiny little Zoom square. My mind races, wondering how she and the rest of the board will come to terms with this fraud reveal, if Gordon knows I fed him those death peanuts, and how severely and unavoidably fucked I am. I need their buy-in to fire Victoria, which I know I'll get, but I'm still scared they're going to berate me for letting this happen. For my complete and utter incompetence. The fraud could be terminal, and no matter how distracted I was by Darcy's death or the raise or the secret discrimination case, Victoria still did this on my watch.

"Hey team," Gordon says mournfully as he joins the video call, ensuring his unnecessarily bandaged wrist is in full view. "Just now getting my sea legs. It's been a rough few days to say the least."

"Are you alright?" Laney asks, completely unaware of what Gordon suffered. She doesn't have or use Twitter, so she missed his zillion-character rant about the careless employees who poisoned him and the latest musings on his imminent manslaughter lawsuit.

"Uh, yeah," he responds with a heavy sigh, clearly milking it. "I went into anaphylaxis at a Thai spot a few days back. I was with Alexis, actually, who saved my life. We were catching up on the stuff we're gonna talk through today. I fell down hard at the restaurant, and uh, I hurt my hand pretty bad."

My mind quickly jumps to the incident and can't recall this part, though I feel relieved he thinks I saved him. Per my memory, though, he slumped down in his chair, slowly, and then crumpled to the ground. It was more of a gentle slither than a hard fall.

"We're so glad you're here, and that you're healthy," I interject, eager to move off this topic as quickly as possible. "Is Jürgen joining, or?"

"I'll catch him up," Gordon replies, unwrapping and rewrapping the bandage for no reason.

I take that as my cue to start detailing what I know about the fraud thus far. I give Gordon and his analyst credit for bringing the issue to my attention, and reassure Gordon, Isabella, and Laney that I had no idea this was unfolding behind my back, and that I inherited the problem from Darcy, who I recently learned was herself suspicious. I haven't received Hazel's files yet—I'm not sure she's online at this ungodly hour—so I show versions of the data and charts Gordon's analyst put together, indicating how the scheme started slowly at first, but ramped aggressively as we barreled toward the Series C. I own up to my lack of oversight and preemptively admit that yes, I was distracted by mourning Darcy and gearing up for the raise, and yes, I put too much trust in my team.

"So you know who it was, then?" Laney asks. Her voice and eyes are soft and empathetic.

"I think so, yes. I just found out about all this yesterday, so it's still early. I need some harder proof, but—"

"Alright, so who is this fucker?" Gordon pries, angry and impatient.

"I'm pretty sure it's our Head of Growth, Victoria. Victoria Solis."

The call goes silent. No one says a word. I watch everyone watch each other in the zoom squares.

Alarmed by the quiet, I fill the silence by detailing my plans to lay off Victoria, reveal the fraud to my employees, and notify everyone that a deeper investigation is pending, in case anyone else was involved. I start to explain my hunch that Victoria has even more to hide, given she was at Burning Man with Darcy, but Laney cuts me off.

"This isn't your fault," Laney says compassionately. "I just want you to know that. What you've been up against here, between taking over as CEO, and you know, losing someone so close to you, it's all very understandable. Before we talk logistics and all that, I feel the need to put that out there."

"Agreed," Isabella chimes in, clearly posted up in the conference room of a luxe hotel or The Battery House. "You have our full support, Alexis. I second what Laney said."

Gordon nods profusely and gives a quick "yup" before subtly massaging his bandaged hand, and I am overcome with relief. My two primary fears were one: that they'd all assume I was complicit or directing the fraud in some way, and two: that Gordon knows I poisoned him, and planned to call me out.

"That said," Isabella continues, twirling her pen between long, French-manicured fingers. "If it wasn't your fault and *you* as CEO, you know, had the best intentions, I'd hate for this to derail our plans, here."

"What do you—" I interject, confused.

"I hear you," Gordon adds, then clears his throat. "Look it uh, it took us a bit to parse through, you know, when we were looking at all the data and the credit cards and the shipping addresses and such. It's something we can potentially obscure, and uh . . . stitch back together. The growth looked totally normal and healthy for a good long stretch."

To my surprise, Laney is silent.

"I worry it wouldn't be fair to you," Isabella says. "And the business is otherwise sound, right? Is it fair to let this tank the raise and even, you know, the company?"

"And your investments," Laney adds, surfacing the subtext. Gordon and Isabella have already dumped tens of millions into Savvy. Admitting to fraud, doing mass layoffs, and killing the Series C would mean a total wipeout. Isabella and Gordon would lose all the money they poured into Savvy, and so would their investors. It would make them look like fools.

"I think it's reasonable to say, or to suggest, that we sit on a potential solution here and regroup tomorrow on our ideal outcome," Isabella concludes, using more coded language than Gordon had. "We can maybe—emphasis on 'maybe,' here—discuss getting you some holdover capital in case the raise takes a bit longer than we thought, given all this."

I sit silent for a beat, overcome with shock and disgust, but also, a tinge of relief. If I do charge forward—firing Victoria but still doing the raise, hiding the fraud with some help from Gordon's analyst and getting some new money in from Isabella—I can keep Savvy alive. I could maybe get Isabella to wire her money by tomorrow, too, which is when I'm supposed to pay Jada. Isabella and Gordon seem fairly invested in keeping Savvy scandal-free and on track for this next massive round of funding, which works in my favor.

"Just so I'm clear," I reply hazily, still wrapping my head around the proposal, "you think it's fine if I just lay Victoria off, take my meetings with Fisher and all those guys, and work with Gordon's team to um, to kind of course-correct what happened?"

"No darling," Isabella answers, "I don't think you should lay her off."

"What? But she—"

"Because first of all, you said yourself you need proof. Which it sounds like you don't have. And second of all, but most importantly, her father is an investor in a few of our funds. We can't afford to lose him."

I freeze. I look empty-eyed into the Zoom squares and start to panic. I can feel the guttural scream brewing again, desperate for release.

"But it's not, it's not fair," I stutter. "I um . . . I'm going to have proof hit my inbox in like, two hours from now. I swear. And I just—I can't work with her anymore anyway, you know? It's a big feeling of betrayal. And if I don't fire her, it's . . . it's setting such a bad example."

"Not if the team doesn't know," Gordon says, too calmly. "Then it's just, you know, business as usual. And firing a key hire like that, your Head of Growth . . . it's not a good look for the raise. At all."

"And if my fund loses Dr. Solis because of this," Isabella adds, her voice soft, "it puts future founders in a horrible position. We take checks from successful people like Dr. Solis so we can give it to female founders like *you*. We only invest in underrepresented founders and overlooked categories, right? He was a big win for us. We can't have a portfolio company fire an investor's kid, especially not for fraud. And especially when you have no proof."

"But—but she killed her!" I blurt out, suddenly, and everyone on the Zoom seizes up. Gordon looks down and starts massaging his bushy eyebrows with his bandaged hand. Laney purses her lips, and Isabella cocks her head so far to the left, it might fall right off.

I wasn't planning on telling them. After all, I have nothing to back me up. The Instagram photo is gone. The Playa's been cleaned up and cleared out for ages now. Darcy's body is buried six feet under in that god-forsaken mermaid wig. There's no hard evidence. There's nothing.

Just dust.

"She killed who, honey?" Isabella asks, her voice still cloyingly maternal.

"She killed Darcy. She was at Burning Man with her. I . . . I saw a picture."

I feel ashamed even saying it, but I was so sure they'd agree to fire her—to evict her from my life. I need them to know the stakes what it really means for her to stay. What it really means to have to see her name on Slack, and in my emails, and to brush past her in the office Darcy and I lived and laughed in every single day.

They were on the bus that night. Darcy called her out on the scheme. Victoria panicked. She shoved her in the chest, and Darcy fell. Between the dust storm and the alcohol and the rampant psychedelics, no one saw it. No one knew.

But I do.

I know she killed my best friend.

"Alexis, sweetie," Laney chimes in, clearly worried. "Are you okay?"

"Yes! Yes, I'm okay! Stop talking like I'm—like I'm crazy or something. I'm just—I'm telling you what I saw." I'm nearly screaming now and hear the bedroom door creak open. I can see Ethan's half-asleep, confused reflection in the hallway mirror. "It's not just that she faked these orders. She did other crazy shit to me! And Darcy! Like crazy person shit! She texted me for *weeks* and pretended to be someone else so she could monitor me and what I knew about the fraud and the murder and she—"

"Alexis, sweetie," Laney says quietly in her cream cashmere crewneck, the California sun beaming warm, bright light into her office. "It's too much. This is all just far, far too much. I don't know where we go from here?"

"What I think Laney's trying to say, Alexis," Isabella cuts in, "is that you're overwhelmed. Clearly. You're overwhelmed and overtired. I wasn't sure if you, you know, just hadn't dabbed some concealer on yet. But your under eyes do not look good. Have you been sleeping?"

"She hasn't," I hear Ethan proclaim from behind me, his messy hair and scruff peeking through my square in the Zoom. I swiftly kick him in the shin, praying it's all out of view, and he drops to the floor in pain, clutching his lower leg and cursing me under his breath.

They can't think I'm impaired. They can't think I'm unqualified. They can't think I'm lost, or crazy, or tired, or weak.

"I'm fine," I declare with a smile, realizing, with a knot in my stomach, that they'll never believe me. That I'm stuck. That I'm trapped in this never-ending nightmare where Victoria wreaks havoc on my business, my life, my sanity—and there is no recourse. There is no justice.

"Why don't we do this," Gordon finally chimes in, his eyebrows sufficiently disheveled now. "Alexis—you take the day off. Yeah? Okay? Good. You've been through a lot in the last few days, what with me nearly dying at your feet, and this fraud stuff, and God knows what else with just, you know, with whatever else might be going on at home."

Ethan's still on the floor and looks up at me, his eyes fixed and stern.

"Yes, take the day," Isabella adds, forcing a smile, "maybe take the night with your, uh, your fiancé over there—"

"Boyfriend," I interject. "He's just my boyfriend."

"Right, well, you take the day with him, let him take care of you, and let us regroup on next steps. I promise you Alexis," Isabella says, serious now, "you've taken this thing to fifty million, and you really—you wowed hundreds of investors on stage the other day. Despite everything you've been up against. We've got your back."

"You're a phoenix!" Gordon exclaims while leaning back in his chair, clearly smug with his use of the word.

"Yes, you're quite resilient," Laney shares calmly, before sipping from her one-hundred-dollar MacKenzie Childs mug.

"What the fuck was that?" Ethan screams from the couch, holding a pack of Trader Joe's frozen gnocchi to his lower leg.

I stare into space and don't answer, at a loss for words on where to start. Tears swell in my eyes, my mind too overheated and overwhelmed to replay the details of what I know, and what I saw. My heart is filled with shame—over the fact that I emotionally cheated on Ethan with an impostor for weeks on end, then physically assaulted him—and with exhaustion, because all I want is the pure peace of being left alone.

"Whoa, whoa, whoa," Ethan says, rushing over to sit beside me at the kitchen counter as soon as he sees my lip start to quiver. "It's okay. Baby, I forgive you. I know you're dealing with a lot. Have you eaten? I'll order us something and we can talk everything out."

The thought of putting food in my drained, dead body sounds like labor. I half-heartedly tap on caprese and lemon pasta when Ethan hands me his phone for delivery from our favorite Italian place.

Over a crusty spliff I find in a nearby ash tray, I mentally prepare to tell Ethan about the confrontation at Victoria's, the fraud, and the

Instagram photo of her on the Playa. He's overheard too much, and I can't get away with keeping all of this from him any longer. The tobacco and weed singe my lungs and for a moment, I feel release. Over my next few hits, I outline the Instagram shot of her on the Playa, and my suspicions, the board's recommendation to "obscure" Victoria's fake orders, and their assertion that we preserve her employment and barrel toward the Series C. I remind him that Jada plans on going to the press tomorrow if I don't wire her the money she's owed. Just saying it quadruples my heart rate and immediately kills my light but much-needed buzz.

"But you don't know it's her for sure? The fraud or, the accident or whatever?" Ethan asks.

"I *know* it's her."

"But you don't have proof?"

"I saw a photo of her on the bus with Darcy! And the fake orders came from IP addresses in Chile and Southampton!"

"But can you trace them to *her* specifically? And like, are we really saying some photo proves she's a murderer? Seems far-fetched to me. I think . . . yeah, I think you're probably overtired like what's-her-face said."

He bites his cheek, eyebrows raised in concern, like a lawyer who doesn't believe me. I briefly imagine him making Partner, doing this same bit at a deposition or in court, and making the opposing counsel squirm. Ethan can reek of skepticism when he wants to.

"You can't fire her if there's no proof of anything," he says with a sigh, shaking his head and side-eyeing my joint. "And maybe cool it on the weed? This whole thing is already messing with you. I know you were drunk the other night at dinner with my family."

"Ethan," I reply firmly, puffing my joint with purpose now. "No, I wasn't. And I'm not doing this with you. We can't go back in time, and a bunch of bad shit happened at once with you, too. It's not like the Savvy thing—"

"I'm just saying that—"

"I don't care. It doesn't matter. It's not my fault Victoria did this. None of this is my fault."

"No, I know it's not your fault. But if you don't have proof then I—"

"No! *'But'* nothing! I need a partner right now, not a fucking lawyer. I know I don't have proof from the bus. I know this is all a shitshow. But I'm going to handle it. I'm going to fix it. Everything will be fine."

"Alexis!" he screams back, combing his hand through his hair to calm down. "It's not fine. *You're* not fine. Look at you for fuck's sake! You've lost, what, fifteen pounds in four weeks? You don't sleep. You're never sober. You're either hopped up on Adderall or drinking or both."

I wince.

"What?" he asks, even more aggressive now. "Do you not agree?"

I instinctively pause to breathe in through my nose, and out through my mouth.

Maybe I know he's right. Maybe I am rotting. Maybe I'm unhappy. But maybe a part of me knows, deep down, that Ethan has no role to play in me getting better. That the voice inside, the one begging me to be alone, isn't screaming because I'm drained or irritated—it's because yes, I am broken. And because I know now, for certain, that Ethan will never, ever fill the cracks.

"I'm sorry. I'm going," I blurt out, bolting to put on my Uggs.

"Wait, *what*? The food's not even here yet. We can—look, I'm sorry, okay? We can talk this out. You just dumped a lot on me, you know. I don't know what to say."

"Is it so wrong to just want, '*I'm sorry you're going through this,*' '*How are you feeling, and how can I help?*' '*You're so strong, Alexis. I know you'll figure this out?*'"

I start crying uncontrollably.

"I'm sorry, okay?" he says, crying now himself. "I have a lot on my plate, too. I still haven't told my mom, and I can't bring myself to start applying out. I feel like a fucking idiot. I feel like I'm nothing."

"And what if I responded to that and said, '*The pressure's making you rot. You're a mess. This is ruining you.*' Would that feel good? Is that what you want to hear?" I grab my keys and head toward the door.

"She's gonna go ballistic," he says from the kitchen, fighting through tears. "And she's gonna ice me out again. She's gonna—"

"You're so pathetic! Oh my god!"

Seeing him like this—raw, shaking, blubbering like a baby—curdles my mounting resentment and within seconds, turns it into something worse: disgust. I loved both him and his potential, but clung so hard to the latter, that at some point, the Ethan before me stopped being enough. I poured years of love into this man, certain that if I gave him the unconditional love that she couldn't, I'd release her hold on him. It's true that he never asked me to love him like that. He never asked me to fix him. But doesn't it count for something that I tried? Doesn't it count for something that I wanted to?

"Please just stay with me," he says, his face in his wet hands, and with one last look at him, I can feel it, that I've finally given up.

"I still love you, but I'm sorry, your mommy issues can't be my problem anymore. I just don't have the capacity."

I throw the door open, arising from my rot, as the talk track in my head grows louder and louder and I try trusting it, one word at a time.

I'm sitting cross-legged on the floor of Darcy's office with her MacBook on my lap, and my phone in my hands. I cautiously type

The Raise

Dr. Wes's real phone number into my dial pad and take stock of my surroundings before I place the call.

I take a deep breath and imbibe the familiar smell of wood and fig. I scan her desk, remembering how she'd tap her long acrylic nails on the table when she was thinking through a tough decision or figuring out how to word something in an email. I glance at the empty trash can and suddenly see it overflowing with Chipotle soda cups and leaky salsa sacs and cracked tortilla chip from the nights we'd stay late to plan layoffs or prep annual reviews. I spot the faded red wine stain on her peach blush area rug from when we urgently opened a bottle as our last round of funding hit Savvy's account.

I stand there for a moment committing the entire scene to memory. I've lost so much so quickly. I can't bear the thought of Darcy's stuff disappearing along with her.

Not yet. Maybe not ever.

I hit the green "call" button on my phone and take a deep breath.

"Hello?" says Dr. Wes, and I feel a new wave of embarrassment. That my Dr. Wes was never him, was never real.

"Hey—yeah, um . . ." I reply, unsure of what to say next. "It's Alexis, Darcy's—"

"Alexis," he laughs, and it sounds warm and grizzly. "I know who you are."

"Right," I sigh, and let out a chuckle. "Yeah."

"How've you been holding up? It's, uh, it's good to hear from you." His tone is curious but concerned, a quiet acknowledgment that he's confused. My outreach is clearly unexpected. I wonder if he knew Darcy kept their relationship a secret. From everyone. From me.

"I'm not great, actually," I admit, and it feels so good to say it. My voice starts to quicken as I try explaining myself. "That's kind of why

I'm calling. I mean, I know this is super random, and I don't want to make this weird. I really don't. I know you're probably busy, but I—"

"Whoa, there. Slow down. Is everything okay?" He sounds like a TV Dad. Like Coach Taylor.

"No?" I whimper.

"Okay, okay," he says, his buttery, calm voice betraying a slight smile. We both laugh again for some reason. The exchange suddenly feels so surreal, it's almost silly. Darcy—his secret lover, and my business partner—is dead. She fell off a decorative, double-decker bus in the middle of the desert, a million miles away from us both, the two people who knew her and loved her so deeply. Our shared laughter seals us in the twilight zone, a place we never thought we'd be. Without her.

"I don't really know how to say this," I continue, collecting myself, "or how to ask this. But, well, if something bad was going on, do you think she'd put Savvy at risk to stop it? Or, I don't know, do you think she would've done whatever it takes to keep Savvy going? I guess that's what I'm getting at."

"It depends on what the bad thing is, I guess. What's going . . ."

"It's bad."

"Okay, well. Can you . . ."

"I'm not going to tell you the details. I don't want to get you involved. It's better that way, I think. But it's bad."

He grunts. "Like WeWork bad or Enron bad?"

"Closer to Enron bad, I'd say."

"Alrighty then. Well, that's, uh, well that's a pickle."

"I had nothing to do with it. Obviously. And *she* had nothing to do with it," I rush to clarify, desperate to preserve his impression of her. Desperate to keep her on his pedestal, where she belongs.

"I assumed as much. She was a killer, that's for sure, but I don't think she had 'Enron' in her."

"No, I know. That's why I'm freaking out. Because I don't, either."

"Then I think you know your answer."

I hang on the line in silence, processing what Dr. Wes just said. I know he's right. I know I should follow my compass, listen to my gut—whatever 'woo-woo' way you want to put it. But I still don't fully trust myself. Maybe my Saturn hasn't returned quite yet.

"But what do you think *she* would do?" I pry, hoping for a silver bullet. Praying for someone else to hand over clear instructions—some definitive answer. Just like I did with Victoria, and our growth, which proved a total disaster.

"It doesn't matter what she'd do," he says matter-of-factly, like he's never been more sure of anything.

"Of course it matters. It was her company."

"It was *your* company, too. It *is* your company. And you're the one in charge," he urges. "And more than that—you're the one with all the information. You're not giving me anything—which I totally get, and maybe agree with—but Darcy doesn't have the full scoop, and neither do I. You're, you know, asking me to spit out an answer when I don't have any data to inform or shape that answer."

"Right, but—"

"And regardless, you're different people. You're leading how *you* lead. You're building how *you* build. And she trusted you, and the ways you did both those things."

"She did?" I ask, my voice audibly shaking before I release a full, unexpected heave that fills the entire room.

"Alexis, come on," he reassures me, his voice soft and kind. "She'd cosign on whatever you think is right. But she's not here anymore."

"I know," I reply, still crying, her office cradling me like a bassinet. "I just miss her so much. And she was so . . . she was so mean to me. Before she left. It didn't end how I wanted it to end."

"Look," he says, his voice a bit shaky now, too. "I don't know what happened between you guys before, you know, before the accident. But last I saw her, she was here agonizing over some letter to you. We almost missed our dinner reservation because she was so in it. I don't remember exactly what she said, or what she was writing about. I've wished," he chokes on the words, and I know he's crying, too. "I've just wished so badly that our last few moments together came into sharper focus. That happens sometimes, when someone dies. You suddenly see it all more clearly."

"Yeah," I tell him, as gently as I can, and all I want to do is fly to Boston to give him a hug. To give him her green suit. To give him her makeup or office heels or her collection of dead vapes. I want him to have as much of her as I have. I want him to have a piece of whatever's left. "It's happened for me with some things. Some days I can remember everything."

"Well, you're lucky. I'm still in my fog, I guess. I wish I remembered more."

"What was it like? To be that close with her?" I ask, because I'm sure he remembers that.

"I don't need to tell you this, of all people" he sighs, collecting himself. "But yeah. Darcy was . . ." he trails off, looking for the right word to summarize their thrilling chemistry, how she made him feel, the "Big Love" Darcy thought would never come, that arrived mere months before she left us all alone, empty, and a little broken for the rest of our lives.

"She was transcendent."

By the time I get to Darcy's grave, the sun is setting. The sky is pink and blue like cotton candy and light burns through the clouds like glowing orange lava. Darcy would've called it a "stock photo of a sunset."

The Raise

I blacked out the entire Uber ride here. I felt like after talking to Dr. Wes, I had to get to Darcy as quickly as possible, and at any price.

I lean my back against her tombstone like it's the cold wall of the Jetto bathroom and rest my vape on the grass below like it's the tiled floor between us. I close my eyes and breathe. I feel like I can't keep running, like I don't know how much longer I can live in her honor.

What is a life if you don't put your needs first? What is a life if you're living it for someone else?

Even though I'm broken, even though I'm more overwhelmed and anxious and scared than I've been since I was twenty-two, I no longer feel desperate for some sort of life blueprint, for someone else to show me the way. Look where it got me.

In the short-term, mirroring someone else who has it all figured out feels good, and feels like relief, but in the end, all you've done is betray yourself. You've sacrificed your own identity. You've packaged up your misery and loneliness and insecurity and fear and sold it to a noble custodian, someone you think has the power to hold you, and repair it all.

But the truth is, the custodian is lonely, too. She's insecure. And she's fearful. At least, sometimes. To give her that power and apply the weight of taking care of you, of healing your wounds and telling you who to be—it's not fair. It's not right. Victoria was wrong, and Darcy never told her I was smothering or needy or that I put her on a pedestal and made her feel like she might fall at any moment. But that doesn't mean it wasn't true.

I turn around to face her tombstone—Darcy Lyons, 1988–2019—and kiss the top, like my mom kisses my forehead. My lips feel cold against the fresh stone, my tears dripping and slipping off its sloped edges.

I may not be found, but I'm not lost anymore.

I may not have direction, but I know where I can't go.

By Alexis Ecker
October 4, 2019
7 min read

Why I'm Shutting Down Savvy

After seven grueling years and the death of my beloved business partner, it's time to say goodbye.

Mere weeks ago, my co-founder and best friend Darcy Lyons died in what was believed to be a freak accident at Burning Man.

Within days, I was the new acting CEO of Savvy, leading the team, gearing up for our Series C, and doing my best to steer a workforce in mourning. The last month or so has been the most demanding, tragic and difficult period of my life. And I know many employees at Savvy feel the same. Losing Darcy was a gut-punch. It was an earth-shattering event for so many who loved and admired her, and who worked alongside her.

Trying to persist has been quite the feat, but we did so in her honor, and because we believed in Savvy and its future.

In record time, we added hundreds of thousands of users to our platform and shared our success on the biggest and brightest stage in our industry, at TechCrunch Disrupt. I'm honored I got the chance to show Savvy to the world, and tell Darcy's story of innovation, grit, and resilience to a community of our peers.

Recently, though, it came to my attention that there are people and forces that have been using fraudulent tactics behind-the-scenes to make Savvy a success. I will not go into full detail here, but I can communicate with the utmost confidence that Darcy did not and would never stand for this. She lived a life of integrity and believed that hard work, determination, and collaboration were the keys to making Savvy a billion-dollar business. This fraud now undermines everything she has done, and has cast a dark, painful shadow on the company she dreamed up at the age of seventeen, and then, against all odds, went on to actually build. I would like to state here, on record, that I too was unaware of the fraudulent tactics used to boost Savvy's growth.

I am disgusted and ashamed.

I inherited Savvy in all its glory and its mess, and as the new CEO, I've come to my own conclusion on how to move forward, and what happens next.

With a heavy heart and extreme distress and disappointment, I hereby announce that I am shutting down Savvy, effective this Friday at 9PM EST.

Full-time staff will get two months of severance. It's all we can afford. And unfortunately, we are not able to cover your healthcare as of the end of this week, but you can visit this link to find alternative, affordable options.

This is not how I wanted things to go. It's not how I wanted things to end. In an ideal world, I'd be able to offer a more generous package, but I can't, because I had to reserve part of our runway to compensate someone we let down.

Before Darcy passed, we turned away a qualified candidate and discriminated against her so we could "look good" to investors, and "tell the right story." As two non-technical women founders, we were constantly patrolling how seriously we'd be taken, how closely we approximated the "stock photo" image of an executive leadership team, which typically boasts lots of old, educated white men. This candidate was not an old, educated white man. In fact, she was a young, educated, brilliant, Black woman. We let our concerns for how we'd be perceived, and our obsession with feeding investors the people and patterns they believed in, overshadow the obvious fact that this candidate was perfect, deserving, and beyond ready for the role. Her settlement check has already been wired, and I have apologized to her privately. I feel great shame and remorse.

Due to the fraudulent behavior that's come to light, and our dwindling cash balance, I regret to inform our customers, and all of you, that there is no asset here. A part of me wanted to go into cockroach mode and start over, lay off a majority of the team and rebuild with a tight-knit group of loyal supporters. I wanted to do it for our community of smart shoppers, the ones who love and use our platform every day. I wanted to do it for my ego. I wanted to do it for Darcy.

But I don't have it in me. That's not how I want to or should spend my time right now, given all I need to process.

To my employees: your shares are now worth nothing. But your work experience is worth a lot. If you'd like, you can list your name, email and LinkedIn in this spreadsheet so other employers or hiring managers reading this can find you and hire you for your next exciting role.

To our board and our investors: thank you for believing in us, and wanting us to win, even against all odds, and sadly, in some cases, at all costs.

And to Darcy, our fearless leader, the glue that held it all together: I know this hurts you, even in death. I know this is never what you were building toward, never the outcome you expected or prayed for on your grueling fundraising trips, during tense investor pitches or in high-stakes strategy meetings. You put up with the bullshit of being underestimated and overlooked not because you saw the light at the end of the tunnel, but because you were building the tunnel yourself, with your brains and your bare hands. You will forever be a role model to women everywhere who want to put their potential to the test and shoot for the moon. You will forever be remembered as Savvy's mother, leader, and protector, and you will forever be beloved by everyone who worked for you, and everyone you knew. You changed me and my sense of self, my sense of how much I could grow, how far my skills could expand. I loved you like a friend, a sister, and a partner for life, and I will honor you endlessly.

I will not be taking calls or requests from the press and will be available in my office from tomorrow morning through Friday night to consult with my employees and wind down our business.

This is not what I'd hoped for.

17

Three Weeks Later.

I roll up the wine-stained peach carpet in Darcy's office as my mom's new maltipoo, Bono, nips at my feet. She always wanted a dog when we lived with Simon, but she didn't trust him. "I always worried daddy would tell us it ran away," she says, building cardboard boxes in the corner, "when really, he squished it dead or something. From yapping too much or peeing on the floor. And then I'd find it wrapped in a tallit, buried somewhere behind the pool."

I take a break from packing up Darcy's stuff—her business books, her printed contracts, the press clippings her mom would mail to the office—and lay down on the ground, staring up at the ceiling. Bono prances over to give me a full-face bath, licking forehead to chin, and while I'm more like my dad than my mom when it comes to animals, I think of Bono's lifeless body stuffed in the dirt, and my heart aches.

After publishing the Medium post, I spent days fielding calls from alarmed employees and angry investors, scanning belligerent, viral tweets from customers outraged by the shutdown and the hiring discrimination. I pulled multiple all-nighters analyzing and organizing

Hazel's documents, which finally hit my inbox, and reading takedown pieces about me and Darcy in *The Cut*, *Vanity Fair*, and *Business Insider*. I never went back to the Park Avenue apartment I shared with Ethan—I just holed up at my mom's. She played back-to-back Oprah audiobooks to try and calm me down, claiming it worked for her "every time," but even Oprah's soothing, centered voice couldn't shake my sense of unease.

My entire world had collapsed. My closest friendship. My relationship. My company. It was a world that took nearly a decade to build, and less than two months to destroy.

"Whaddya wanna do with this?" my mom asks with one hand on her hip, the other removing postcards and magazine cutouts and "save the dates" from Darcy's corkboard. She's holding up a polaroid of me, Ethan, and Darcy, all smiles at our third or fourth holiday party.

"Toss it," I say, still on my back, lightly disassociating. I don't know if I wronged him, or if he wronged me, but there's no use in keeping a photo of me with two people I'll never see again.

Ethan called me from his parents' house a few hours after the Medium post hit the wire, to see if I was okay, but then launched into questions about my salary and healthcare, given it was clear I was tanking the company. I recalled my Minetta Tavern rendezvous with Janine and her insistence that I dial back my workload once Ethan made Partner. In a way, the unspooling of Savvy made her wish come true. I had a sneaking suspicion that I was on speakerphone, given the tone and content of our conversation, but I couldn't be sure. But I decided my mistrust was enough of an issue—the inkling that Janine would always be there, woven into the fabric of our relationship, a grating voice inside his head that I could never silence or replace. So I told Ethan the truth: that I hadn't given myself severance, that I would have healthcare for only a few more weeks, and that it was over between us—but that I hoped he would make Partner somewhere else some day, somewhere he could start over with a clean slate.

I heard loud, competing voices in the background of the call, and then the line went dead.

Well, I guess Janine finally learned the truth.

My mom waddles over in her five-inch heels and lays down next to me.

"How are you feeling, babygirl?" she asks, genuine concern and affection in her voice.

"I'm okay," I say, and I mean it. I've become somewhat of a hermit—sleeping in, cooking, writing, and reading. Before, I felt most at peace when I was running at hyper-speed. Perhaps because there were all these signs along the road that I didn't want to see. But now, I enjoy long walks up and down the city—with a hat and dark sunnies on to shield my face, of course. I was the talk of tech, Wall Street, and Twitter for one whole news cycle. It feels like now half of Manhattan knows my face, and not in the good way.

"I wanna bring back the silicone Cheetah gloves," my mom tells me, stroking my hair. "I feel like they'd do well this time, you know? Every time we snack and watch crime I'm so worried we'll stain the couch. Maybe you can help them go viral?"

"No," I say, high off my new ability to set boundaries, using that big scary word women don't know they can say without punishment. "I'm in a good spot now with Hazel and the admin work. I don't think I can handle more than data entry or doing her invoices right now."

"Okay, sweetie," she answers softly, still petting my head. "I understand. I just want you to get back on your feet whenever you're ready. You have so much to offer."

She's not wrong, but if I've learned anything, it's that you have to be wise with who you offer your magic to. It's not like I blame Darcy for what happened to me, for my loss of self, my codependency, my inability to see where she started and I stopped. But on some level, especially thinking back on Stop the Bleed, and asking her for help I never got, I think she took slight advantage of my love for and reliance on her. I don't think it was malicious, but still. Having me in her pocket—enamored, impressed, and aiming to please—furthered her goals for the company.

I like working with Hazel because it's perfectly mindless, but also because she's the only tether to Darcy I have at this point. We met for cocktails once I emerged from my catatonic state, and I've been working for her part-time ever since, doing executive assistant type stuff. She's easy to talk to and never seems irritated or bored when I share funny misadventures Darcy and I experienced while building Savvy. Hazel has her own clear ambitions, but I don't make them mine, which feels new and nice and safe.

Victoria and I, on the other hand, haven't spoken in three weeks, and the last time we chatted was a terse exchange over email, when she asked for some stats she needed for her resume.

I never responded.

I'm not sure what she's doing now, if she jetted back to Santiago or the Hamptons or what, but I don't care anymore. I continued pilfering and taking my mom's sedatives for the first few days I stayed over, numbing myself to the pain of what happened, and what I did, and the fact that I'm back at square one with no real direction or ambition of my own. It felt impossible to process what Victoria had done—how her obsessive need to prove herself, to seem successful in her own right, drove her to the point of fabricating that success and derailing the thing Darcy loved most. Initially, I couldn't accept that all of this—Savvy falling apart, erasing everyone's employment, losing all our investors' money—was Victoria's fault, and not mine. I descended into a depressive episode. I couldn't leave my mom's bed. All I wanted to do was sleep and smoke and hit the "off" button on my thoughts. But my mom caught onto my drug use pretty quickly, because moms always know. She sat me down, hugged me hard, and said it was time to detox, and that she'd help. The next day, she hid the drugs and handed me a blank journal, something I could use to process without the pills. After a few weeks of journaling and a handful of sessions with my new therapist, I'm finally starting to accept that in an impossible situation, I did my best. And in not compromising my values for a system that has none, I took a short-term hit—or a bludgeoning—but long-term, sunsetting Savvy was the only choice I could live with.

But it's not easy. Isabella is suing Savvy for fraud, mismanagement, falsification of business records, and inadequate training. The paperwork came in immediately, and Hazel kindly offered to find a litigator looking to build her credentials who would represent the company on the cheap, one of her friend's daughters or cousins or something. I accepted the intro and e-signed our engagement letter, then let my computer die.

Luckily, I have Hazel's documentation and details on the fraud and where it was coming from. I pray Victoria gets her due, but I have a hunch Isabella will choose to protect Dr. Solis, her investor, and refuse to accept or believe that Victoria is or could ever be liable for Savvy's downfall.

I have to live with the fact that no one—not Isabella, not the rest of the board, not the police, not Ethan, not even my mom—will understand the depths of Victoria's depravity. I must carry the knowing with me every day, just like I carry Darcy's memory. They're intertwined now, like a bloody braid.

My mom's plucking goo and crust from Bono's eyes when a muffled ping rings from Darcy's deck. I stand up, find my phone, pick it up—and freeze.

It's a text.

From *her*.

> **Victoria:**
> 📎

I quietly swipe my screen and open the link she shared, and my stomach drops when I see the headline.

PRESS RELEASE: CRAFTED ADDS VETERAN RETAIL EXECS TO C-SUITE; WELCOMES VICTORIA SOLIS AS CRO, DANIEL DELANCEY AS CTO.

I skim the announcement, my heart racing at an Adderall-induced pace. But this time, I'm substance-free.

"What's wrong, honey?" my mom asks, suddenly sitting up from the floor, like she can detect my discomfort without even seeing my face.

As I sit frozen, balking at the news, another ping comes in.

"Nothing, mom. Do you mind grabbing me a La Croix from the office fridge?"

"I can't believe you drink that crap. It tastes like Dial soap. *Blech*." She pushes herself off the ground and dutifully exits the office, and I open my phone.

> **Victoria:**
> Resilience.

I take a deep breath and debate whether to reply, but realize I have nothing to say.

My mom returns with the La Croix and a crumpled lemon Luna Bar. I take a big bite, and my thoughts squirm about as I crunch. I'm curious what everyone else thinks of Victoria's new job at Crafted. I'm sure she posted it everywhere, and it's getting tons of praise. She finally got the Chief Revenue Officer job at a billion-dollar company. She can finally make her dad proud, or so she thinks. Let's hope she doesn't run the Savvy playbook to juice Crafted's orders. Even though I despise Marz, I wouldn't want anyone else to experience what I've been through.

I click my phone to black and survey the room and our progress. Most of Darcy's stuff is packed up, the cardboard boxes addressed to her mom in Long Island. Her desk is clean and empty and ready for Housing Works to pick up along with the rest of the office. A few employees called dibs on pieces in the foyer and conference rooms, and I'm happy to oblige. It's the least I can do.

There's only one more area to parse through: Darcy's office closet.

I toss my Luna Bar wrapper in the forty-two-gallon garbage bag my mom and I slung on the door handle, then make my way to the tall armoire.

I take a deep breath and pry it open.

Immediately, Darcy's smells—her skin, her neroli perfume, her coconut vanilla deodorant and mild, salty sweat—hit my nostrils and make me want to cry. I paw her soft emerald suit, her Burberry trench, her Khaite leather jacket, and purse my lips so I don't erupt in tears. My mom can't see me cry. It breaks her every time.

I gently remove each garment from the hangers and pass them to my mom to fold and secure in a box for Darcy's mom. With each motion, I think of Savvy: all the brands we helped, all their beautiful clothes, the customers who loved them and wore them with pride. I flash back to Darcy in the vintage Burberry trench, laughing hysterically in the car after I backed into a pole at a gas station right before an important pitch. I think of her wrapped in the Khaite jacket after our celebration dinner at Eleven Madison Park, our arms linked, our stars aligning.

And I feel lucky. I feel so lucky. Because unlike Dr. Wes, when it comes to Darcy, I remember everything.

The rack of clothes now empty, I can see the bottom of the armoire in clear view. And that gift bag is still here—the one I knocked over when I "borrowed" the emerald suit before Theo's fortieth birthday party. I pick it up and spot a small metallic scribble I didn't notice before.

My name. In silver sharpie.

I stumble backward and unconsciously put my hand over my mouth. I sit down in Darcy's chair and put the shiny black gift bag on the desk, and stare at it.

"What is that?" my mom asks, distracted. She's rustling through her purse and pulls out a doggy bag. Bono shat on the floor.

"Just a gift of some kind. I found it in there," I say, and point to the closet.

"Well, open it! It's not like she'll know you took it . . ." she replies, then shrugs her shoulders.

I grip the top of the bag and put it in my lap before gently opening it at the lips. I take a deep breath and remove what's inside.

There's a folded-up piece of computer paper, and a book by Jamie Frisco. Her second. The one called *Everything I Know and Everything I Didn't* about her second act as an investor, and the qualities she's seen in the most admirable and successful founders.

"It's a book? Lame!" my mom exclaims, before heading out the office and toward the kitchen. "I was hoping you'd find a nice piece of jewelry or something."

But what I did get is so much better.

It's a typed letter. From Darcy.

Lex,

I have a lot to say and I wasn't sure if I was even gonna write this or give this to u. U kno its hard for me to talk about this stuff and my emotions and I legit weighed whether I should dictate to one of the admins and have her piece it all together lol but I figured im a grown ass adult and I can handle writing a few paragraphs, amirite? That said, Ill probably rewrite this note a zillion times before I ever send it but here we go.

Im rly sorry for how I reacted w the whole stop the bleed thing and I should have listened to you in the lead up when u said u needed help on the project. That wasn't fair to u and putting u under that pressure and not giving u what u needed, and then flipping out on u, wasn't ok.

U r fully capable of doing insane and impossible things and for that and so many other reasons it has been such a gift to work w u. But I guess for that reason I also assume you can handle it all. I definitely take on a lot and just kind of grin and bear it but I shouldn't expect the same of u. And maybe I shouldn't even expect that of me in the first place. I was rly on the fritz w gordon and the raise and I put my needs and savvy's needs ahead of having any empathy for u and I shouldn't have done that. For some reason u feeling overwhelmed, overwhelmed me, and my reaction was to shut u down bc I couldn't handle my own shit. I rly regret it and I just want u to know that.

I feel like I don't say it enough but im so proud of u. And so grateful for u. Not bc u helped make this insane crazy company happen (of course, that too) but bc ur belief in me has changed my life in so many ways. Before I met you, and before we started working together—especially during the Marz stuff, I had this shitty mean voice in my head putting me down and telling me I wasn't good enough. Im still kind of unpacking how it got there and who put it there but what matters is over time, that voice got replaced by you encouraging me or telling me im a baddie or whatever and Its almost like I can barely hear it anymore. Like its dropped to a faint whisper.

Im excited to keep hustling and doing this crazy shit w you when I get back. I got u this book because I read it, and I could only think of you. I know you also struggle with the same shit. Feeling like it's all too much or ur not smart enough or whatever, and it killed me the last few days knowing I made those feelings worse.

Ur amazing. Seriously. I think maybe if you read this it'll help you see what I see. And maybe we can murder these stupid mean nagging voices together. Maybe that will never happen lolol but whatever, just take this as my gesture of like: I know I fucked up.

And im sorry.

I already told the recruiters to start looking for rly good ops people so we can take some stuff off ur plate after the raise, because I want you in more of a leadership role. More front and center. I know you can handle it.

I know it prob took a lot for u to even ask me for help, and I know u needed it, and im so srry again I didn't listen.

SEE U AFTER ~THE BURNNN~ BITCH!!!!
Xo,

D

I read the letter again and again and again. This must be the letter Dr. Wes was talking about—the one she was writing the last time he saw her. I can't believe it.

My tears hit the ink and make some words turn blurry. I find myself smiling while I clutch the letter to my chest and, to my surprise, start hysterically laughing.

I have never loved anyone as hard as her.

I have never needed anyone more.

My connection to her felt urgent, violent, essential, and pure.

But no matter how many supportive Slacks I got, or how many late nights we spent giggling together, or how many doors she opened for me—it never felt like enough. I always felt anxious, and less than, and wanting. If she kept something personal from me, I felt automatically betrayed. If she kept me out of early investor pitches, I felt automatically inferior. If she delegated to Victoria, I felt undermined and overlooked. I didn't take her actions at face value. I didn't interpret our time together, and her decade-long commitment to me—to us—as a sign of our mutual devotion.

Why?

Because Darcy's letter is right. I couldn't see what she saw.

That she loved me. That she needed me, too. And that if we don't see our own value, it's hard to believe that anyone else truly values us.

So maybe two broken people can fill each other's cracks, after all.

Because both in life, and in death, she filled mine.

My mom reenters the office, Bono prancing at her feet, and gives me a look that says she knows everything. She sees it all. It's a moment that reminds me of Darcy—how we could lock eyes in a meeting, from across the room, and say a million thoughts and feelings in total silence.

"Are you ready to go, babygirl?" my mom asks, and I notice a Savvy tote filled with La Croix hanging off her stubby little arm.

"I'm ready," I reply, and for the first time in a long time the girl I hear sounds convinced, and convincing.

I think finally, maybe, I believe her.

Acknowledgments

Thank you to my mom. Strategizing this book and feeling my way through its themes started way back in 2019, with you, over Kim Crawford sauv blanc and rambling voice notes. Thank you for then, and for reading pages in 2021, when we were quarantined on that European cruise for your birthday, and for holding me like a baby in 2023 when the future of this book seemed so uncertain. I kept going because you knew I could.

Thank you to my agents at CAA for believing in me, and to Abby Walters specifically for giving me pivotal edits and feedback. And thank you to Sammie for making the introduction to the team.

Thank you, Becky and Elias, my non-fiction agents for my first book, for giving me such an incredible and rare opportunity. You told me that book was only my first, and you saying that gave me a hunger and motivation to try something new and to keep writing.

Thank you to my early readers and supporters: Hannah, Olivia, Jon, Paige, Jana, Nick, Kendall, Dave, Sarah, Rae, and Jana, and all my friends who have cheered me on the last five years. I love you.

Thank you to the full cast and crew of *The Raise* for the work you put into our cinematic trailer and the world-building we've done together. Eva, *The Raise* has been such a blessing—to partner creatively, laugh together, see you shine in your element. I am just so happy we did this. Thank you for making my dreams come true. Sofija—the way you hold everything down, plan so meticulously and produce to perfection sets a standard for everyone around you, including me. Thank you for your heart and for your excellence. Anyone who works with you is extremely lucky.

Thank you, Alison, for your creative direction, my stunning cover, my gorgeous website, my social campaign—the entire visual universe. I am blown away by you and feel so honored you worked with me on this. My hand-drawn logo for Cashmere Street Press means more than you will ever know.

Thank you to my brother Ben for always acting so casual with me when I'm frantic or panicked or in a flop era. Your assumption that I'll just figure it out is often what pushes me to figure it out. I love you so very much and we will always have each other.

Thank you, Dave, my current boyfriend, for reading one-sixth of the book when you were still trying to win me over. And thank you for loving me, supporting me, and trying to make my life easier.

Thank you, Alana, for everything.

And thank you Leigh Stein, my dear friend and book coach, for taking my years of scheming and brainstorming and character mush and helping me turn it into a plot. I am so happy I read *Self Care* and stalked you on Twitter. Reading your work, you unlocked something inside me that needed to be unleashed and then I got to work with you? On my book? It was a *dream*.

And lastly, I want to say this: Lady Gaga famously said nearly six-hundred times on her *A Star is Born* press tour, "There can be 100 people in the room and 99 don't believe in you and you just need one to believe."

In her case, it was Bradley Cooper. In mine, it was me. I was the one.

So, I want to thank myself for pushing when no one else would. For believing *The Raise* deserved to happen. For believing when no one else did.

Made in United States
Orlando, FL
01 November 2025